He looked at her,  apologize, but the face silenced him

Seeing his yearning reflected in Lynn's gaze tipped Jax over the edge, into drawing her close, into stroking her, into learning her curves...

Then she saved him from himself by turning quickly away. He stared at her back, hoping that accidental touch hadn't offended her.

When she spoke, her voice sounded a bit husky. "I'll ask the boys about it. I doubt they did it, but they could have some idea of who might have."

He cleared his throat. "Good idea." But all he could feel was the precipice he hovered on, and the desire to carry her over it with him. With difficulty, he banked his internal fire.

This woman deserved better than a short-term tumble in the hay. She was a long-term type of woman.

No way could he be that for her, especially when his own ideas of marriage were so polluted by his past. He couldn't trust himself.

Dear Reader,

Writing this book turned out to be especially enjoyable in some ways. It's not often that I get to delve into family relationships, and this family was particularly fun.

Regardless, many of us have a family member who turns up drunk at Thanksgiving (or other holiday) and we hope that they fall into a drunken stupor on the couch before anything embarrassing or awful is said.

Well, there's no family member like that in this one, but there *is* a relative who causes a lot of problems out of jealousy. Even he was fun to write.

Then there is the other, a stranger who intends murder. I hope none of us meets someone like that.

Rachel Lee

CONARD COUNTY PROTECTOR

Rachel Lee

Recycling programs for this product may not exist in your area.

ISBN-13: 978-1-335-73803-5

Conard County Protector

Copyright © 2022 by Susan Civil-Brown

Harlequin Enterprises ULC
22 Adelaide St. West, 41st Floor
Toronto, Ontario M5H 4E3, Canada
www.Harlequin.com

Printed in U.S.A.

Rachel Lee was hooked on writing by the age of twelve and practiced her craft as she moved from place to place all over the United States. This *New York Times* bestselling author now resides in Florida and has the joy of writing full-time.

Books by Rachel Lee

Harlequin Romantic Suspense

Conard County: The Next Generation

Snowstorm Confessions
Undercover Hunter
Playing with Fire
Conard County Witness
A Secret in Conard County
A Conard County Spy
Conard County Marine
Undercover in Conard County
Conard County Revenge
Conard County Watch
Stalked in Conard County
Hunted in Conard County
Conard County Conspiracy
Conard County Protector

Visit the Author Profile page at Harlequin.com.

For my wonderful family

Prologue

"Guilty."

In a hearing room, the General Court Martial has concluded. The judge announces the verdict of the five jurors, a unanimous decision of *Guilty*.

It is the only word the defendant hears. It rolls through him like deafening thunder. He knows what it means: he has been convicted of war crimes, to be stripped of his rank, his time in grade, any future retirement. He will go to prison.

He stands at attention, outwardly accepting the judgment. As he is taken away, he looks at his sister, standing straight in her Marine uniform. He sees his own fury reflected in her eyes.

The defendant believes he has done nothing wrong. It was war, after all. He was just doing his job.

An unjust verdict.

It should have been *Not Guilty*.

Chapter 1

Jasmine and Adam Ryder's wedding reception in the Conard City Park had become quite an affair. White fairy lights had been strung among the autumn trees, placed by neighbors and friends far beyond the number of strands originally planned by the bridal pair. They cast a glow that illuminated an open grassy space and many of the wooded paths through the park. The trees had begun to don their autumn cloaks and the fairy lights brightened them from beneath as the evening took over from daylight.

Long folding tables groaned beneath food as potluck dishes were added to the original offerings of sandwiches, sliced cheeses and crackers. Plastic flutes glimmered golden with champagne, poured from magnums, and bottles of beer poked out from ice chests. Stacks of paper plates had been replaced by blue plastic with matching utensils.

Voices filled with laughter and happiness nearly drowned the brass quartet from the community college.

The bride, dressed in a white wool dress, had shed her short veil and donned a thick white wool shawl, her black hair and blue eyes gleaming. She gazed around at the magical setting and murmured, "Wow." Then Jazz Ryder looked at her new husband, Adam.

"Wow," he agreed, taking it all in.

His best man, Master Gunnery Sergeant Jackson Stone, stood beside him. Dressed in his Marine Corps blues, Jackson, or Jax as he was familiarly known, had been glad to fly across the continent for this wedding. Adam had been his only real friend here since early childhood.

"I guess," said Jax, "that I won't have to make one of those ridiculous speeches."

Jazz laughed. "At least you don't have to recall any of Adam's funny moments from years ago."

The three of them, along with the bride's identical twin sister, Lily, had already made a joke about the similarity of their nicknames: Jazz and Jax.

The ad hoc gathering had mostly ignored any idea of formal clothing, except for a few in their Sunday best. The rest unapologetically wore jeans and boots.

As the evening chill descended, no one seemed to care. What had started as a small reception had turned into a huge party, the kind of event Conard City enjoyed.

Jax watched the bride and bridegroom begin to move among the crowd, greeting everyone they could, thanking them for this outpouring. Then he eased to a quiet area, aware that his uniform stood out, and he didn't want to draw attention away from the couple. This was *their* night.

He didn't stand alone for long. "Hello, Jackson."

He turned his head, looking down at a small elderly woman who held the leash of a harlequin Great Dane that seemed almost as large as she was. An odd pairing.

"I don't suppose you remember me," she said. "I'm Edith Jasper."

His memory of her surfaced. "Miss Jasper! You taught senior English."

The woman's smile broadened. "I think you're old enough to call me Edith now. You were so quiet. I always wished you'd speak up because you were one of my best students."

Jax didn't know how to answer, especially because he'd had no idea.

Edith patted his arm. "You've come a long way. Now meet my dog Bailey."

Jax held out his hand, palm up. Bailey sniffed, then seemed to grin. "Big, isn't he?" He hardly had to bend to stroke the huge dog's head.

"People keep expecting him to knock me over or drag me, but he's a good boy. He's always known my limits. Anyway, it's nice to see you again. Now get out there and meet more people who remember you."

He doubted many of them remembered him at all. He scanned the crowd casually, wondering how Adam was taking all of this. Adam had confided that after three tours in Afghanistan he'd come home with some PTSD and couldn't stand to be in crowded places for long. Cities could be torture for him, although this one boasted a population of only around five thousand. Small in some places, but large enough in Wyoming, where the biggest city had a little over sixty thousand residents.

Jax wasn't aware of any PTSD on his part, but that might not mean anything. Experience in the Corps had taught him how to master his mind so, while the threat might be lurking somewhere inside him, he didn't know it. But then he hadn't been wounded like Adam.

"Hello, Jackson," said a redheaded woman as she approached. She wore a silky green dress that slithered over her ample curves.

She clearly remembered him, but he couldn't place her. She appeared to be about his age.

"We nearly dated in high school."

Dated? Astonishment filled him. He'd never come close to dating in high school but instead had avoided it. Not that anyone had expressed interest back then. "Nearly?" he repeated.

She pursed her brightly lipsticked mouth. "Well, you used to smile at me across the classroom. You liked me then. I'm Madge Kearny, remember?"

Jax racked his brains. "It's been a long time…"

She laughed flirtatiously. "Too long. You went and joined the Marines before anything could happen between us. You…"

She was interrupted by another woman, one with thick, long auburn hair and bright green eyes, dressed in a gray slacks suit. She was smiling and said, "Now, Madge, let Jackson get his feet under him." She turned to Jax. "I hear you're staying for a little while."

"Thinking about it." Carefully neutral. Women were drawn to this uniform like flies to honey. He didn't credit himself with any of their attraction.

"You see, Madge?" the woman said. "You'll have plenty of time to get reacquainted. Isn't that Joe over there looking for you?"

Madge scowled at her and flounced away.

The woman laughed quietly. "Always on the hunt, that one. Hi, I'm Lynn Macy. You won't remember me, but

I was three years behind you in school. You and Adam were close, as I recall."

"Yes."

"I'm sure he's very glad you were able to come." Her smile grew gentle. "Trust your own memory. I bet a lot of people would like to claim you as a buddy now."

Then she moved off into the crowd, leaving him feeling uncomfortable in a whole different way from Madge. He kind of liked it.

Lynn glanced over at Jackson Stone while she fell into conversation with Judge Wyatt Carter and his father, Earl. The two of them had played a big part in helping her keep the house her late husband, Matt, had willed to her.

My, Jackson had changed, she thought. From diffident, introverted string bean to a well-filled-out man who stood confidently. The years away had served him well in that regard. And although she hadn't known him directly, being three years younger, everyone knew *of* everyone.

A group of men over by some trees began to sing a bawdy song. *Drunk*, Lynn thought. Then she heard a gravelly voice behind her.

"I hope I don't have to get official tonight."

Lynn recognized the voice immediately. Sheriff Gage Dalton. She turned, smiling, and saw that his redheaded wife, Emma, had her arm through his.

Emma shook her head. "This guy never gets a night off. Come on, Gage. There are enough deputies around here tonight to handle drunkenness."

It was true, Lynn thought. Quite a few of them, in street clothes, were enjoying the party, and it wasn't as if Gage would have to stand in himself. "I'm voting with Emma," she said.

"Me, too," both Carters said in unison.

Gage shook his head, the burn scar on his cheek making his smile a bit lopsided. "I'm being ganged up on."

"Your wife would like you to take a night off," Emma said on a laugh. "Come on, Gage. The judge has ruled."

That caused Wyatt Carter to grin. "Yeah," he said. "Ruling from the bench."

As the Daltons walked away, Earl Carter, a plump lawyer, leaned toward her. "Is Luke leaving you alone?"

Luke was her late husband's brother-in-law. "He stops by once in a while. I know he's unhappy with the legal decision."

"Damn," said Earl. "It's not your fault Luke and Matt's father left the house to Matt. As I recall, Jed Macy had his own good reasons for that will. Loose cannon, that boy Luke."

"Dad," Judge Carter said. "This is supposed to be a happy night. Don't go reminding Lynn of bad things."

Lynn spoke again. "It's okay, Wyatt. You two helped a lot. I can deal with Luke's resentment."

And she could, even if she suspected Luke would like her to fall off her roof while she was repairing shingles.

Well, he'd never hurt her. Too much of a coward.

She moved along, speaking to friends and acquaintances she'd known during her entire life in Conard County. It was a great gathering.

When Lynn arrived back at her house, she noticed the lights showing from the second floor of her house. Her college roomers seemed to be burning the midnight oil. Probably upcoming exams.

She stepped through her front door, hearing dueling music from above. Apparently, they'd taken advantage of her absence to turn up the volume. Amused, she moved

to the dining room to look once again at the list of remodeling items she planned to buy soon.

This project was more than Matt's legacy. Remodeling and repairing this house had become her most enjoyable activity. Matt's father had let it run down, and
when he died, Matt had been in the Army, unable to do
much about it.

Lynn had tinkered with things while Matt was away
but hadn't wanted to make major changes until he ap-
proved. Now it was her project alone and she felt as if she
were spreading her wings, finding new interests and new
things she loved to do. Even a few years ago she couldn't
have imagined herself taping and mudding drywall, re-
vising the house's layout and handling a circular saw with
the ease of familiarity. Or painting a three-story house,
her biggest project to date.

Now the four upstairs bedrooms took roomers com-
fortably and her own apartment was complete. Her next
project would be dealing with the water damage in the
living room, a bad surprise when she'd ditched all the
ancient furniture.

Pleased with her steady progress, she climbed the two
flights of stairs to her own apartment in the attic. She'd
turned the overhead trapdoor into a stairway, one she'd
built herself specifically for this purpose with a door at
the bottom.

As she flipped on the lights, she looked around, loving the warmth she'd created in the large attic. What a
discovery it had been when she'd finally explored what
she had thought of as storage space.

All the walls and high-peaked ceiling were covered
with gleaming wood that she'd stained and polished; the
floors were built of wider wooden planking to match.

Two full-size windows graced the ends of the attic, allowing plenty of light to enter.

She'd turned it into her own studio apartment with a bath in one corner, a small kitchenette under the back window and her bed in a corner. She'd discovered comfy chairs and ottomans discarded up here, but bright yellow upholstery and some new springs had fixed them up as good as new. Colorful rag rugs dotted the floor.

She wouldn't have changed anything about it now even if she'd initially been uneasy about her decisions. Matt would have loved it, too, she was certain.

Its only problem was that it could get chilly in the winter, and she'd dealt with that by installing an electric fireplace that added to the coziness on cold nights.

She showered quickly—at least the three boys below had left her enough hot water—donned her flannel pajamas and crawled into bed with a good book on her tablet.

She felt sorry for Jackson Stone, though. He'd been a standout at the reception and she wondered how many people would now claim to be his long-lost friends.

Of which he'd had none back when he'd lived here. Despite how confident he appeared now, perhaps his personality hadn't changed that much, considering how he'd stood aside at the reception.

But dang, he was sure an attractive man.

Chapter 2

The fire at the La-Z-Rest Motel started around 2:00 a.m.
A smoke detector squealed a shrill, nearly deafening,
alarm.

With flames licking two walls of his room, Jax managed to pull on his camos, grab his laptop and his Marine
blues, which hung in a garment bag. With them and his
desert boots in hand, he raced out into the chilly night
to join the other guests who gathered across the highway
to watch the burgeoning conflagration. A crowd grew as
truckers left their rigs to gawk, too.

He laid down his laptop and suit bag so he could jam
his feet into his boots and tie them. Then he stood and
watched for a few minutes with the others as fire trucks
arrived and tried to put out the blaze. The old motel appeared to have been built from wood that had grown
tinder-dry over the years, and the fire had taken over
the whole building.

Someone was watching everything they'd worked for going up in flames. He had no desire to rubberneck a tragedy.

While the firefighters began to work, he turned and headed into the truck stop diner. Engines growled all around him as he opened the door and stepped in to be greeted by delicious aromas.

"You okay?" asked the grillman, a lean, tall man of middle years. Over his white T-shirt and jeans he wore a denim apron, and on his head a white baseball cap. "That fire…"

"I'm all right. I hope everyone else is."

"Yeah, it's bad. Well, there's just me here tonight, and I suppose a lot of hungry people are going to show up shortly, so before I get rushed, what'll it be? Coffee's fresh, menu's limited at this hour."

"Hamburger? Fries?"

The man grinned. "You're in my ballpark. Want any pastry, let me know." He snorted. "At least I don't have to cook *that*. I'm Hasty, by the way. You grab a seat. I'll be right with you."

Jax did so, laying his suit bag over one brown vinyl-covered bench and putting his laptop beside him on the other.

By the time Hasty brought Jax his meal and a mug of coffee, others had started to trail in.

Hasty spoke, jabbing a finger at the parking lot full of trucks. "We're not usually too busy at this time of night, so I let my whole staff take off for the wedding. That's why I'm the only one here, and from the looks of it, I'm in for it. Bad snowstorm in the mountains out west. Too many switchbacks coming down the other side, so they're all waiting."

Jax nodded.

"You that Stone guy everybody's talking about?"

Jax felt momentarily taken aback. He glanced toward the growling trucks, wondering how the drivers could have heard.

Hasty chuckled. "Might surprise you, but some of my customers are locals. They like my food. Anyway, a few came in for a midnight breakfast and mentioned you. If it *is* you."

"It is." Jax held out his hand. "Jackson Stone."

Hasty shook his hand with a firm grip. "Pleased to meet you. But a sad way to do it." Then he walked away to deal with the steadily growing crowd at the counter, the fire on everyone's tongue. Because Hasty was alone, the truckers carried their own meals to tables.

Jackson figured he was going to spend the night here before deciding what to do in the morning. A diner wasn't the best place to sleep, but as he recalled, the La-Z-Rest was the only motel for many miles. Right then he didn't know if his rental car had survived. He doubted it. Sure as hell, most of his clothes hadn't.

Then he laughed at himself. He'd survived worse conditions, conditions that came without a hot meal or a roof.

He got a second meal at the counter, and Hasty heaped on a larger order of fries.

Back at his table, he ruminated over the day. It had been good to see Adam so happy. The last time they'd met it hadn't been pretty. A bunch of insurgents had been firing from a clifftop at an allied convoy, and Jax's unit had taken them out. Once they'd secured the area, he and his squad had slip-slided their way down to the convoy, where bodies lay about, some of them badly burned in the raging fire that had taken a troop transport and a Humvee. They offered as much aid as they could while waiting for choppers.

Then he'd turned one man over and recognized the face of Adam Ryder, his lifelong friend. Badly shot up, close to death. For the first time on the battlefield, Jax had felt tears wet his cheeks. *My God, Adam.*

Jax dragged his thoughts away from a memory best forgotten, instead rambling over the wedding, a pleasant affair. More than pleasant, actually. When he'd learned that neighbors and friends had gone over-the-top with food and decorations, he'd been surprised and then realized he shouldn't be. Even in his shy youth, he'd known that people here took care of one another. Besides, a big party was probably the best entertainment around.

And those two women. That Madge had been pushy, really pushy, and he was quite sure he'd never given her any cause to think they were an item. He hadn't been an item with anyone back then, hadn't wanted to be. All he had wanted was to be *out* of this place.

But Lynn Macy had been very different, jumping in to silence Madge before he was forced to say something rude. And then walking away casually, pressing him not at all. Just friendly. And quite beautiful. His gaze had wandered over her, taking in a compact figure that a gray slack suit couldn't fully conceal. Much more attractive to him than Madge.

Through the window beside him, he could see only the truck parking lot. He wondered if the fire was out, then wondered why it should matter to him. He'd lost only some clothes. Others had lost a whole lot more and he couldn't help.

Full of good food and strong, hot coffee, he finally turned his head to look around the diner. The truckers were happy enough to wait at the counter and carry their own food to their tables, but not as quick to clean up. Even paper napkins had been left crumpled on tables and plates, although there were plenty of trash cans around. Too many new arrivals were simply shoving dirty dishes to one side to make a space for themselves.

No way was Hasty going to be able to deal with this while grilling nonstop, and his staff shouldn't have to face this mess when they came in the morning. Nor should *he* be sitting on his duff.

Annoyed by the mess, he rolled up his sleeves and got to work clearing tables. With a bus bin full, he went to the counter.

"Hasty, what can I do with these?"

Hasty looked over from the grill where he had six burgers frying along with potatoes and onions. He raised his brow. Then he grinned. "I thought you guys never volunteered."

"Sometimes I buck the rule. So where?"

Hasty pointed with a jerk of his head. "Dishwasher's in back. Just shove the pan on the counter beside the dishwasher. I'll get to it all later."

Jax didn't leave it at that. He knew how to use the commercial dishwasher, even though it appeared to be as old as Hasty. He sprayed away remaining food, then put cups and plates on the rack. As each rack rolled through the hot wash and rinse, he went to clear a few more tables.

Lead by example. That had long been drilled into him, and it seemed to work here as drivers began to clear their own tables and stack dishes at one end of the counter. Jax was amused. He hadn't intended this, but it was good to see nonetheless.

At last, just around dawn, the traffic tapered off. Hasty even had time to take a smoke break outside the door. Jax stepped out with him, needing some fresh air.

"Thanks for all that help. Want another meal?" Hasty

asked him. "This time on the house. I'd give you a steak if I had one."

Jax smiled. "Just plenty of coffee, if you don't mind."

Hasty flashed a grin. "Now, why would I mind? You saved me in there. And my staff, come to that. They'd have wanted to put my head on a pike if they came to work and saw that mess."

"Could you blame them?"

"Hah! Couldn't say I would." Hasty ground the cigarette butt beneath his heel. "Gotta get back to the grill, and you start thinking what you want to eat besides coffee. Not like you have any place to go right now."

It was true. Jax stood staring up at the sky, breathing the refreshing night air that was tinged with the smell of wet ash, wondering why in the hell he'd wanted to come back to this one-horse town. It wasn't as if it held many good memories.

Across the highway, impossible to ignore, rose the blackened skeleton of the motel. One fire truck was still there, dousing the remains to make sure embers wouldn't start another fire.

He saw the sheriff, Gage Dalton, approaching him just as dawn began to redden the eastern sky. Aside from meeting him briefly at the reception, Jax remembered him from his childhood before Gage took over from the old sheriff, Nate Tate. Back then he'd been called *hell's own archangel* by locals because of his fire-burned face and his darkly determined isolation.

Dalton shook his hand. "Gotta ask you some questions about last night."

No surprise, given that he was newly arrived. "Fire away."

"At my place, if you don't mind."

His place. The Sheriff's Office. Momentary uneasiness niggled Jax. "Let me get my gear."

It was still early, but a few people were about, eyeing Jax curiously as he rode in the front passenger seat of the official SUV. He wondered how that would hit the grapevine, which was as effective in this town as any in the military.

Inside, walking through a squad room in serious need of upgrades with only the computers looking like recent models, he followed Gage down a back hallway to his office. The desk had a computer on one side and a stack of papers on the other.

"Have a seat," Gage said, waving him to a seat facing the desk. Gage walked around it, wincing as he settled into a chair that creaked its age.

Gage smiled, that lopsided smile that looked as if the scar tissue on the side of his face wouldn't allow him more. "So you're a master gunnery sergeant now. Do I call you Master Guns?"

Jax shook his head. "How about just Jax?"

Gage's smile widened just a shade. "Then call me Gage. No formalities here." He leaned forward, wincing slightly again as he rested his forearms on the desk. "I remember you just before you left. You were so thin you looked like you'd blow away in a strong breeze."

"Never happened."

Gage laughed. "I'm looking at you, aren't I? Listen, I didn't want to talk to you because I suspect you of anything. I'm just collecting any information I can get about the fire. In case it was arson."

Jax nodded without surprise, having considered the possibility because Gage wanted to talk to him. The idea disturbed him. "Was it?"

"Don't know yet. I'm moving ahead before any memories fade or change. You know how malleable memories are?"

"I do." He'd had more than a little experience of that, watching how Marines' minds could grow and change a story in the telling and retelling and then totally believe it.

"Some welcome home," Gage remarked. "Anyway, what do you recall?"

"The back wall and side wall of my room flaming. Fire was creeping toward the door. Well, creeping isn't exactly right. It was moving fast."

"That place was tinder, all right. And then?"

"I jumped into my camo, grabbed my laptop, suit bag and boots. Out of there faster than a bat out of hell."

"I hear you didn't hang around to gawk."

Jax shrugged. "Why would I? I've seen plenty of fires and all I could think was it was sad for the owners. Everyone got out, I hope?"

"The guy next door to you didn't."

Jazz stiffened. "Damn, if I'd known..."

"If you'd known, we'd have more than one crispy critter."

Jax wasn't offended by the black humor. A familiar survival mechanism. Dealing with ugliness had to be handled somehow for sanity's sake.

Gage continued. "You ought to understand as well as anyone that courage is sometimes useless."

It was true, but for the first time Jax let feeling emerge from his lockbox. He knew all about what fire could do to a person. Too much. It sickened him. "I still feel bad about it."

"Of course." Gage nodded and leaned back. "So you didn't hear anything, see anything?"

"Not that I'm aware of. I'll rack my memory, but frankly I was dead asleep."

Gage nodded. After a moment, he asked, "What are your plans?"

Jax heard the subtle implication in the words. He was an unknown factor in this town and therefore suspicious. Naturally. "None yet. I suppose my car is a total loss."

"Between the fire and the water hoses, not to mention axes, there might not be enough left for a scrapyard."

"The rental company is going to be thrilled."

Gage shrugged. "I'll give you a police report for them. So, *are* you staying in town?"

The implication was not as subtle this time. Jax spread his hands. "Has a new motel sprouted anywhere?"

"Hardly. Listen, I know a lady who runs a rooming house. As I recall, she has a spare room or two."

Great, Jax thought. He was going to be stuck in this town for a while. Any plan he'd had of going to Denver to look for quarters for himself had gone up in smoke with the fire.

Without asking, Gage riffled through an old-fashioned circular card file. "Old sheriff used this," he remarked. "Too much trouble to move it to the computer, especially since I've been adding to it because I can't mess up cards."

Soon Gage was speaking into the phone. "Hey, Lynn, you got a room for a guy who got burned out of the motel last night?"

Jax could hear a woman's voice faintly, first sounding appalled, then quieter.

"Thanks, I'll bring him over. Jackson Stone. Yeah, ten minutes, if that's okay?"

Gage hung up. "You got yourself a room. Ready?"

* * *

Jackson Stone? For some reason, Lynn was surprised. At some level she must have known he was staying at the motel but had been shocked nonetheless when Gage told her. She'd only just heard the news about the fire from one of her roomers, a college student named Will. Will sported a bright orange thatch of red hair, a ton of freckles and an infectious grin. He hadn't been grinning earlier when he delivered the news.

Dang, Lynn thought. That motel was a local landmark, having stood since the 1950s, back when long road trips had become popular. These days it survived on truckers who occasionally didn't want to sleep in their cabs.

She had two rooms of her own left, both reasonably ready, but unlike her students, who were given a list of items to bring for themselves, mostly bedding, Jax would have none of that. Diving into an upstairs closet, she checked to make sure she had enough spare sheets and pillows.

Since she had two empty rooms, she decided to give him his choice.

When the front doorbell rang, she didn't bother to tuck her work shirt into her jeans. She had a lot to do today. Instead she got an unexpected and unwelcome surprise.

"Mom!"

Nancy West stood there, smiling. Behind her, her rental car blocked the end of Lynn's driveway. "Hello, sweetie. It's been too long."

The same thing her mother always said, even though it hadn't been *that* long, and Lynn offered her usual response. "Why didn't you call and let me know?"

"This trip was a whim."

They always were, Lynn thought as she stepped back

to allow her mother inside. The woman wore a beige business suit and low heels. Her short salt-and-pepper hair was perfectly coiffed. Nancy always presented a flawless appearance.

She walked in, scanning her daughter with faint disapproval, then looked around the entryway. "I can see you've been busy. Do you still have those college kids staying with you?"

"Three," answered Lynn, wishing she could make this situation vanish. Her mother had objected to her taking roomers since the start. She loved her mother, but the frequent criticisms, implied or overt, were enough to make her gnash her teeth.

"Well, I hope you have room for me! I'm your mother, after all."

Lynn contained a sigh. "The room you usually take. At the back of the ground floor. Make yourself at home." As Nancy always did.

Nancy West beamed. "My bags are in the trunk." She handed Lynn the keys then said suddenly, "Oh, who's that?"

Lynn turned to see the sheriff's car pull up. "A new roomer," she answered.

"In a sheriff's car? I hope he's not a criminal..."

Nancy's voice trailed off as she saw the tall, broad-shouldered man in belted camouflage climb out carrying a suit bag and a laptop case.

"Ooh," murmured Nancy. "A soldier."

"A Marine," Lynn corrected her. Already she was starting to feel a little annoyed. *Ooh?*

"They're all the same." Nancy laughed lightly.

"I wouldn't tell a Marine that."

Nancy eyed her. "Do you already know him?"

"Jackson Stone. I grew up with him. Now, let it go, Mom."

"Funny," Nancy mused as Jax approached. "I don't remember him."

Few people honestly remembered him, Lynn thought. As he reached the foot of the porch steps, Lynn called out, "Hi, Jax. Work your way around my mother and come in."

He smiled. "I appreciate this, Lynn."

"My pleasure. Just drop your stuff in the living room. We'll have some coffee before I show you to your room."

"Coffee sounds great. I'm addicted."

"Tea for me," Nancy said brightly.

"Of course." Knowing her mother, Lynn figured Nancy didn't want to miss one bit of this interesting development, especially since it involved a handsome man in uniform. She offered Jax another smile. "I just need to get Mom's bags from her car first."

"I'll help," Jax said promptly. He took his laptop and suit bag quickly into the empty living room and returned. "Ready."

Lynn walked with Jax to her mother's car and unlocked the trunk. Before she could move, Jax hefted both large suitcases, then carried them into the house behind her.

"Where do you want them?" he asked.

She pointed. "The bedroom in the back, please."

It was all Lynn could do not to frown. She'd planned to give that room to Jax, the only room with a private bath. Trying to keep her face smooth, she walked into the kitchen.

Nancy followed, her heels tapping, "How nice to have a man around," she said.

"It's temporary and I'm in no hurry to have a man around. What kind of tea do you want?"

"Earl Grey, please."

Lynn started the electric kettle, salvaged the teapot from an upper shelf, then turned to begin making coffee.

Jax returned to the kitchen. "I wasn't sure if I should put the suitcases on the bed, so they're standing beside it."

"Thank you so much!" Nancy beamed. "That's fine."

Nothing like a man to perk her mother up, Lynn thought. Instead of being annoyed, she suddenly felt amused. This might be fun to watch.

The Earl Grey was perfectly steeped just past three minutes, the way her mother preferred it. No milk, no sugar. The coffee wasn't far behind.

They sat at the long wooden refectory table that filled the middle of the kitchen like an outsize island and provided extra counter space. The only seating it offered was benches. Lynn planned to use it in the dining room when she was finished with the repairs and painting. The table was a fine piece and just needed some love to remove all the cut and burn marks. Or maybe she'd leave it looking distressed. There was plenty of time to think about it.

Nancy looked around. "You really need to do something about this kitchen, Lynn."

"With my roomers using it all the time, I'm not terribly concerned about it. They seem happy. At some point I'll get to it."

She looked around anyway. The room hadn't been remodeled at all since Matt's mother had done it at least three decades ago and she hadn't changed out the appliances. Those definitely needed replacing, especially the fridge, which *had* to be ready to die at any moment. As it was, she had to clean it out often. Her boys, as she thought of them, were pretty good at cleaning up after themselves, but the fridge? Some of the things they left forgotten were gross enough. A dead refrigerator would only make it worse.

There were plenty of knife cuts on the green laminate countertops despite a ready stack of cutting boards. She'd have to get something more impervious to carelessness. And she was honestly tired of the green everywhere.

"Maybe my next project," she told her mother. "I'll see."

Jax spoke. "Are you remodeling?"

Nancy answered before Lynn could. "Constantly. I think she keeps busy to suppress her grief over Matt."

Lynn clamped her teeth together to avoid snapping. "I enjoy it" was all she said. She thought she caught a glimmer of sympathy in Jax's dark eyes. For what? Matt's loss or her mother's bald assessment?

"How long are you staying for, Mom?"

"A few weeks."

An unsatisfyingly vague answer.

Nancy spoke again. "What do you do in the Army, Jax?"

Lynn cringed. *Here she goes again.*

"Marine Corps," Jax corrected her with a half smile. "I give a lot of orders, shoot a lot of guns and take my Marines to hell. And you, Mrs. West?"

The kitchen was suddenly as silent as a grave.

Later Lynn took Jax upstairs and pulled clean sheets and pillows out of the linen closet for him. Towels, too.

Jax thanked her again for the room and told her to just drop the linen on the bed. "I know how to make it up."

"Bathroom is down the hall—you can't miss it. Sorry you'll have to share."

"Like I never have before?"

"I bet you have. Anyway, I give my students strict rules about keeping it clean. I hope they haven't let me down. Every couple of weeks I check it out, mop the floor, maybe scrub the tub if they haven't in a while. No guarantees about what you'll find right now. Certainly no spit and polish."

"Wasn't expecting it. Now how much rent do I owe you, Lynn? Seriously."

She flushed. "Nothing. I wouldn't charge anyone who'd been burned out of their only bed."

He shook his head. "How much? Please."

She looked straight into his rugged face and dark eyes and sensed the pride in the man. No handout would be acceptable. She told him what she charged each of the boys. "But that's monthly. If you don't want to stay that long…"

He shook his head. "I'll get it to you later today," he promised. "I don't think I melted my ATM card or it would be fused to my butt."

She laughed, truly amused. Then she left him and headed back downstairs to try to keep an eye on Nancy. When her students came home later, they were apt to get the third degree.

A pleasurable little shiver ran through her, though, as she descended. Jax was certainly an attractive man.

And she wished even more that her mother hadn't chosen this time to visit.

Jax easily remembered the way to Freitag's Mercantile on Main Street. A few people on the street studied him curiously, but left him alone. That was fine. All he'd ever wanted when he'd lived here was to be left alone. Except by Adam.

Their friendship had begun early when their mothers, both ranch wives, had gotten together on occasional

Saturday afternoons for a coffee klatch. He and Adam had no other friends out there in the wide-open spaces and had cemented their relationship, even though Adam was a couple of years older. At first, Adam had acted as an unofficial babysitter, but when Jax grew old enough to have a strong interest in playing with miniature cars and making roads in the dirt, they'd become fast friends. Jax grew up a little faster in those early years by keeping up with Adam, and nothing had ever disturbed the bond between them.

So what was he doing here, now that Adam had gone off on his honeymoon? Damned if he knew, except that the sheriff didn't want him to leave. He should have been on his way to Denver this afternoon or tomorrow.

He just hoped Adam enjoyed himself. He'd confided to Jax that cities, large towns, large crowds, always made him jangle, made him hyperalert. He was going to dive into all of that for Jazz, to make her happy.

Well, Adam must have taken part in the planning. Maybe he was ready to step out and see what happened.

In Freitag's he found everything he needed to get him through a week or so. Jeans, of course, some sweatshirts and hoodies for the growing autumn chill, and underwear, a long-sleeved shirt. At the last minute he added a medium-weight navy blue jacket and leather gloves.

With his purchases packed into a new black duffel bag, he crossed the street to the bank to get the rent money for Lynn as he'd promised, then headed back to Lynn's house. He was glad that his wallet and cell phone had been in his camo pocket when he'd dashed out of the burning motel. The cell phone had become an essential item for military personnel who might need to be reached at any time.

Well, he was stuck here for a while, even though his

plans had been vague at the best. Gage Dalton had made that clear, however obliquely.

Well, why not? He'd been a loner as a kid and had suddenly showed up in town for the first time in fifteen years. Then the place where he was staying burned to the ground.

If Jax were the sheriff, he might want to keep an eye on himself, too.

The thought almost made him smile.

Chapter 3

By midafternoon, Lynn could have cheerfully packed her mother back into her car and sent her home. Even the process of making dinner had become a headache.

"Why don't you have anything decent in the refrigerator?" Nancy demanded, peering inside. "Soda. Left-over pizza. Milk."

"The boys…"

"You live here, too," Nancy said as she opened the freezer. "Toaster pastries? Frozen waffles? Frozen dinners? Lynn!"

"Mom, the boys…"

Again Nancy interrupted as she began to look through the cupboards. "Look at all these sweet cereals. You need something with bran in it. Don't you ever cook?"

Lynn rubbed her temple with her hand, feeling the approach of a headache. "I live upstairs, not down here."

"No, you live in your *attic*. What is wrong with you?"

This was a full-bore attack. Her mother rarely criticized so harshly, preferring sly innuendos or brief, tart remarks, but the woman was on a tear.

"I *like* my attic," Lynn said firmly. "If you'd come up and take a look, you'd see how nice it is." Not that she really wanted her mother to go there and start criticizing her private space.

"I'm not climbing two flights of stairs. You know my arthritis…"

"I'm sorry. How could I forget?"

"Because you hardly keep in touch!"

Lynn nearly gaped. With Nancy dropping in for irregular stays multiple times each year, there hardly seemed to be any point in Lynn traveling to visit her.

Nancy put her hands on her hips. "You've become as bohemian as those boys you rent to. I suppose you'll expect me to eat at that diner again."

"That diner has some great food," Lynn said, wishing she'd just learn to shut her own mouth and let Nancy run out of steam. "Anyway, since you're here, I'd planned to go to the market and get things you'll like for your meals. Are you still off eggs?"

Nancy waved her hand. "Turns out they're good for you in moderation. I'll come with you to the market."

Feeling almost desperate, Lynn shook her head. "You need to unpack. I *am* capable of grocery shopping." *And I need a break.*

Nancy merely shook her head and started the kettle boiling. That was another thing that annoyed Lynn. Her mother insisted on a whole pot of tea, then would drink one single cup because it only tasted good when it was freshly made.

Lynn escaped. Hopping in her car gave her a temporary sense of freedom and she was grateful for it. Lord, had her mother been that bad the whole time she was growing up?

It was possible she hadn't noticed it as much when she'd been wrapped up in school, in her shop classes and her friends. Now she was getting distilled Nancy.

And Nancy would make it difficult to get on with her remodeling project. Always.

No wonder her dad had bugged out when Lynn was fourteen. Her mother was a born micromanager.

Then she felt ashamed. She shouldn't allow her frustration to make her unkind. Still, she often thought marrying Matt had been her wisest decision ever. Not only had she loved him deeply, but she'd gone away with him whenever she could follow him to his current station. A stronger, more independent Lynn had emerged.

Thinking of Matt saddened her deeply. The grief came more rarely now, but sometimes when it struck her, it speared her as badly as it had during the first weeks and months.

Sighing, she climbed out of her car at the grocery store, retrieved her reusable bags from the trunk, and went inside to deal with the prospect of cooking for her mother. Maybe she'd invite Jax, too. His first night, and everything.

Plus, he might be a good buffer.

She nearly giggled out loud. Was that fair to him? No. Would a good home-cooked meal make up for it? Maybe.

Nancy had changed into more casual clothes, a pair of knit blue slacks, a long-sleeved turtleneck pullover in a lighter blue and black ballet slippers.

"If you're going to remodel anything," she said as Lynn brought in the grocery bags, "it should be that bathroom."

"All in good time, Mom." She placed the bags on the trestle table.

"I don't understand why you keep putting me in there."

Lynn faced her. "It has the only private bath on the first two stories right now. *And* there's your arthritis."

For once, Nancy held her tongue.

Jax had decided to jog around town after dropping off his duffel, taking in the sights, trying to see how much he remembered after all this time. He hadn't exactly been familiar with these streets during his youth, having spent most of his time on the ranch and coming in only for school and occasional weekend shopping trips under his father's watchful eye, nor did any of it elicit good memories. It was all simply neutral, even Good Shepherd Church. His parents hadn't been churchgoers, which had been fine by him. He was sure he wouldn't have wanted to be there. Not back then.

He recognized most of the downtown, however, and saw only a few changes. The bakery for one. Then a door with an inscrutable sign that he didn't remember. The corner hardware store remained, probably serving people who needed last-minute items for some project. The lumberyard handled most larger purchases.

Maude's diner still bore the fading name City Café, although even in his childhood everyone had referred to it as Maude's. He was pleased to see it. He imagined that café was such a pillar in this community that the whole town would collapse without it.

There was a small new market for organic food. He wondered how they were hanging on. Something must have changed around here.

Then he saw a boarded-up storefront bearing a sign, Tex-Mex Restaurant, Coming Eventually.

A snort of laughter escaped him. He wondered what kind of problems the owners were dealing with but handling with a sense of humor.

By the time he arrived back at the boardinghouse, he'd learned that nothing held any attachment for him. Not even a hint of nostalgia.

God, what a dork he'd been back then.

Since he was stuck here until the sheriff concluded he wasn't an arsonist, he decided to make the best of it. Otherwise he'd have left tomorrow at the latest, having satisfied his curiosity, having shown any interested parties that he wasn't that dork anymore. The desire wasn't an angry one. Just answering an old need to be *somebody*, even in this backwater.

But tomorrow he could pick up a knapsack, a few supplies, and head toward the mountains to hike. It had always been one of his favorite things when he could escape, hiking in those mountains.

When he arrived back at the house, the first person he saw was Nancy West, stepping out of the kitchen. The delicious aroma of roasting chicken reached him.

"Join us for dinner, Jackson," she said with a broad smile. "We'll have plenty."

How could he politely refuse? "Thanks. I need to shower first."

So that was the way the wind was blowing, he thought with a tremor of amusement. Nancy West wanted to play matchmaker. He suspected her machinations would mortify Lynn.

This could get interesting.

Madge Kearney had her own ideas of *interesting*. They all involved Jackson Stone. She'd tried to get his attention in high school, mostly because she'd wanted to be the first and only girl who could. It wasn't even that she really wanted *him*, but that wasn't the point. Then one day he'd smiled at her and she'd believed she'd crossed the first hurdle. Before anything else happened, he'd left for the Marines.

She was ready to try again, but then that officious Lynn Macy had intervened. And now it wasn't simply a matter of counting coup. He had turned into one hell of a gorgeous man, and that uniform!

Unfortunately, she'd already heard he was rooming with Lynn because the motel had burned down. She'd have to find a way past that before Lynn snared him.

The contest was on.

Much to Lynn's relief, her mother decided to join some friends for cards that evening after dinner. Nancy might have moved away years ago, but she kept some ties with old girlfriends.

Nancy walked out, free as a bird, leaving the dinner cleanup to Lynn. Lynn didn't mind. A brief release from her mother's needling was welcome. And Nancy still hadn't mentioned how long she intended to stay.

She heard a footstep behind her and looked up as she cleared the table.

"Let me take over," Jax said, smiling. "If I could clear up Hasty's diner last night, I can sure do the dishes for a lady who cooked dinner."

"I can do it," Lynn said automatically. *I can do it* had been a refrain of her entire life with Nancy, and it always burst to the forefront when her mother was around. *Look, Mom, I can do it by myself.*

Inwardly, she shook her head. What was it about parents that brought out the child in everyone?

"I'm sure you can," Jax answered. "Hell, near as I can

tell you're rebuilding this entire house. I saw the stack of drywall and ceramic tile on one side of the…dining room, I guess it is?"

Lynn laughed. "Eventually. For now, it's storage."

"So let me help with this. My mother raised me to believe the cook shouldn't have to clean up. Just grab a seat and supervise the putting away."

She sat, still smiling. "If you're up to tolerating my boys."

"Your boys?" He began filling the sink with soapy water.

"My roomers. I suppose that's what I should call them. That or my students. It's what I usually do, but somehow *my boys* fits these three better. Especially Will. You'll see when you meet him. They should be trailing in soon, bringing doggie bags or cold pizza or whatever they think will stoke their fires for a night of studying. So they'll move in on the fridge."

"No problem. If necessary, I'll step out of the way. So how did you get into taking roomers?"

She put her chin in her hand, frankly enjoying the sight of his broad back and narrow hips as he washed. "It helps with my overhead. I'm plowing a lot of Matt's insurance money into fixing this place up. It was his family home and it had started to go to ruin after Matt's dad died and while Matt was away so much. My own little project."

"It hardly looks little. I'm sorry about Matt. As I recall, he was one of the good guys."

"He was." That tide of grief began to well in her, and she tried to push it away. It'd be there later. It always was.

"So what has been the hardest part of this project so far?" Jax asked.

"Gingerbread," she answered emphatically.

He turned from the sink just enough to look at her. "Gingerbread?"

"You see all that fancy trim on the outside of the house, running along all the eaves and the front of the porch? Even the porch railings?"

"Yeah. It's charming."

"Now it is. When I took over, it was a total mess. Try scraping off all that flaking paint and then repainting it. If this place weren't on the historical registry, I'd have pulled it all off."

"How'd it get on the registry?"

"Must have been Matt's father. I don't know. What I *do* know is that I have to keep the outside exactly the same. So the gingerbread remains."

He was making fast work of the dishes. "Pain in the neck, keeping it the same?"

"Only that gingerbread, and I couldn't afford to hire anyone to do it. Painting the whole house except for the gingerbread would have been cheap by comparison. But it looks good now and should stay that way for at least another five years. Which, if I jump on it right away, means I won't have to do the scraping."

He rinsed the last of the silverware. "Towel?"

"In the drawer on the left of the sink."

"Tell me where to put everything."

"Silverware drawer to the right. Just open the cabinets and you'll see where everything else goes."

He nodded and set to work. "What changes are you making? Or are you making any?"

"Well, I finished off my attic apartment, got rid of a lot of ugly furniture and replaced flooring. And I put new drywall in the rooms I rent."

"Why new drywall?"

"Because the walls needed a heck of a lot of spackling, and a ton of old wallpaper needed to be steamed off. Drywall turned out to be easier and less expensive, believe it or not. I was even able to save the wainscoting. Next, I need to get onto the living room. Water damage from before I replaced the roof."

He finished drying the washed dishes and reached for the roasting pan.

Then the boys arrived together. As predicted, all of them carried bags or pizza boxes. Ready to burn the midnight oil.

As a group they came to the kitchen with their loads of treasure and paused.

Lynn made the introductions as Jax was drying the roasting pan. "Will, Barry and Tom," she said, pointing each one out. "Jax Stone. My new roomer for a little while."

Jax stepped to one side after saying hello, roasting pan in his hands. "Help yourselves to the fridge. I can stay out of the way."

But she could see the three lads were a little intimidated. Not only was Jax obviously a mature man, but muscles showed through his sweatshirt and jeans. He was, she thought wryly, clearly not a college student like them.

"Why only a little while?" asked Will of the bright orange hair and freckles. The other two leaned toward the nondescript.

"I got burned out of the motel," Jax answered. "Lynn was kind enough to offer me a room. We sorta grew up together."

Attended the same schools more like, Lynn thought wryly. Several years apart. "And, guys, my mom's visiting. She's in the downstairs bedroom."

The three of them looked a little overwhelmed. They

were used to pretty much having the house to themselves, except for Lynn.

"Great," said Tom cheerfully. "Lynn won't be so alone."

They stuffed some of their goodies into the fridge and carried the rest upstairs with the excuse of exams.

"Ouch," said Lynn as she listened to them thunder up the stairs. "I won't be so much alone."

"Well, you won't be," Jax answered. "Like it or not. Where does this go?"

"I keep all the pans in the oven."

And now came the difficult part, Lynn thought. At this time of evening she usually sought out the peace and privacy of her attic apartment, but she couldn't send Jax to his room. It seemed rude to just leave him on his own down here. Why? He was simply another roomer.

Then he spoke. "I think the sheriff suspects me of arson."

Shock stilled her for several seconds. Then, "Come up to my aerie," she said impulsively. "It's more private."

She could see he was startled, but then she had startled herself.

She led him through the door that closed off her private stairway at the bottom, feeling a bit strange to invite him up here. The only people she'd invited before had been some of her girlfriends.

After she reached the top, she flipped on the lights and turned around to watch him mount the last few steps.

He paused, taking in the entire studio apartment. "I really like this. I never thought an attic could look like this."

"I'm fond of it. I used to think it was just storage space, but then I saw all this fine wood. All it needed was some TLC. Grab a seat. Want a beer?"

"Love one."

He settled into one of the padded armchairs in front of her electric fireplace. As she passed it to give him a beer, she flipped the logs on, producing heat and a warm glow.

"One heads-up," she told him. "No alcoholic beverages in the downstairs fridge. My boys aren't of legal age yet and there's no point in tempting them."

"Not a problem."

She took the other chair, ignoring the recliner to one side. "What's this about being suspected of arson?"

He took a pull on his longneck. "It's subtle. I was gently brought in for questioning, asked about my plans, and then Gage called you immediately to see if you'd rent me a room. That quick offer of a room made it clear."

"Wow," she breathed, astonished. "But was it arson?"

He shook his head. "No one knows yet, according to Gage. He said he's getting ahead of the game before memories change. And I *am* the new guy in town."

"Well, except for the itinerant truckers." She bit her lower lip. "That must have been scary, waking up in a burning room."

"I didn't have a chance to be scared. Besides, I'm no longer as easily scared as I might once have been."

Sipping his beer, he looked around again. "Lynn, you've done a fantastic job with this. I'm surprised you ever leave."

"Work must be done. And despite what my mother said, I'm enjoying it. There's something deeply satisfying about working with your hands and seeing the results. I've also learned a lot."

Jax looked around once more, then turned toward her. "If I'm overstaying, just let me know. This apartment feels private." Like a personal retreat. He'd been surprised when she asked him up here, and he'd seen her own startlement in the way her head jerked, a very small movement. That invitation had slipped out. He'd felt awkward about accepting it, but knew he'd be rude if he didn't. Now he felt uncomfortable staying up here.

She surprised him with a gentle smile. "If you don't feel right about being here, you know where the stairs are. They're hard to miss. In some ways you haven't changed, Master Gunnery Sergeant."

He stiffened a bit. "Meaning?"

"I remember the old days. Somewhat. I *do* remember that you must have felt like a fish out of water. I guess this place is making you feel that way again, because you sure can't feel that way on the job."

He shook his head, feeling almost dissected. "Of course not."

She leaned forward, placing her beer bottle on a small table that stood between the chairs. "I used to be terribly shy," she confided. "I finally found a way around it."

"What's that?"

"To have a role to play. A place where I know exactly what I'm doing and what to say."

He gripped the beer bottle tightly, his gaze straying away to land on a framed wedding portrait of her and Matt that was sitting on top of a bookcase. She must still hurt.

He rose abruptly, looking for a place to put his empty bottle. "I need to go."

"Leave the bottle on the table. Sorry I was so forward."

"No, you weren't. It's okay."

He waved her to remain seated while he strode to the stairs. He hadn't realized anyone could strip him so bare in such a short time.

She'd hit the nail on the head, though. Right on the

head. Master Gunnery Sergeant Jackson Stone had a clearly defined role.

Jax Stone, back in his hometown, didn't really.

Chapter 4

Mom!

The word in her head slammed Lynn from sleeping to waking in an instant. The woman would be downstairs, brewing her inevitable tea, and trying to interrogate whatever unfortunate soul passed by the kitchen. Her boys didn't deserve to be made uncomfortable that way.

Sheesh!

She hurried through her washing up, then, wrapped in her green velour robe with fuzzy slippers on her feet, she hurried downstairs to provide protection for her boys.

As she feared, Nancy was in the kitchen holding Will captive by courtesy, the youngster not knowing how to escape politely.

"Will?" Lynn said briskly. "You're going to be late for class."

Will looked so relieved it was almost funny. "Yeah. Thanks for reminding me, Lynn." He dashed away.

"Such a nice boy," Nancy said, sipping her tea.

"Then why were you giving him the third degree?"

"I was doing no such thing!"

"I know you, Mom. Leave my boys alone."

A frosty silence descended, which was fine by Lynn. God, she needed some coffee before facing more of this. She crossed the icy space to start brewing a pot.

"You know," Nancy said finally, "you can't get to know people without talking to them."

"Questioning descends to a whole other level." Lynn turned, leaning back against the counter while the coffeepot gurgled and steamed behind her.

"Why do you think I was questioning him?"

Lynn swallowed a sigh. She spoke quietly. "Because I know you. You really don't need to discover everyone in Will's family tree, or why he decided to go to the college here, whether he has a girlfriend and what his future plans are."

"It's just ordinary interest. Besides, you've invited three strangers into your home—I'll leave Jackson out of this for the moment—"

"Thank God," Lynn muttered.

"Anyway, I'm a concerned mother. How did you choose these boys?"

"The college chose them. They send me students they believe won't cause me any trouble."

"*Believe*? You don't check into them yourself?"

Lynn turned to pour herself a cup of coffee. This morning she indulged herself in some cream. "Believing the college has served me well over the last two years."

At last, she sat facing Nancy across the trestle table. Her mother was, as always, dressed in high-quality clothes, the businesslike image she'd cultivated since Lynn's dad had walked out. Today her color of choice was a creamy rose with a white scarf loosely wrapped around her neck.

Lynn herself hadn't worn much but work clothes since Matt's death. She liked it that way. Right now, however, given the chill of the night that still clung, she was grateful for her comfortable robe.

Surprising her, Nancy poured a second cup of tea from the same pot.

Lynn sipped her coffee, then put her chin in her hand. More was to come, so she tried a stalling tactic. "How's life in Cheyenne?"

Nancy brightened. "So much better than it was here. There's plenty to do, and I really like working part-time as a paralegal. Which reminds me…"

Of course, Lynn thought. Turnaround. Fast enough to cause whiplash.

"Why must you take roomers?"

"It only makes sense. This is a big house. The rent helps. And honestly, I like the feeling that the house isn't empty."

"You must be burning up Matt's life insurance with all the remodeling you're doing."

Lynn felt her face freeze. Financials were off-limits. "Far from it," she said flatly, trying to close the subject.

"Well, I guess all this work is making the property worth more."

In fact, this house was something of a white elephant in a town that always seemed to be verging on going bust. But she didn't care. It was Matt's legacy, his father's legacy.

"Mom, I like my mornings quiet. Time to wake up."

Nancy smiled. "You always were a sleepyhead."

But at least her mother fell silent, finishing her cup of tea and going to make fresh.

Lynn enjoyed her first and second coffees in magnificent silence, but as her brain slipped into waking mode, she had a question. "Do you have plans while you're here?"

"Just to catch up with my daughter." Nancy smiled. "I'm going to be working."

"That's all right. I'll watch."

Lynn could have groaned. She loved her mother, she really, truly did, but Nancy was easier to take from a distance.

"What's your current job?" Nancy asked brightly.

"The living room. There's water damage to the walls from before I reroofed the house." Right now she was hoping that when she pulled out the old walls she didn't find rotted wood.

Nancy frowned. "You shouldn't have done that roof by yourself."

"I didn't. I just helped." As if she could have brought in pallets of shingles and raised them by herself. Not to mention replacing all the rotting plywood up there. A patch job she could do alone, but an entire roof? She knew her limits.

"I hope you brighten up that room. It's so dark right now."

Fashions left over from the old days. The long-ago old days. Wallpaper that had never been bright to begin with and that had darkened with age. Even the bay window didn't provide enough light to make a difference.

Matt's father had shown little inclination to change anything. So had Matt's mother, come to that. When they'd both died, his father to a stroke, his mother to cancer, Matt had inherited this house that hadn't been updated in over fifty years, maybe more.

Old items, she'd been discovering, could be endlessly repaired if she wanted to keep them. Newer stuff not so much.

"I do hate this green in here," Nancy remarked.

"Me, too." For once they agreed.

Nancy settled in with her fresh pot of tea. "Are you seeing anyone?"

Lynn just looked at her mother. "Do I feel you stepping on my toes?"

Finally, Nancy laughed. "You're right. None of my business. Well, if you don't mind, I'll go to the grocery and get something to cook for dinner. Maybe we should invite that nice soldier."

"Marine, Mom."

"Well, I just don't see the difference. Anyway, I'm off!"

Invite that nice soldier. Let the matchmaking begin.

Alone in the kitchen at last, Lynn giggled. Her mom was such a trip. One that had to be kept under light control, but still a trip.

She wondered if she should warn Jax, then decided he would figure it out himself. It might even be fun to watch.

In the afternoon, while Nancy buzzed around the kitchen wearing an old apron she'd discovered near the back of the pantry, Lynn studied the living room walls, trying to decide where to begin. Obviously all the floor and window molding needed to be removed before anything else, but the ceiling molding should stay if she could save it. Or was she going over-the-top with that? Remembering how miserable it had been to paint all that gingerbread, she wondered how much time she wanted to spend on those ornate moldings that had, unfortunately, been painted. Stripping and refinishing them might take longer than the rest of the room altogether.

Still, she had to find out at least some of the damage behind the plaster walls before she made any other plans.

It killed her to have to remove the plaster, knowing she couldn't replace it, but there was no choice. Water stains marked the wallpaper, especially the outside wall.

Regretting it, she picked up a large hammer and smashed the wall near the biggest stain. Lath greeted her, although she should have expected it under plaster. Oh, man, that stuff was irreplaceable, too. Too bad, she decided. She *had* to know how much damage the leaking porch roof had done. Plaster tumbled around her feet and made a small dust cloud.

"You ought to be wearing a dust mask."

Lynn turned and saw Jax standing in the doorway. "I know," she admitted. "I'm just taking a peek. Trying to determine the extent of the damage. I'm hoping none of the wood frame has rotted."

She noted his dark blue jogging suit. "Been out for a run?"

"Yup. I kinda feel like a prisoner even if I'm not. Strange. Anyway, I'm not used to just hanging around. If you want any help with the demolition, let me know." He grinned. "I'm good at smashing things."

"Too bad you weren't here when I moved the furniture out. That stuff was *heavy*."

He laughed, increasing the level of attraction she felt toward him. Making her heart flutter.

Oh, God, she didn't need this. She wasn't *ready* for this. A man in uniform. A uniform had gotten Matt killed. Guilt plagued her, too, a sense that her reactions to Jax were like cheating on Matt. She told herself the guilt was ridiculous, but it clung anyway.

Jax joined them for dinner that night. Instead of letting Nancy steer the conversation, he turned to Lynn. "How's it going?"

"Well, I made a few more holes, then spritzed some water to bring down the dust level," she answered. "Next I'm going to have to rip out some of the lath. Then I get my snake inspection camera and look inside the wall. My primary concern is that the wood frame might have rotted. Or worse, grown black mold."

He nodded, slicing a piece off his pan-fried chicken breast. "That would be a huge problem. Any idea how the wall got wet?"

"Maintenance wasn't the best before I took over," she answered, helping herself to more asparagus. "Since there was no damage to the wall upstairs, I'm thinking the water came from the porch roof. The flashing was loose."

"That'd do it," he agreed.

Nancy laughed. "I know nothing about flashing."

Lynn answered. "It's the metal that joins the roof to the house and prevents water from getting in."

Nancy nodded understanding. "A bad problem."

"Worsened by the fact that most people don't discover it until they have some interior damage. Or until they replace the roof. The roofer I hired reckoned the roof was well over thirty years old. I'm lucky the damage wasn't worse."

Nancy spoke again. "I still think this house is a white elephant and you should dump it as quickly as you can."

Lynn couldn't answer. Her throat tightened and it became difficult to breathe. Her mother just couldn't seem to understand her emotional connection to this house through Matt. Or how much she still missed Matt.

Jax surprised her. "I don't think it's a white elephant. It's a great house and Lynn is making it beautiful."

She shot him a look of gratitude, suspecting he understood more than her mother did.

While they were clearing the table, Lynn heard a

knock at the front door. "I'll get it," she said, wondering who it might be. She wasn't expecting any deliveries, and with autumn nights setting in earlier, casual drop-ins during the evening were rarer.

She opened the door with a pleasant smile formed on her face, then felt it freeze as she saw her brother-in-law, Luke.

"Hi, Luke."

Even in the kitchen, with the clatter of dishes and running water, Jax heard Lynn's tone change.

"Aren't you going to invite me in?" a man's voice said.

"We're just finishing the dinner cleanup, Luke. This isn't the best time."

"Hey, I'm family."

"That's a matter of opinion."

The man's voice spoke again, wheedling. "Look, you won the lawsuit. At least be nice."

That did it. Jax wiped his hands on a kitchen towel and stepped into the small foyer. A man of average height with shaggy blond hair brushed his way past Lynn, forcing her to close the door behind him or let the cold night in.

"It's settled, Luke," she said tautly. "There's no more to say."

Luke looked past her. "What's this? A bodyguard?"

"Is there a problem, Lynn?" Jax asked. He stood with arms akimbo and sternness filling his face, the way he looked at troublesome men under his command.

"It's just Matt's brother," she said over her shoulder. "No threat but a major nuisance."

"Is that any way to talk about me?" Luke asked. "The issue is settled, now it's time to make up."

Lynn threw up a hand impatiently. "I don't feel like

making up, Luke. You put me through legal hell for two years while I was still grieving. All because you thought you should have part of an inheritance your father and my husband didn't want to give you."

Luke frowned. "That wasn't fair, either."

"Maybe not. But it wasn't my decision and I'm sticking by Matt's. So what do you want?"

Luke spread his hands. "Like I said, we're family. Time to make amends."

"Not yet and not now," Lynn replied firmly. She reached to open the door. "Next time call first."

Anger reddened Luke's face, but he followed her implied order, stepping out into the darkness. Lynn slammed the door behind him.

Jax watched her turn, then look uncomfortable. "Sorry about that."

"What was going on?"

"Oh, I can tell you," Nancy said from the kitchen doorway. "Dishes are done and I'm making fresh coffee for the two of you. And how about some key lime pie? It's just about defrosted enough for serving."

Jax didn't want to turn down the invitation. Nancy amused him. "Sounds good to me. Lynn?"

Her cheeks had pinkened. "I behaved rudely."

Nancy shook her head. "You weren't rude. That slithering snake doesn't deserve the time of day."

Jax raised his brows and wondered if Nancy would share the story behind this. *Slithering snake?* The phrase made him want to laugh, but now he honestly wanted to know what was going on.

One thing he'd discovered in a rush: he didn't like to see Lynn upset like that. Nor did he like to hear her apologize for a situation she hadn't created.

With the three of them seated at the trestle table, Jax

noted that the passage of Lynn's anger and embarrassment had left her looking incredibly tired.

Maybe it wasn't his place, but he asked anyway. "Who was that guy?"

Lynn didn't answer but Nancy did. "Her brother-in-law. *Ex* brother-in-law."

"Ex?"

"Matt's brother."

Lynn spoke wearily. "Mom, don't."

"Why not? Everyone in this town knows the whole ugly story. Just sit there and eat your pie. Jax has a right to some answers because I think he was prepared to defend the battlements." She eyed Jax favorably.

"It's a hideous story," Lynn said quietly. "Let's not."

"Let's do," Nancy said firmly.

Part of Jax wanted to shut Nancy down when Lynn clearly didn't want to discuss this. Another part wanted to know what was going on, why Luke had tried to barge in that way. And since he was going to be around indefinitely it seemed, he wanted to know what Lynn was up against in case he could help. But he'd also noticed there was no good way to stop Nancy when she had her mind made up. The two women were alike more than they probably knew. Stubborn.

Nancy served him another slice of pie. He hadn't realized he'd wolfed down the first. Stuffing his mouth to keep quiet, he supposed.

"At its root," Nancy said, "it's all very simple. When Matt's father died, he left the house to Matt. Not a single thing to Luke."

"Why not?" Jax couldn't resist asking.

"Luke is a ne'er do well, a ladies' man, a wastrel. Burned through every dime he ever got, apparently lives off whatever woman he happens to be with at the time.

Then there was a short prison sentence for drug possession. I think those boys' father had had enough. So he left it all to Matt. Probably hoping that Luke wouldn't get Matt into his financial mess because he owned half the house."

Jax could understand that, but he could also understand how that must have made Luke feel. There couldn't be anything quite like the sting of being cut out of your own father's will.

"Anyway," Nancy continued, rising to refresh coffee cups and her own tea, "Matt apparently didn't feel much different about Luke. Their dad's will didn't change a damn thing. Luke was still running around, mooching off women and friends and living the high life on other people's dimes."

Jax looked at Lynn and saw her nod sadly.

She spoke. "He was so messed up, Jax."

"Still is, from what I hear," Nancy said. "Anyway, if Matt had wanted to, he could have given Luke half stake in this house. Evidently he didn't, because he left everything to Lynn."

Jax nodded understanding, but he was beginning to see how this story was playing out. Terrible for Lynn.

"The long and the short of it," Nancy said, "is that Matt was hardly cold in the ground before Luke filed a lawsuit to gain half ownership in this house. He lost his appeal just three months ago."

Lynn sighed.

"And now," Jax remarked, "he wants to be friends."

"Exactly!" Nancy's answer was emphatic. "Not likely, not after dragging my daughter through a legal mess when she should have been grieving."

"I *did* grieve," Lynn said flatly. "He couldn't prevent that. But more than once I just wanted to throw in the towel and let him have it. But Matt's wishes…" She trailed off.

Jax now saw Lynn in a different light. She wasn't just a vivacious widow with a project. She was a strong woman with a mission. Remarkable.

He repeated a phrase he'd heard more than once. "Nobody ever grows younger from a lawsuit."

He saw a faint smile crack Lynn's weary face.

"This Luke sounds vengeful," he added.

Lynn shook her head. "All hat and no cattle. Apparently he's past being nasty to me."

"I wouldn't count on it," Nancy said. "For heaven's sake, Lynn, he's been taking women for a ride since he was eighteen. Hardly does a lick of work from what I've heard. Mark my words, now he'll be all sweet, trying to get something from you."

"Well, he won't," Lynn answered firmly. "I'd have been a softer touch before the lawsuit, before he grew nasty with me. That ship has sailed."

Later, upstairs in his room, listening to the sounds of music and voices from the students' rooms, Jax turned the story around in his head.

Bad enough to lose your husband without his closest relative dragging you into court. He was glad Nancy had ignored her daughter and explained the situation.

But he felt awful for Lynn. In a town this small, Luke would be hard to escape. And the streak of vengeance he'd already displayed boded ill.

Damn!

Chapter 5

In the morning, Jax received an unexpected phone call while he was out taking a walk near the junior college. He was officially on leave, all his friends knew it, and phoning for casual chats wasn't customary. It had to be official, he thought grimly as he tugged his phone out of the breast pocket of his camo.

The call came from Lieutenant Hugh Briggs, a prosecutor with the Naval Judge Advocate's office. The two had become acquainted after the war crimes trial of Theodore Albright a year or so ago.

"Master Gunnery Sergeant Stone," Hugh said. "Briggs here."

The use of his military rank rather than his first name put Jax on immediate alert. He responded formally. "Something wrong, Lieutenant?"

"Well, that depends on how you look at it. This isn't an official call, by the way, so let's skip the ranks. I used yours just to, ah, get your complete attention. Because while this isn't official, neither is it a joke. Put your ears on, Jax."

"Copy."

"You alone?"

"Right now. I'm walking through cattle country. Any mooing you hear isn't me." His tension wasn't easing any despite his joking. Briggs needed to get to the point.

Hugh laughed. "Got it. Wide-open spaces populated by prime rib and T-bone, huh?"

"The cattle might have a different idea."

"Might could be," Hugh answered.

Silence crackled a bit with static while Jax stood still, waiting.

"Okay," Hugh said. His voice had tensed. "There's something I want you to be aware of. Again, it's not official. No determination has been made."

"Understood."

"You remember the court martial? When you were a juror?"

"Yeah. The only one I've served on, not something I'll ever forget." The photos alone had twisted his gut, and he'd seen plenty in battle. The testimony from Albright's fellow soldiers had made them even worse.

"Well, here's the thing. Again, no one's certain, but the first steps are being taken in an investigation. An investigation that might take months or years, so a heads-up is the least you deserve."

Jax's insides tightened, a tingling crept along his spine. Not fear, he knew fear intimately. Preparedness. "Shoot."

"Two of your fellow jurors are dead. The first was put down to suicide but the second one… Let's just say questions arose. Two jurors within such a short time frame struck a few people as suspicious. Maybe not, maybe a coincidence."

"How likely would this be, Hugh? One in a million?"

"Marines are mostly young and healthy as you know, and while military suicides are sadly common, the second death wasn't easily explained away. So just listen. Like I said, an investigation will take next to forever. There were people in Albright's own squad who denied he'd done anything wrong despite the testimony from others. People who consider him a brother. You know the dynamics."

Indeed Jax did. Brotherhood was forged on a battlefield. He'd thought it stunning that any of the squad had stepped forward with their stories of atrocity. But they had, which made the acts even more sickening. When your brothers-in-arms condemned you, it was bad. Worse than bad. Maybe evil.

"I'm in the back of beyond, not in Denver yet, Hugh, if this is a warning."

"Consider it one. Like I said, no proof, but dangerous to ignore. And when has being in the back of beyond ever protected anyone from a determined Marine? Remember that."

"I guess I should thank you, Hugh."

"As long as you don't shoot the messenger. Just keep high alert. Don't let your guard drop. These two guys were near a military base. You're hanging out there somewhere like a staked-out goat."

After the call disconnected, Jax stuffed his phone back into his pocket and resumed walking, but his head was turning over what Hugh had just told him.

He was quite sure Hugh should have kept his mouth shut, but had decided to buck the rules to call him. Which in itself meant plenty.

Someone was killing jurors from the trial? It was mind-boggling.

And entirely possible.

The idea so offended him that his stomach turned hollow. Then rage crept in. Everything in the code should prevent this. But apparently someone had gone well past the code onto a plane of his own.

Above the law.

When he returned to Lynn's house, he heard some hammering from the living room and poked his head in to see what she was up to. She was knocking out more plaster, but wearing a mask this time. She had also pried out some narrow strips of wood.

"How's it going?" he asked casually.

"Well enough. I'm kicking up too much dust. I need to cover that door with plastic, but I didn't get out my ladder." She shrugged and gave a small laugh. "I don't know why, but I'm tripping over myself today, doing things out of order."

"Got that plastic anywhere?"

"In the next room." She brushed her hands together and stood looking at the mess. A Shop-Vac stood nearby, but she didn't reach for it.

"You find anything wrong?"

"I need to check a few places after I pry out some more of the lath. When the dust settles, I'll bring my laptop and camera in here and start looking around. Cross your fingers for me, Jax. I don't want to have to replace the framing."

"Fingers crossed," he assured her. "I'd like to help if you'll let me." As if he'd be around long enough to do anything majorly useful.

"Bored?"

He could almost see her smile behind her dust mask. "I like to keep busy." Certainly true.

"Help is always welcome."

He glanced around. "Where's Nancy?"

"You mean because she didn't leap out at you?" Lynn asked drily. "She headed out with some girlfriends. Tea at the bakery or something. Anyway, I need to clean up."

He stepped back from the doorway. "Let me get that plastic up for you." He scanned the wide door frame. "Looks like I won't need a ladder."

"Quit bragging about your height."

He flashed a smile. "Accident of nature."

Twenty minutes later he had the heavy plastic stapled up across the top, locking in all the dust.

"Thanks, Jax. I really appreciate it."

"Always glad to be of service." He paused, wondering what he was thinking and why he was going to ask. "Like to join me for lunch at Maude's?"

She tilted her head to one side. "Yeah. I would. Sounds good. Let me get rid of this dust and we can go. I'll only be a minute."

Jax certainly wasn't the introverted high school student any longer, but he was still reserved. Very reserved. His face revealed little, if anything, and sometimes she wondered if his feelings were as well contained as everything else.

Probably.

She didn't waste a lot of time up in her apartment, just washed her face and hands, brushed plaster dust out of her hair and put on fresh jeans and a bright blue flannel shirt. After a quick look in the mirror, she grabbed a blue bandanna to tie back her auburn hair.

That would do for Maude's. Pulling her jacket from a

hook by the attic door, she met Jax in the vestibule. Still wearing his camos and desert boots, with an olive web belt around his waist, he held one of those billed hats with an eight-point crown. Matt had told her about them. *Utility cover*. Different from the other services.

"Sorry to keep you waiting," she said.

He shook his head. "You didn't. I expected you to take longer."

She flashed a grin at him. "Thought I was going to do all that girlie makeup stuff?"

That drew a smile from him. "You don't need it and I'm glad you didn't."

Nice compliment, she thought as they stepped outside. He put on his cover while she pulled on her jacket. The breeze had stiffened and grown chillier.

"I guess Jazz and Adam had their wedding just in time," she remarked, zipping up. "Winter's breath is blowing. Do you want me to drive us? Are you cold?"

Jax shook his head. "I'm fine with walking if you are."

They strode along the sidewalk at a fairly brisk pace that felt good to Lynn. She worked hard physically, but nothing like the stretching her muscles enjoyed from walking.

The sun peeked from behind a cloud and cast buttery light everywhere.

"I've sometimes thought," Lynn remarked, "that I can tell the season by the color of the light. Silly, I guess, when the sun is at the same elevation in both spring and fall. But something about autumn sunlight seems more golden."

"That's an interesting thought. I never really noticed."

She shrugged. "I'm weird."

"I wouldn't say so."

They turned a corner, getting close to the diner.

"Heard anything about the cause of that fire yet?" she asked.

"No," Jax answered. "But it probably takes time to make a determination."

So calm, she thought. Stable, without any apparent emotional ups and downs. He didn't even seem in a rush to learn about the fire that might have killed him. Inevitably she wondered if this was training or if this was the real man. But how could she ask? None of her business.

But that didn't keep the question from escaping anyway. "Does anything excite you?"

He stopped walking and he transfixed her with a pair of very dark eyes. "When it matters, a helluva lot."

"So the fire doesn't matter to you?"

"What matters is that someone lost their livelihood and one poor bastard lost his life. As for why, that's not for me to discover. I'm used to awaiting the outcome of investigations."

Lynn shrugged inwardly as they approached the diner. He was right, of course. But among friends she was used to hearing speculations of all kinds, and sometimes talking things to death.

Jax evidently wasn't like that. Which meant that even casual conversation might be difficult with him.

They stepped inside Maude's and conversation came to a sudden halt as everyone at the tables turned to look at Jax. *The grapevine must be afire*, Lynn thought with amusement. The prodigal returns? Or just, *Hey, have you seen what that strange kid has become?*

Lynn had to stifle a giggle. Maybe when she caught up with one of her friends she could find out.

Conversation, along with the clatter of crockery and flatware, resumed as fast as it had halted.

Lynn pointed out a table near the back and headed that

way, unzipping her jacket as she went. Jax had already removed his hat, and when they sat, he placed it on the far end of the table.

Maude's daughter, Mavis, a stocky woman, arrived promptly with coffee mugs and the plastic menus.

"Thanks, Mavis," Lynn said.

"Might be a few minutes," Mavis grumped. "We got busy."

"That's good, right?"

"Depends on who's making us busy."

As she stomped away, Lynn looked at Jax to see the corners of his eyes crinkled with amusement.

"I know," she said. "I wonder what's been going on here."

"Your guess is probably better than mine."

Maude and her daughter were the county's most famous grumps, but Lynn had never heard them complain about their clientele. She looked around the room, wondering what subsurface currents she couldn't detect.

Jax spoke, interrupting her thoughts. "I wonder if Maude has half a rhino on the menu."

She grinned. "That hungry?"

"For some reason, yeah. I promise not to embarrass you, though."

"As long as you don't eat that rhino raw, I won't be."

He laughed quietly.

Wow, another laugh, Lynn thought as her heart did that fluttery thing again. Maybe he wasn't as staid and sober as he usually seemed.

Mavis returned carrying a brushed aluminum carafe. She slammed it on the table in front of them. "It's hot and fresh."

Lynn looked at the carafe in amazement. "When did you get these?"

"Last week. Ain't nobody got time to be running around filling coffee cups all the time. I figure that'll take care of you, but if you need more, I'm not invisible."

A laugh escaped Lynn, and Mavis completely astonished her by winking. "Bringing up Ma," she said quietly, then stomped away with their orders.

"I guess I missed something," Jax remarked.

"Only that Mavis is bent on changing her mother's ways, I gathered. The carafes must be the start."

He nodded, smiling faintly. "A good one. I never came here much when I was a kid. I don't exactly remember the way things were."

"They certainly didn't include insulated carafes. Mostly slamming coffee cups. And now you can get a latte, too, if you want."

He nodded. Well, Lynn thought, there didn't seem to be much to say about it. Conversational dead end.

Their burgers arrived, thick and juicy. Jax had ordered two of them, along with a side of broccoli. Lynn had chosen the side salad. In between them stood a heap of hot fries. She could have laughed at the way Mavis had decided they were going to share them.

They'd hardly started eating when a familiar voice said, "I hope you don't mind me joining you," Madge Kearney said sweetly. "The place is too crowded for me to find my own table."

"Help yourself," Lynn answered with a smile, indicating the chair beside her. But instead Madge took the seat beside Jax. Lynn stifled an urge to laugh.

Madge wore a red dress with a low neck, allowing her ample cleavage to show. A bit too much for the weather and this diner. Over the back of the chair she'd hung a red jacket.

"Oh," said Madge, "those burgers look heavenly. Mind?" She helped herself to a fry.

Lynn looked at Jax and thought she saw a smile in his eyes. Did that mean he wasn't fooled or that he was enjoying the unexpected attention? She'd have to wait it out and see.

For all Madge claimed the burgers looked good, and freely helped herself to another fry, she ordered the chef salad.

"Have to watch my figure," she said on a girlish laugh.

Jax glanced her way. "Physical work tends to do that, too."

For an instant Madge looked miffed, but then her face smoothed. "I bet you do a lot of that," she said to Jax.

"You might say so. Lynn does a lot, too."

Madge's gaze drifted toward Lynn. *My*, thought Lynn, *she's angry with me*. Not that it mattered.

The salad arrived quickly, along with an icy diet cola. Madge returned her attention to Jax after she speared a small piece of lettuce. "You were burned out of the motel?" she asked.

"Yes," Jax answered when he'd swallowed and could speak politely.

Lynn bit into her juicy burger and dabbed her chin unapologetically. Good stuff. And with her mouth full, she had an excuse not to speak or let her tongue run away with her.

"How ever did you find Lynn's place?" Madge asked after another nibble.

"The sheriff arranged it." Jax wiped his own mouth with a napkin and looked at Madge. "I'm under suspicion, you know."

Madge's eyes widened.

Lynn wondered why he'd chosen to say that.

Madge cleared her throat. "But you wouldn't have…"

"I might have," Jax answered flatly, then took a big bite of his burger.

"No one could think that!" Madge protested. "You only just got back here and you were always so—" She broke off without finishing, as if trying to find a nice way to say something.

Jax turned his head to look at her. "I've been away a long time, Madge. It *is* Madge, right?"

The woman nodded.

"Funny, I don't remember you. Are you sure you remember me? Or just the reclusive guy who never talked and came home wearing Marine blues?"

Now Lynn could really have laughed. Jax was handling Madge very well. Madge fell silent and returned to pecking at her salad. She probably wanted a stiff drink about now. Whatever her hopes with Jax, they'd just moved further away.

Jax finished his burger and broccoli and devoted himself to eating some fries. "I think a piece of pie will be in order."

"Not for me," Lynn answered. "This burger is huge. You were the one who wanted half a rhino."

He flashed her a grin, then returned his attention to Madge. "So what do you do, Madge?" he asked.

Madge, who had been moving steadily from feeling abashed to feeling angry to judge by her face, turned toward him with an artificial smile. "I work at the dentist's office."

Jax nodded. "Hygienist?"

Madge sighed, her voice somewhat muffled. "Receptionist."

"I bet you brighten up the front office."

Madge just shook her head, threw a few bills on the

table and rose. "See you around, Jax," she said, nearly purring as if to make up for her earlier silence and missteps.

"Sure," he answered indifferently.

As Lynn and Jax walked back to her house, Lynn said, "You handled Madge well."

"Did I? I just wanted to be polite without stirring up anything. You said she was always on the hunt."

"She is and has three divorces to show for it."

"*Three?* In so few years?"

"Busy little bee."

"I guess so." He shook his head.

"Anyway," Lynn continued, "you're welcome to borrow my car if you want. Now that you're here, you must want to do something besides hang around my place. Take a look at the old ranch or something."

"I'm not sure about visiting the old place. And I'm only in town because of Adam. Why is your mother living in Cheyenne?"

Lynn shrugged. "My dad took off when I was fourteen. Mom had always felt constricted here. She wanted some bright lights, I gather. Anyway, as soon as I met Matt, she moved away. She seems happy in her new life."

"But not so much she isn't bugging you."

Lynn laughed. "I guess not."

Later in the day, while Lynn was busy drawing up a remodeling list, Jax had time to do some serious thinking about the call from Briggs that morning.

A suicide and a disturbing death, both of jurors in the Albright trial. As Hugh Briggs had said, the suicide, unfortunately, wasn't terribly unusual. War left deep scars that some simply couldn't endure.

But a second death? Hugh was right about Marines being young and healthy. An OD on drugs wouldn't have started an investigation. Something else had happened. Something serious enough that it couldn't be passed over, nor the link to the trial overlooked.

He would have liked to know what had caused this consternation, but if someone was out to kill jurors, he'd been sloppy with that one. He also knew that no one, but no one, not even Hugh, would share any of the details of the investigation.

Hugh had already crossed a line by warning him. He was also correct that Jax's whereabouts could be discovered. He'd been required to provide a general outline of his plans, although his listed time here was two days for a wedding, then on to Denver.

The information was supposed to be confidential, but that protection wasn't impossible to get around. Nor, in the ordinary way, would it matter.

But this time it might.

Inevitably, his thoughts turned to the hotel fire. No, he told himself after a moment. It was only his second night in Conard City. Very unlikely anyone could have found him that fast.

But Hugh's words rolled around in his mind. Don't discount a determined Marine.

Maybe he should find somewhere else to stay until the sheriff made it clear that he could move on. He sure as hell didn't want to draw Lynn into any kind of mess.

Certainly not a deadly one.

Chapter 6

Luke didn't give up easily, as Lynn saw yet again when two days later he arrived at her door. Wrapped in a drab jacket, his too-long blond hair ruffled by the frigid breeze, he looked chipper despite the cold-reddened tip of his nose.

"Just a cup of coffee, Lynn," he said with a smile. "I promise."

She wanted to close the door in his face. This guy had more annoying persistence than a fly, but Nancy's voice emerged from the kitchen.

"Let the boy in, dear. Might be time to find out what he wants now."

Lynn had to swallow a laugh. Count on Nancy.

"I don't want anything at all," Luke protested as he stepped inside. "Just to talk."

Right, Lynn thought. Her mother was correct. Maybe they could suss out Luke's motives.

"Are you a coffee or a tea man?" Nancy asked Luke as he and Lynn entered the kitchen. "Lynn has this place so torn up I can't invite you into a living room."

"Coffee is fine and so is the kitchen," Luke answered. He settled at the trestle table, and much as Lynn didn't want to sit, she took a seat, too.

Luke looked at Lynn, his gray eyes clear and innocent. Lynn wondered how many women he'd practiced that look on.

"You're doing quite some remodeling," he said.

"She certainly is," Nancy answered, filling two mugs and setting them down. "And this place needed it. It had gone to rack and ruin."

Not quite, Lynn thought, but she saw no reason to dispute her mother's judgment. None of Luke's business.

"You're really lucky," Nancy continued, "that you didn't inherit half this mess."

"Am I?" Luke's smile remained, but his eyes hardened a bit.

"Of course you are! Your father didn't maintain anything at all. But why would he after your mother died?"

Lynn didn't like the direction of this conversation and diverted it. "Mom, Luke was hurt. I can understand that. Let it go, please."

Nancy sniffed, but remained quiet.

Lynn returned her attention to Luke. "I haven't heard. What are you up to these days?"

"Oh, I've got a job out at one of the ranches. Keeps me busy."

Lynn doubted the job was full-time or that it involved any physical labor. That wasn't Luke's style. "What about a special someone?"

Luke's smile broadened. "She's a teacher. Jillie Banton. Know her?"

"Vaguely, I think. Cute." And maybe not so bright. Lynn wondered why so many women were attracted to men like Luke. Too many seemed not to mind supporting a layabout. A far cry from hardworking. A far cry from a househusband. Hah! She could just imagine Luke chasing kids, cooking, cleaning, doing laundry. Oh, yeah.

"I'm glad you have someone," she said lamely.

"She puts a smile on my face." Luke sipped coffee. "So, Lynn, are you restoring the entire house?"

"Most of it needs some restoring. Some serious water damage on the living room wall, too. I need to get in there and find out how extensive the damage is."

Luke shook his head. "That could be a pain."

"She needs to get around to remodeling this kitchen," Nancy said tartly. "It's impossible to keep counters truly clean when they're full of knife cuts. And don't forget the burn marks."

"I haven't forgotten, Mom. One thing at a time."

Luke nodded sagely. "An awful lot for one woman to take on."

One *woman*? Luke had no idea how close he came to having his head torn off.

"That big guy," Luke continued. "He's that Marine, right? How long is he staying?"

Lynn shrugged. "I'm not sure. He came for Adam Ryder's wedding. And he used to live around here."

Just then, the front door opened and her three roomers entered the house with laughter, carrying their laptop cases along with bags that emitted delicious aromas.

"Hi, Lynn," they called out, then stepped into the kitchen.

"Room in the fridge?" Barry asked, holding up a bag.

"You know there always is."

Nancy looked as if she weren't so sure of that. Lynn wondered if she'd gone out to plunder the grocery.

All three of them politely greeted Luke, then after the mysterious bag disappeared into the fridge, they stampeded up the stairs, laughing once again.

"High-spirited," Luke remarked.

"Noisy," Nancy added.

Lynn spoke. "They lighten the atmosphere in this place. I enjoy them."

Luke hung around awhile longer, possibly hoping to cadge a dinner invitation, one that Lynn would never offer him. She'd seen his ugly side during the lawsuit and wasn't going to risk facing that part of him again. Gone were the days when she'd tried to make him into family because of Matt. He'd pretty much shredded that goodwill.

She felt a twinge of conscience as she closed the door behind him, wondering if she was being too unkind, then decided not.

Luke had been pleasant enough during her marriage to Matt, not that he'd ever visited that often. But pleasant. Until a few days after Matt's funeral when he'd dropped the pretense.

Lynn wasn't terribly suspicious by nature, but during the legal battle she had concluded that all that niceness had been meant to get a share of Matt's estate if anything happened.

It had happened, the very worst, and Luke had taken off the gloves. Even though the law had sided with her, Lynn still felt emotionally bruised. While she stood amidst the wreckage of her life, Luke had come after her with both barrels blazing.

Now he wanted to make up? Too late. Far too late.

Sighing, she decided to help her mother make dinner. She wasn't ready to face the mess she might find behind that living room wall. Since it wasn't collapsing, she could wait another day.

"Where's Jax?" Nancy asked as Lynn peeled carrots and potatoes.

"What? Is he your type?"

Nancy laughed but added, "I thought he might be yours."

"Hardly. Uniforms are a put-off for me now."

"I guess I can understand that. I just wanted to invite him to join us for dinner. Seems the courteous thing to do."

He was also just a roomer like the others, Lynn thought, but didn't say so.

Because he didn't exactly feel like a roomer.

"So where is he?" Nancy asked again.

"I have no idea. He has the right to come and go as he pleases."

That ended the subject. Thank God.

Several blocks away, in the house she owned thanks to the settlement in her first divorce, Madge was still smarting from the way Jax had treated her at lunch.

As if she were a stranger. She wasn't! She'd seen that look he'd given her toward the end of their senior year. And they'd been together in school all those years.

It had to do with that damn Lynn Macy, she decided. If Lynn hadn't been there, the entire conversation would have gone differently. She was *sure* it would have.

She had to find some way to take Lynn out of the picture. Some way that would make her utterly unappealing to Jackson Stone.

While Madge's mental wheels spun, she made herself

another daiquiri, her preferred poison. More elegant than beer or a shot of whiskey, she believed.

Yup. There had to be a way to remove Lynn from the competition. She just needed to figure it out.

Sitting back in the comfy wing chair she'd inherited from her second husband, she sipped her drink and inhaled the lime aroma, imagining herself in an elegant bar.

Madge pretended a lot. She just didn't realize it all the time.

Jax had changed into workout clothes and gone for a long run. He had the worst feeling that everything hung in a state of stasis, that more was going to happen, but he had no idea what or when.

Or maybe that was leftover mission-think. He couldn't imagine a more generally peaceful locale than this county. Sure, bad things happened, but most people still left their doors unlocked.

It wasn't as if nothing had changed since his departure fifteen years ago. It had almost surprised him to get broadband Wi-Fi at Lynn's house. The internet might have been around for a long time, but when he'd lived here, most people had to go to the library to use it.

The town, however, looked a little more ragged. The years hadn't been kind. He took in the paint that had faded on some houses, in places peeling away, and all he could do was admire Lynn's determination and her faith that her work would be rewarded.

Or maybe the work itself was reward enough. He wondered if he should ask.

But there was a strong part of him that still hung back from asking questions he had no right to ask, from putting himself forward.

In the Corps he was fine. No problems, set rules, set

limits. He knew who he was. Out here in the hinterlands he felt a touch of that young boy returning.

Enough of that, though. That wasn't him any longer.

He thought about going by the ranch house where he and Adam had cemented their relationship over all those years. When they had been the only friends out there in the wide-open spaces.

But no, there were bad memories there, too, like his father's brutality. Only later did he realize the man had no right to whip him like that. Only when he was eight and happened to be home had he learned how violently his father had treated his mother.

He'd heard her crying one night, "Samuel, no! Please..."

He'd crept from his room and peered from the top of the banister to see what was happening. He'd seen too much, his father pummeling his mother even after she fell to the floor.

At the time he'd had no comparison. He thought that was the way things should be, especially when he heard it happen repeatedly. But he hated it. He also never spoke of it, not even to Adam, for fear of getting his mother into more trouble.

Maybe that had birthed part of his reticence, his introversion. Did it matter now?

All he knew was that when he was sixteen, his father had sent his mother to the hospital with a broken jaw.

And that was when Jax, string bean that he was, had learned to stand up to that ugly, abusive man. Never again.

His mother had left shortly after she got out of the hospital. His dad had started drinking himself into a stupor all the time. When Jax left for the military, everything was lost. The ranch foreclosed, his father settling the last of it by eating his shotgun.

And not one sliver of sorrow had troubled Jax.

He'd kept in touch with his mother for a few years until cancer took her. That *did* sadden him, but he figured she was better off.

No, he didn't want to go back to that place. It was seeded with some great memories, but also with many more memories he didn't want to flood him.

Off-limits.

Instead, it was easier to think about a Marine stalking him. Far easier. *That* was the kind of threat he could handle.

Lynn's roomers went out again for dinner and dates, she gathered. She was happy, however, when she heard Jax return. It was not at all like the comings and goings of her boys.

The pork tenderloin was almost done, roasting with potatoes and carrots. The aroma made her mouth water.

Nancy beat her to the kitchen door. "Dinner, Jax? There's plenty."

Lynn hid a smile. She'd never doubted that Jax was also on her mother's menu. She did, however, notice that he hesitated before answering.

"Don't put him on the spot, Mom."

"I'm sure the man knows how to decline, Lynn."

Jax must have heard her warning to her mother, Lynn suddenly realized with a sinking feeling. Oh, hell. She didn't want him to think she was reluctant to have his company, but she also couldn't dash out there and press him further about eating with them.

She needed to learn to keep her mouth shut. And ignore the niggle of hope that he would accept the invitation. She enjoyed his company, reserved as it was, more than she should.

"I'd like that very much, Nancy," Jax answered. "I need to change and wash up first."

"There's time," Nancy answered brightly.

When his boot steps disappeared upstairs, Lynn looked at her mother. "You *do* have a thing for him."

"I do not. He's way too young for me."

"No December-May relationship then?"

Nancy snorted. "I don't need a trophy husband. I'm enjoying my freedom way too much."

Lynn hoped it was true that Nancy was enjoying her freedom. She certainly seemed like it. But *trophy husband*? She nearly laughed out loud.

She turned from the sink, where she was washing a few prep dishes, and was annoyed to see her mother placing a couple of candles on the table. Candles and holders that Lynn had put away a long time ago.

"Too much, Mom."

Nancy stood back, surveying the table that at present held only dark green place mats. "Do you think so?"

"I know so."

"But it's so boring."

"Fine, but it's better than a romantic candlelit dinner. Cut it out."

Nancy sighed, but for once didn't argue. The candles and holders disappeared back to their place in a corner of the pantry. "We need a tablecloth."

"Sure, and who's going to wash and iron it?"

"They make those that don't wrinkle."

"I don't need a tablecloth. I usually eat in my apartment upstairs. By myself."

"But you never know…"

This time Lynn didn't bother to answer.

Nancy was good at laying out food, however. By the

time Jax joined them, the sliced tenderloin sat on a platter surrounded by browned potatoes and carrots.

Lynn set the places with the best unchipped dishes she could find and flatware that was scratched with age. No point even thinking about it. It was all she had.

"Dinner smells great," Jax said appreciatively as he took his place at the table.

"Something to drink?" Lynn asked.

"Just water, please. No ice."

After Jax had tasted everything, he remarked, "I don't think I've ever had pork this tender."

"Lynn cooked it," Nancy said. "I just helped."

Lynn resisted rolling her eyes, hearing the subtext *Lynn not only remodels but she can do the feminine thing, too. She can cook.* What was up next? Her mother extolling her virtues as a laundress?

She glanced at Jax and caught the twinkle in his eyes. He must have heard the subtext, too.

"It's really good, Lynn," he said promptly, obviously taking the hint.

Lynn hurried to change the subject. "Did you have a good day, Jax?"

"Fair to middling," he answered. "I wandered a bit, thought a bit about the past." And about the present threat, but he wasn't going to mention that. No way.

"Did you visit the old homestead?" Nancy asked.

"No."

The word was flat and forbidding. Lynn looked at him, and other than a slight tightening around his eyes, she saw total impassivity. He'd locked something away deep inside him.

"I'm sure you can borrow my car if you want to get out there," Nancy offered.

Lynn wanted to tap her mother's leg under the table. She wasn't getting it. Jax's single word had said enough.

"Very kind of you," Jax said after a moment. "But I think not." He resumed eating. A minute or so later, he asked, "How was your day, Lynn?"

"Wasted mostly," she admitted. "I couldn't face looking into that wall yet, so I puttered around taking some measurements for new kitchen cabinets and counters. And no, Mom, I'm nowhere near ready to do that. Just thinking about it."

"Sounds productive to me," Jax replied.

"You should consult me about the counters," Nancy said. "I've had experience with all the different types and, believe me, some are vastly overrated. Fashionable, but hard to take care of."

"I'd like to hear about that sometime," Lynn said, heading off potential hostilities. Not that a discussion with her mother would ever become hostile, but it could sure turn difficult.

"Have you heard anything from Adam and Jazz?" she asked Jax.

He smiled. "On their honeymoon?"

Nancy spoke. "I think it's so odd that Jasmine is called Jazz and Jackson is called Jax."

"We joked about it at the wedding," Jax answered. "Pure coincidence."

While the food was wonderful, Lynn wished this dinner would be over. Tension crept across the table as Nancy prattled on about things best left alone, everything from Jax's family to his reasons for not wanting to visit his old home.

As the dinner progressed, Jax grew more monosyl-

labic, offering no explanations. And why should he? It
was no one's business but his own.

Lynn smothered a sigh and was glad when she could
at last stand up and start clearing the table. Jax immediately rose to help.

"Mom, why don't you go find something on TV? Or
a good book. You worked so hard on this dinner."

Nancy smiled, looking from Lynn to Jax as if this
were just what she'd hoped for. "A great idea, Lynn. I'll
see you in the morning."

"Not if Jax can escape first," she said under her breath
when Nancy disappeared.

To her astonishment, Jax laughed. "Too bad she's out
of luck."

Lynn's heart stumbled. "Oh?" she asked, wondering
why she should even care.

"I doubt either of us can be maneuvered as easily as
she seems to think."

He had a point. Relaxing again, Lynn stacked scraped
plates beside the sink. "It doesn't bother you?"

He shook his head and began washing dishes. "It
amuses me. Don't let it bother *you*. But I wonder if she
has any idea how transparent she is?"

That drew a laugh from Lynn. "I'm not sure."

"It doesn't matter. Just relax. I've handled far worse."

Like Madge, Lynn thought. But Jax was subtle. She
wondered if Madge understood that she'd been given a
major brush-off.

The woman's nerve astonished her, though. She knew
Madge was a flirt, always looking for another man, as if
she had no other way of measuring her own self-worth.
But claiming an old friendship when there had been none?
That seemed more problematic than her usual flirtations.

Shaking her head, Lynn started drying dishes.

* * *

Later, upstairs in her private aerie, music from her boys' rooms rising quietly through the floor, Lynn sat with her tablet on her lap, her eyes focused elsewhere even when the screen darkened to save the battery power.

A small fire burned in her electric fireplace. Warm lamplight filled the room, but she wasn't seeing any of it.

Jax had been tense. Not overly so, but she felt the difference from when he first arrived. It couldn't be Madge; she wasn't important enough to disturb him.

Remembering how abruptly he had responded to her mother about visiting his old home, she felt the tension that lay there. At least inside him.

Given how silent and distant he had remained the whole time he'd lived here, at least according to those who had known him better than she had, maybe something other than his nature had driven him to keep his distance.

Rumors flew around this town endlessly, but she'd heard none about Jax or his family. Not a single whisper, which would lead her to believe they'd been boringly ordinary.

Then there was Adam, his friend since before he'd started school, from what she *had* heard. Wouldn't that be a good memory? Something he could recall out at the old ranch?

Why wouldn't he want to follow those pathways in his past?

As she sat there, she grew increasingly convinced that something truly bad had happened to Jax. Something he had locked inside his silence and introversion.

She stared into space for a while, then sighed. He'd never tell her, and she was probably all wet anyway.

Speculating about his past wasn't going to do a damn bit of good.

Instead, she forced her thoughts to the kitchen she'd begun measuring today. No small project, especially since she wanted to do more than replace countertops and appliances. She envisioned gutting the entire room, rearranging everything, adding more cabinets and counter space. The electrical work was going to be expensive, never mind the rest of it.

But if she was going to do it, she was going to do it right. Make it a workable space, rather than a cobbled-together room from an earlier time when the minimum was enough, when a table had to substitute for counters.

Definitely more cabinets because those along the one wall beside the sink simply weren't enough. A built-in dishwasher rather than water-wasteful handwashing.

The measurements she'd taken today hadn't been of what was already there. They had been measurements of the space and the beginnings of rough sketches of how she could change the room without sacrificing too much of the area.

A nice diversion, especially since she had other tasks that were far more pressing like that damn living room wall.

She looked down at the tablet on her lap but didn't turn it on again. Instead she leaned her head back and thought about Matt.

Matt, that wonderful guy who'd swept her off her feet. His smile, the sound of his laughter, his warm hands caressing her. Her other half.

She'd gotten to the point where she could think about all the good things and mostly ignore the horror at the end. The blessing of time.

But as she dozed off, Matt's face became mixed with

Jax's. The two came together seamlessly as if part of her whole. And in dreams, there was no reason to feel guilty.

One floor down in his own bedroom, Jax stretched out on the bed with his hands behind his head. He pictured Lynn upstairs in her attic and felt his body stir.

With each passing hour, his attraction to her grew. He didn't seem to be able to prevent it, but he sure as hell could ignore it. He had to. He was convinced that, after Matt, Lynn wouldn't want to get involved with another military man. And he had no intention of leaving the Corps early unless a severe enough wound or injury made him unfit for duty. In five years he'd be able to retire if he chose, but he often thought about extending past that.

He'd be only thirty-eight, and that seemed too young to hang up his uniform.

Nor did he believe he'd be any more acceptable to Lynn because he'd just been given command of recruiting centers in Denver. The position was an honor and physically safe, but it could end at any moment if he was needed in the field. Nope, not secure enough to offer a woman widowed by war.

He shook his head at the unwanted direction of his thoughts. Why was he thinking about her in the long term anyway? They hardly knew each other and he sure as hell wasn't going to have a fling with her. Leave it alone. It could never be. Don't allow these feelings to strengthen.

He thought about Madge for a few minutes, a safer place for his mind to wander. He was still astonished by her insistence they'd had something going in high school. She seemed to be stalking him, judging by the way she'd joined his table at Maude's. It wouldn't be the first time that had happened since he'd put on the uniform.

But that was a minor matter. The problem would end when he left.

Which turned him in a different direction. He was pretty much stuck here until the arson investigation was completed, which meant he was going to have to deal with Madge and the amusing Nancy for longer. He kind of liked Nancy West and her determination to push Lynn to her way of thinking, especially since Lynn clearly wasn't going to allow herself to be pushed.

He wondered, though, how much Nancy sometimes embarrassed Lynn. The question brought a faint smile to his face. Two strong-willed women. They must clash quite often.

The amount of work Lynn had put into this place impressed him. She must be at it nearly all the time. He envisioned her on ladders, scraping and painting all that gingerbread, and there was a lot of it.

He bet that standing in the front yard, he'd have gotten a very nice view of her butt.

Ah, hell. He rolled over, trying to squash the images.

Better to focus on the call from Briggs. Could he be right that someone was out to kill the jurors in the Albright trial? Maybe so, since an investigation had begun.

With his eyes closed, it was too easy to remember that trial. Too easy to see the photographs, too easy to hear the testimony from men who had served with Albright. Those who accused Albright were clearly unhappy about doing so, but equally angry that he had ordered them to kill unarmed civilians. Those who had steadfastly stood up for him had insisted that he had done nothing wrong. It was war, after all.

Those who had accused him had probably killed their own careers and knew it. After that, no one would want to serve with them again because they had violated the code of brotherhood, no matter how justifiably.

Good men had risked everything to stand up for the right. Raising their voices to say that morality had its place even in the midst of war.

Yeah, war was an atrocity-making situation. Atrocities happened because they couldn't be avoided. But to *intentionally* commit them?

No.

The jury's deliberations had taken some time. None of them wanted to convict a fellow Marine of war crimes. The whole idea of convicting one of their own had run counter to their grain. They'd spent a lot of time looking for exculpatory evidence, as if there was any.

They'd spent almost none considering whether Theodore Albright had committed the acts for which he was standing trial. The evidence and testimony were too undeniable.

The inescapable verdict had been rendered with heavy hearts. No sense of satisfaction at all. No sense of self-righteousness. As disgusted as Jax was that Albright was a Marine, he had taken no pleasure in convicting him.

If someone really was killing jurors, he doubted Albright was directly behind it. He was in too much trouble already and still had the hope of an appeal.

Ah, hell. This train of thought wasn't helping, either. Sleep was determined to elude him.

Then he remembered Luke Macy. He didn't like the guy at all and didn't trust him. Nancy had it right when she'd called him a slithering snake.

Imagine him wanting to be friends now with Lynn after a lawsuit. The man had made her life hell, and Luke, after losing the case, should have gone away with his tail tucked. The man clearly knew no shame.

What could Luke hope to gain now? Money? He doubted Lynn had much to spare with the cost of re-modeling this house. But Luke might suspect otherwise, given that she was spending so much.

God, he was surrounded by messes. With his face in the pillow he nearly laughed. And he'd thought he'd be bored hanging around here?

It was a damn TV drama.

Chapter 7

In the morning, over toast and eggs, Lynn announced, "It's time to get started on that living room wall whether I want to or not."

Jax, who'd made breakfast for the three of them, lifted his head. Nancy was busy shaking hers.

"What can I do to help?" he asked.

"Catch me when I collapse," Lynn answered wryly. "God, I'm dreading this."

"You should call a contractor," Nancy said.

Lynn sighed. "Like it or not, I can do this myself. And it may not be as bad as I fear."

"I hope not," Nancy replied. "But since you're going to be banging around and stirring up dust, I think I'll go out."

Lynn nodded. "Might be for the best. Meeting friends?"

"I'm going to call them, maybe arrange for lunch or an afternoon tea." Nancy favored her with a smile. "Have you looked outside yet? Cold and gray. A good time to stay indoors and visit. Before lunch, though, I may go shopping at the Mercantile."

"I doubt they'll have anything to suit your style," Lynn couldn't resist saying.

Nancy waved a hand. "You never know. Sometimes the larger world actually reaches this far."

"Just don't buy anything for me."

Nancy laughed. "Banish the thought."

Lynn looked at Jax. "She keeps wanting to dress me up." It had been an ongoing argument since Lynn's childhood, and Lynn still wasn't sure she'd won it.

"Hopeless cause," Nancy replied tartly. "Anyway, I'll stop at the grocery on my way home. Maybe I'll find something tempting."

"I could thaw the chicken that's in the freezer."

"No," Nancy said. "I most definitely do not want chicken again."

Dishes done, Nancy sailed out the front door dressed in emerald green wool.

"That's how she wants you to look?" Jax asked after the door closed behind Nancy.

Lynn smiled at him and shrugged. "She used to want me to wear frilly things. Maybe she still does. I'm just practical, and that suit she was wearing is *not* practical."

"Not for what you're doing."

She gathered up her inspection camera from the toolbox she kept in the dining room and grabbed her laptop as well.

"Everything the camera sees will show up on my computer screen," she said, then looked at Jax. "I'm sorry. You probably know that."

"As a matter of fact, I do. One of the lessons of my job."

God, he looked good this morning, Lynn thought. Yummy. Scrumptious. She was glad he was wearing jeans and a sweatshirt, not either of his uniforms, so she wouldn't swoon.

Hah! *Swoon.* Where had that word come from? Besides, she was still struggling with a feeling of guilt. Anyway, Jax was leaving soon and she didn't want a fling. That went against her nature.

Together, they traipsed into her living room, letting the plastic over the door fall behind them.

"Have you made enough holes?" Jax asked, pointing to the gaping spaces in the wall. He grinned.

Lynn laughed. "Enough that this wall could never be patched now. But I knew that when I started." She'd also pulled pieces of lath out of all those walls, enough to peek inside. They were dark holes right now.

Little light fell into the room through the window. Nancy had been right about the day's grayness. Looking outside, Lynn saw the wind blowing autumn leaves from the trees.

Oh, well, winter always came as sure as the sun rising in the east.

She turned on two of the work lights that stood on tripods, then knelt, opening her computer and starting the correct program.

Jax squatted beside her. "Want me to feed the camera in while you watch the screen?"

Lynn nodded. "That would definitely save me some time."

"I doubt it, but it'll make me feel like less of a fifth wheel."

She plugged the camera into the port on the side of her computer and saw the curtains show up on her screen. "It's working. Okay, let's go."

"Just tell me which way you want me to turn the camera when it's inside."

"Dang," she said, feeling butterflies in her stomach. "I don't think I was this worried when I first discovered the water damage on the wall."

He had dropped to his knees, holding the camera, and agreed. "I imagine dealing with the roof was easier than having to reframe this wall would be."

"By far. I really don't like unpleasant surprises, like seeing the water stains when I evicted the old furniture. New walls, and the flooring is warped as well. I need some good news in here."

"We can hope." He turned to the wall. "Ready?"

Not really, but she'd put this off long enough. "Go ahead."

Grimly, she returned her attention to the screen. Fiber optics ran through the cable, not only returning the image but delivering light at the camera end. She was now looking at studs.

"No insulation in here?" he asked.

"None. These old houses rarely had any, unless they used newspaper. No thanks."

"Tinder," he agreed.

At her direction, he ran the camera through the entire bay, up the studs as far as the camera would reach, then back down again and across the bottom plate.

So far so good. She blew a sigh of relief. There was a little blackening of the wood at the bottom, but nothing major. Maybe it was good there'd been no insulation.

Five more holes and she was satisfied. "No new frame required."

She switched off her computer and sat back on her bottom, braced by her arms. "What a relief! Now I can just go ahead with the drywalling."

"And insulation? Will you add any?"

"Blown in, like I did upstairs. Easy-peasy."

He laughed as he coiled the camera wire. Sitting cross-legged, he faced her. "You have an interesting idea of easy."

Lynn shrugged. "Why? Because I'm a woman?"

"No, absolutely not. Just because most *people* wouldn't undertake this task."

She liked the way he was smiling at her, liked the tingle inside that ran all the way to her toes. Once again she felt sideswiped by the attraction she felt. Wow!

All that because of a smile. She averted her gaze and tried to reach equilibrium. God knew how she'd react if he ever touched her. She closed her eyes, envisioning herself turning into a puddle. A hot puddle.

It had been a very long time since she'd felt like that.

She jumped up suddenly, shaking herself. "I need to get the mail."

It was a good excuse to run, except he followed her. Before she reached the curb, however, he'd taken over an Adirondack chair and leaned back, crossing his legs, one foot on the other knee.

It *was* chilly out here, she thought. She wondered if Jax was thinking about sitting out on the porch long enough to turn blue.

She pulled the door of the box open, started to reach in, then squealed and jumped back.

Jax leaped instantly to his feet and charged down the short sidewalk. "Lynn, what's wrong?"

She pointed, her hand shaking. "Snake. There's a snake…"

Jax peered into the box and saw a small snake coiled inside atop some mail. Maybe two feet long, max? How the hell did it get in there? And why? He could certainly understand Lynn's shock.

He started to reach in, but Lynn cried, "Stop! God, it's a rattlesnake!"

He glanced over his shoulder. "It might look like one, but it's a milk snake."

"How can you be sure? It has a diamond pattern!" Her eyes were huge.

Her fear was natural, especially in someone who probably didn't see many snakes. "I recognize this type of snake, even used to play with them sometimes when I was a kid. Not that the snake appreciated it. Anyway, at most I'll get a little bite."

Moving slowly, he was able to get his fingers around the snake just behind its head. "It's logy because it's so cold. It's okay, Lynn."

Jax pulled the snake from the mailbox, holding its head, and watched it coil slowly around his hand and forearm. "See? It's trying to get warm by wrapping around me."

"Ugh." But she leaned closer to look. At last she said, "It's kinda pretty. But I don't like snakes."

"A lot of people don't."

"Aren't you going to kill it?" she asked when he took two steps down the street.

He paused to look back at her. "I don't know how it got in your mailbox, but it doesn't deserve to die for it. I'm going to find a safe place to let it go."

He felt her eyes on him as he walked down the street, thinking this snake needed a decent space with some tall grass to hide in. He'd seen one by the college, he thought.

But he couldn't imagine how it had gotten into her mailbox. Someone must have put it there.

* * *

"A prank," Lynn said decisively when he at last got back to the house. "It had to be a prank."

She'd changed into a green sweater, but still had her arms wrapped around her. Jax wondered if she was cold or still shaken.

"Your roomers pranking you, maybe? Or some neighborhood kid?"

To some people the snake might be funny, especially kids in their teens. He hadn't gotten the impression from her roomers that they'd do something like this to her, but it was possible.

She spoke again. "Well, it's obvious that creature couldn't have crawled in there on its own. But I don't think my boys would prank me that way."

He shook his head. "Can I make some coffee? And I know from experience that young men can get up to the craziest things."

As indeed he did, having commanded many of them during his term of service as he rose in rank.

"Why? Did you do crazy things?"

He put a filter into the basket while he chuckled. "I didn't, but I'm in the military, remember. Plenty of young people. I've been working with them all along, had to discipline some of them for acts of utter stupidity."

He turned to reach for the canister of coffee as she turned toward him at the same instant and brushed his arm against the peak of Lynn's breast. He froze, then snatched his hand back. *Hell!*

He looked at her, getting ready to apologize, but the expression on her face silenced him. Somehow her green eyes had turned almost smoky, and her lips had parted.

Stillness filled him in the instant before his blood surged.

Seeing his yearning reflected in her gaze almost tipped him over the edge, into drawing her close, into stroking her, learning her curves...

Then she saved him from himself by turning quickly away. He stared at her back, hoping that accidental touch hadn't offended her.

When she spoke, her voice sounded a bit husky. "I'll ask my boys about it. I doubt they did it, but they could have some idea of who might have."

He cleared his throat. "Good idea." But all he could feel was the precipice he hovered on, and the desire to carry her over it with him. With difficulty, he banked his internal fire.

This woman deserved better than a short-term tumble in the hay. She was a long-term type of woman.

No way could he be that for her, especially when his own ideas of marriage were so polluted by his past. He couldn't trust himself.

Lynn, wrapped in a hot haze, knew she had to escape before she did something she'd regret. Like throwing herself into Jax's arms. Was that desire she'd seen in his eyes? Electric tingles were coursing through her own body, but she doubted what she'd glimpsed in him. No man since Matt had looked at her like that. Which was how she wanted it. Right?

"I'm going upstairs for a little while," she said, trying to regain command of her voice.

Then she hurried away. Hurried to solitude. Hurried toward a chance to get a grip on herself. Fled from needs she wasn't ready to handle.

By the time she reached the sanctuary of her attic, she began to feel ashamed of herself. She'd never been one to run from anything, but she was running from perfectly normal feelings. Feelings that didn't have to come to fruition.

And she felt some guilt. Guilt because of Matt. Guilt because she had the niggling sense that she was cheating on Matt as if he were still alive.

God, she was a hot mess.

To an extent, her mother was right, damn her. She *had* been burying her grief in all the remodeling. But she loved the work, and while it kept her preoccupied, there were the long nights when it did not. Not at all.

She flopped on one of the comfortable chairs she had reupholstered but ignored the matching hassock. She was too agitated to fully relax.

Matt's photo, in dress uniform, stood beside her bed on one side. Their wedding photo occupied the bookshelf. On the other end of the bookshelf she had built along one side of the room, there was another enlarged photo of Matt smiling at her. There were also five photo albums filled with prints of pictures she'd taken of him and he of her, plus all the cell phone photos she'd had turned into prints. They included his childhood photos, such as they were, as well as hers. Even a few other relatives, long since buried.

A family history of sorts, and she still looked through them. Especially the photos of Matt and the two of them together.

Each time she did, she felt a mix of happy memories and heartache.

So much of her life had gone with him. Too much.

These days the happy memories came more often. A good thing, because for a while, Matt's death had banished them all. She could still remember that period when the world had turned gray and life had felt too difficult to live. The light had gradually returned, and along with it a desire to live.

But the words *you need to move on* still irritated the hell out of her. She was moving on at her own pace, and nobody telling her to, however kindly meant, had helped at all. In fact, they'd implied something was wrong with her because she hadn't moved on the way others believed she should.

She had a tight-knit group of friends who'd remained blissfully silent except to listen to her and sympathize. Never suggesting how she should handle her sorrow. But there were plenty of others, causing her to narrow her world to a small group of people.

That was probably bad for her, but here she was, buried in work she loved with little spare time on her hands. Although when her mother was here, she had almost no choice about making the time.

She sighed, looking again at her favorite photos of Matt and smiling. He'd been wonderful. Oh, he had his faults like everyone, but she'd had hers, too. In her mind, however, he was as close to perfect as anyone could be.

She remembered the day she'd met him. Oh, she'd seen him around school, knew who he was. Conard City was small enough that no one could escape notice.

But that day, as she'd crossed the college campus in Laramie, he'd walked toward her in his ROTC uniform. A handsome figure, drawing her gaze. But then he'd stopped in front of her.

"Excuse me," he'd said politely. "You're Lynn West, aren't you? I'm Matt Macy."

She'd smiled. "I recognized you."

"Well," he said, taking a deep breath, "every time I see you, I want to date you. How about some coffee?"

Three months later they were engaged, and six months after that meeting on campus, they'd married.

Almost a fairy tale.

She cherished that memory, hugged it close to her heart. *Fated*, she often thought. For a while.

She didn't think she'd ever have that feeling again and wasn't at all sure she wanted to. Not all fairy tales had happy endings.

She turned her thoughts to Jax. A mystery, really. She knew almost nothing about his past except that he'd been reclusive. In fact, unlike a great many people she knew around here, she didn't know Jax at all.

Best to keep away, she told herself sternly. Wearing a uniform by itself didn't make him trustworthy. Neither did feeling a strong attraction to him.

She glanced at the clock on one of those bookshelves she'd been staring at and realized the afternoon was waning. Her mother had gone out with the express determination not to eat roast chicken tonight. Lordy, what might she have brought home?

Time to get down there again, face her demons and help deal with dinner. And maybe save Jax from the third degree.

Nancy had gone all out. She smiled as Lynn entered the kitchen and said, "Wait until you see!"

Lynn braced herself. "Just tell me it's not raw oysters."

Nancy wrinkled her nose. "I know you hate them."

"Slimy and salty," Lynn agreed. "I'll leave them to those who like them."

"I'm sure they'll be grateful. No, I found some decent shrimp and I thawed them for shrimp cocktail. I *know* you like that."

"One of my favorites." Her mouth watered at the mere thought.

"Then, being in a mood, I got some frozen lobster tails and some fillets. Surf and turf tonight, my dear."

Lynn plopped down in a chair, astonished. "Wow," was all she could say. "Just wow. Can you afford it?"

"I have a healthy bank account these days. Lawyers are generous to paralegals. Which they should be, considering how many things we deal with for them. Halfway to lawyers ourselves. Anyway, I hope Jax doesn't have a seafood allergy." Now Nancy looked a trifle worried.

"Mom, he's a roomer, not a guest. He doesn't have to eat with us. Where is he?"

"Said he was going out to run, get rid of some excess energy. He must have a lot of it."

"Probably isn't used to being cooped up," Lynn remarked.

"Maybe not. Anyway, my dear daughter, tonight I cook and you relax."

Lynn grinned. "Sounds good to me."

Madge was still angry about the brush-off she'd received from Jackson Stone. He'd been rude, overtly or not.

Worse, the sheriff had evidently thrown him into Lynn Macy's arms by putting him in Lynn's rooming house.

It was all too disgusting. Smarting, she planted herself in Mahoney's bar and drank perhaps too many daiquiris. She'd always loved frozen daiquiris. They went down so easily and smoothly, and Mahoney always made them the way she liked, with extra lime to give them a bite.

Well, there had to be a way to undermine Lynn before she and Jax really got together. It wasn't as if Lynn wasn't pretty enough, even though she didn't have Madge's endowments.

At some point, maybe during her fourth daiquiri, a man sat down beside her. She turned her head and saw Luke Macy.

"Guess you've been burned, too," Luke said.

"Whadya mean?"

"Lynn. Stone. But mostly Lynn."

"Yeah, she's too much. And *so* not feminine. I don't know what your brother ever saw in her."

Luke smiled charmingly. "Me neither. Cute, I guess, but that's it. Can you believe her depriving me of my inheritance?"

"Yeah. I can't believe that. What's wrong with a little sharing?"

"That was my thought. Not too much to ask. It was the Macy family home, after all."

"You got that right." Madge finished her daiquiri and tapped on the bar for another. Mahoney paused, then nodded. But first he drew some drafts for the other people.

"Let me get that for you," Luke said when Mahoney brought the drink, then looked at Mahoney. "Put Madge's drinks on my tab, and any more she has."

Mahoney rolled his eyes, as if that tab was getting too big, but said nothing.

"*Lynn* should be buying us drinks," Luke said as he took a pull on his own bottle of some fancy brand of beer.

"She ought to be doing more than that."

Luke raised a brow. "What did she do to make you so mad?"

"Jackson Stone," Madge answered. "He was mine and now he's at *her* house."

"I didn't know that," Luke remarked thoughtfully. After Madge had finished half her daiquiri, he spoke again.

"You know," he said slowly, "maybe if we pool our resources we can take care of both our problems."

Madge looked interested. "I'm listening."

Nancy's invitation to dinner was framed in a way that, short of an allergy, Jax couldn't refuse.

"I made something special for dinner tonight, Jax. And I bought enough for three. Surf and turf. I'd hate to waste any unless you're allergic to shellfish."

Lynn's cheeks heated. Her mother certainly had a talent for getting her way.

"I like shellfish," Jax answered, smiling faintly as he looked at Lynn and probably saw her heightened color.

Damn, she'd thought she'd gotten past the blushing stage years ago. Well, Nancy. 'Nuff said.

"How do you like your steak?" Nancy asked.

"Medium rare. I just need to wash up. Be right back."

Lynn wished her mother would let her help, even though surf and turf was an easy meal to put together. Her mom had already found her cast-iron grill, which would sear the meat perfectly.

But sitting there on her hands like a queen didn't suit her, and less so when she was irritated. Not because Jax would be joining them, but because her machinations must be apparent to Jax as well. A few more days of Nancy and he'd probably head for the hills.

If the sheriff let him anyway.

Before long, Nancy served the three of them a beautiful dinner. Drawn butter, too, although Lynn seldom bothered to clarify the butter on the rare occasion she treated herself to a lobster tail.

"This always used to be a favorite of Lynn's," Nancy said as she joined them at the table. Behind her, the counters and the stove looked as if a whirlwind had hit. Lynn wondered if her mother made such messes at home. And if she cleaned them up.

Nah, she probably ate a lot of her meals at restaurants.

So what had brought this on? The candles weren't on the table, so dinner couldn't have been intended to be romantic. Not that it could have been with her mother there.

Lynn gave up her irritating reflections and settled in to enjoy her meal. Her mom had been right—it was always one of her favorites and enjoyed so rarely. Maybe she was being unfair to Nancy, acting out of a reflex from over the years rather than this moment.

"It's perfect, Mom."

Jazz seconded her and Nancy beamed. "I'm not the best in the kitchen, but I do some things well."

Then she turned to Jax, diving in yet again to a clearly sensitive area. "I don't remember hearing much about your family while I lived here."

Jax's face stiffened. "Nothing worth telling. Ranch life is hard."

Nancy nodded as if she knew, when she'd never ranched a day in her life. "Hard on a boy, I imagine."

Jax didn't respond.

Lynn decided it was time to change the subject. "Still haven't heard anything from Adam or Jazz?"

He shook his head. "I guess they're having a great time."

Lynn smiled. "I certainly hope so."

Nancy spoke. "I don't think I ever met Jazz on one of my visits."

Lynn turned to her. "You met Lily, though."

"Oh, yes. And her darling daughter, Iris. And Jazz?"

"Lily's identical twin. Jazz came for a few weeks while Lily was working in Europe to keep an eye on Iris. That's when she and Adam met."

"Ooh, a fairy tale. I love those."

Jax took the wind out of Nancy's sails. "Very little is a fairy tale, Nancy. Those happen in books. And have you noticed how many of the old tales have unhappy endings? They were meant as lessons."

Nancy was taken aback. "I wasn't thinking of those, certainly."

"Of course not." Jax resumed eating while Lynn grinned inwardly. The man knew how to drag her mother back to reality.

Lynn spoke to prevent the silence from growing awkward. "I don't think some of those fairy tales should be read to children. I don't understand why people think fairy tales of that kind are meant for kids. They're folk tales intended for adults."

Jax nodded agreement.

Nancy delicately sliced a small piece from her steak. "A lot of them have been turned into children's books." She sounded defensive, a rarity.

"You're right, of course," Jax answered. "And probably softened by the storyteller and artist."

That certainly softened Nancy. She began smiling again.

The rest of the meal passed without any more uncomfortable moments. When they all professed themselves satisfied, there wasn't a morsel left.

"Compliments to the chef," Jax said with a smile.

"It was wonderful, Mom," Lynn agreed. "Now let me take care of the cleanup since you wouldn't let me help with the cooking."

That pleased Nancy. "Oh, good. My favorite TV show comes on in a half hour."

Nancy vanished into her own room and Lynn looked

around the kitchen, her lips quirking. "I think she never heard of the chef's motto *clean as you go.*"

Jax laughed. "Likely not. Well, you're not alone with this."

They cleared together—then they followed their new routine of Lynn scraping, Jax washing and Lynn drying. Then he scrubbed all the pans, halting only when he came to the cast-iron grill. "Any special directions for this?"

"Scour only with water, heat dry on the stove, then lightly oil the surface."

Then it was all done, dishes dried and put away, the grill sitting on the stove top.

"Someday I'm going to have a built-in dishwasher," Lynn remarked.

"You'll have to tear this kitchen apart."

She laughed. "Exactly what I intend to do. Thanks for all your help."

"No thanks needed."

Then that moment happened again. That moment of hot connection as their eyes met. An instant when Lynn felt as if she were turning into syrup. His dark eyes seemed to blaze with a banked fire.

Oh, God, no. No.

He dragged his gaze away as if she had spoken aloud. "I wonder if the sheriff will let me go soon."

A warning? she wondered. To her horror, her heart sank. "You have to get back so soon?"

He nodded his head. "I'm taking over a new posting in Denver. I was planning to hunt for a place to live before I go on duty."

"Well, this must be bollixing things for you."

He shrugged a shoulder. "There *is* the internet. I need to go look online. Good night, Lynn."

Right after he headed upstairs, her boys came in,

laughing and talking among themselves. She was grateful to hear them because there'd been an instant where this house had felt so empty.

"Hey, guys," she called and went out into the entry. "You know anything about a snake in my mailbox?"

Their eyes widened and they all shook their heads.

"What happened?" asked Barry. He was a handsome twenty-year-old with light brown hair and blue eyes.

"I went out to get the mail and was shocked to find a milk snake inside the box. Probably a prank, but I wondered…"

"Wondered if we'd prank you," said Tom. He was mostly identifiable by a large nose. "Nope. I don't think any of us would pull something like that. But we can ask around."

Lynn just shook her head. "There are plenty of younger people around here who *might* think it very funny. I didn't really believe it was any of you, but I thought I should ask."

They all nodded, then headed upstairs.

In spite of herself, Lynn felt a niggle of suspicion. They had more cause to want to prank her than any other youngster around here.

But it seemed so unlike them.

As the night deepened and the streets emptied, Terri Albright walked around the town. This wasn't a place where she could blend in as a tourist, so she kept to the darkness, dressed in dark clothes but being careful not to look suspicious.

She was angry. Angry beyond words. She was going to kill Jackson Stone for what he had done to her brother. She could hardly wait for the moment and hoped she could do it at close range so she could see the light go out of his eyes.

But even as she relished the idea, she knew she had to be cautious. After Stone there were two more jurors, and she didn't want to make Stone's death so obvious that the entire Naval Criminal Investigative Service crashed down on the problem. Bad enough that her friends had mentioned there was already a quiet investigation.

She'd tutted along with all of them. How awful that anyone would want to kill men who'd only been doing their duty. Unbeknownst to her friends, she didn't think it awful at all.

What was worse was that she couldn't get to those nine men who'd testified against her brother. Too many. Eyes were apt to focus on her, but if she left those men alone she could still look innocent, for surely she would have gone for them. Right?

Instead, she'd have to be satisfied with watching their careers crash and burn. Rats, all of them. Violating the unwritten code on which so many lives depended.

But the jurors could have turned the outcome, and for that she would never forgive them. They should have seen her brother for the honorable man he was, a man acting under the pressures of war. Doing things many others had done.

Anyway, she hated this damn town. It was too small to make her comfortable, too small to carry off the murder of Jackson Stone except in the most indirect way possible.

She'd hoped by setting that motel fire, she'd drive him on his way to his new posting in Denver. A larger city would make her mission easier. Safer.

Instead, he had planted here and was now living in a rooming house filled with other people. Harder to reach than at the motel.

Maybe if she'd set a bigger fire he'd be dead already, a clearly accidental death.

But she'd been focused on pushing him to Denver. She blamed herself for that slip. Poor planning, inexcusable in a Marine.

Okay, then. She'd messed up. She wasn't going to mess up again, however. Unless she saw an opportunity in this ink spot of a town, she'd have to wait for Denver.

A wait wouldn't be easy, though. She'd waited long enough already.

Chapter 8

Three days later the cause of the motel fire still hadn't been discovered. Gage Dalton said the inspector was leaning toward arson but hadn't yet discovered the means.

Jax was stuck a little while longer. He chafed under the restriction, then wondered at himself. He was a Marine for Pete's sake, used to following orders, even ones to stay in place.

But this was different. When those orders came, he'd either been in a combat situation or otherwise occupied.

Point was, he'd been busy. Busy enough to make the hours pass. Here there was little of interest to preoccupy him. Moreover, since Hugh Briggs's call, he'd been forced to follow procedures for a threat he didn't honestly believe would reach for him here.

That chafed, too.

He needed to be working out, at least. He was avoiding open spaces that might make him an easier target, so that meant running up and down the streets of this small town.

A quiet town, except for a few brawls at Mahoney's. Folks here were pretty well rooted in their familiar lives. Good for them, not good for him. It made him wonder if recruiting would be a good fit for him. But at least then he'd be able to work out decently and frequently. At least he'd have a command to watch over again.

Right now he was rootless with nothing to do.

Well, except for Lynn and her mother. That Nancy West was something else. Her supposedly covert attempts to get him and Lynn together were fun to watch. He doubted she had any idea just how transparent she was. No, not likely or she wouldn't be doing it. And the way Lynn's eyes sparked or her jaw tightened... Well, Jax felt a lot of sympathy for her.

Lynn, though, was becoming a problem for him. The more he saw of her, the more he wanted her. Now, when he went to bed, he was acutely aware that she was one flight of steps away. Sleep eluded him because he couldn't help fantasizing.

God, he needed to break the back of this before he became addicted. She was a military widow, unlikely to want to become involved with a Marine. She was planted here in Matt's family home, on a mission of her own, a mission that demonstrated how deep her ties to her late husband remained.

Then there was himself. After the way he'd grown up, he couldn't trust himself. What if he carried the seeds of his father? What if somewhere deep inside him all that violence wanted to emerge?

He should stay away from the house more. Stay away from Lynn more. Except there was nothing in Conard City to keep him busy.

Well, she'd begun to tear down a whole lot of plaster and was about to begin pulling out the lath. Surely she'd want help with that, and it would give him a good chance to use muscles that ached for something, anything, heavy-duty to wear them out.

He'd probably sleep better at night, too.

Sighing, he shoved his thumbs into his jeans pockets and turned toward the rooming house. The autumn was steadily sliding into winter, more rapidly now, and the light jacket he wore over his sweatshirt wasn't quite warm enough.

Too bad. He'd experienced far worse cold in Afghanistan.

Since Jazz and Adam's wedding such a short time ago, leaves had been pulled by the wind from the trees, scattering them everywhere. A brightly colored path. Overhead, the remaining leaves still wore their autumn cloaks, but a lot of bare branches showed through now.

Before long the world would shift into browns and grays. Right now, the sky had the rest of the world beat with its gray layer of clouds.

Suited his mood anyway.

As he walked, he kept scanning rooftops and the taller green pines. Threat could come from anywhere, although the Marine in him suggested that it wouldn't be a gunshot. Not here, not in such a quiet place.

But he didn't know the mind of his enemy. Knew nothing at all about the person behind these murders, the person who even now might be coming for him.

If they were inexperienced in tactics, they might just try it, planning to escape fast. If they'd started that fire, they'd certainly not thought it through. As fast as that motel had gone up, they could have done a much more successful job of arson.

Not that he wouldn't have escaped anyway, unless smoke had overcome him in his sleep. Possible anyway.

He had serious doubts that the fire had been intended for him. On the other hand, who would have wanted to burn down that local landmark? Someone who thought they'd been overbilled?

He snorted. Nope, the other possibility was a firebug, but where were the other fires?

When he got back to the house, he heard pounding and crashing from the living room. Yup, Lynn was hard at it. He poked his head in past the plastic and saw her surrounded by pieces of plaster and a ton of plaster dust. She held a sledgehammer and took another swing. More plaster pieces, more dust. At least she was wearing a dust mask.

"Want any help?" he asked.

A lock of auburn hair had escaped her blue bandanna and, as she turned toward him, she brushed it back, smearing the side of her forehead with white dust.

"Anything you want to help with," she said from behind her mask. "There are extra masks in that box beside the door."

"Be right back." Then he paused. "You need a drink or some coffee? You can come out here and we can deal with that first."

"Right now I'd like a double shot of bourbon, neat." Then she laughed. "Sure. I'll wash up a bit at the sink."

He caught sight of her brushing as much dust as she could from her jeans and green plaid shirt.

Hopeless task, he thought with a smile as he headed to the kitchen. Nancy wasn't there. Well, she probably had more ways to occupy herself around here.

She had friends to visit. He didn't. The only statement he'd wanted to make had been at the wedding. Done. And despite Lynn's comment that a lot of people would want to claim friendship with him now, not a one had tried. He was still a stranger to them, drifting through.

Not that it much mattered to him one way or the other.

The coffee finished brewing just as Lynn entered the kitchen.

He eyed her. "You clean up well for a snowman."

She laughed. "I slapped myself with a few rags." She went to the sink and began washing her hands and forearms. "Man, this stuff gets yucky when it's wet."

"Got an alternative?"

She shook her head. "These clothes are going in the trash when I'm done, though. I don't want to clog up anything."

He poured two cups of coffee and placed them on the table. "Time for a break. Then I'll swing the hammer if you want. Or I'll start cleaning up."

"The cleanup's going to be a pain. I still can't believe there's no mold inside that wall. Talk about luck."

"I agree."

"But sadly that lath has to come out, too. I'm not even going to try to replaster the wall." She dried her hands and arms on paper towels and came to join him at the table.

"Where's your mom?" Jax asked.

"She said something about shopping." Lynn smiled. "I hope she goes to the grocery because I haven't spared a single thought about dinner."

"I can go to Maude's and pick up something," he volunteered.

"It may come to that." She shook her head. "I often don't think about these things when I'm in a mood to work."

"I can take care of myself, Lynn."

She eyed him with a faint smile. "I'm sure you can. But there's my mother."

"That woman is a trip. I'm enjoying her, though."

"Ahh," she said after taking a sip of coffee. "Ambrosia. Thanks for making it."

"Well, I wanted some, too," he answered, drawing a laugh from her. "It's grown a lot chillier out there."

"My cell phone was pleased to tell me we might see some flurries later. Jazz and Adam tied the knot just in time apparently."

"Well, they could have stood out there in a gentle snowfall, looking like something out of one of those globes."

She grinned. "It wouldn't have been as beautiful with everyone bundled up in coats."

"Currier and Ives?" he suggested.

"Hah! Listen, how about a sandwich? I just realized I haven't eaten since breakfast."

He rose at once. "I'll make them. Just point me and tell me what you like."

"I was thinking peanut butter."

"Can do. One or two for you?"

"One please. Bread in the breadbox over there."

Lynn watched Jax as he made the sandwiches, thinking his every move suggested he was a man in excellent control of his body. Smooth and easy. Not the slightest misstep. No wasted motion. Impressive.

Well, everything about him was impressive. Matt had been impressive, too, but in a different way. It wasn't just the military bearing, or the comfort within his body, which both men shared. It had also been Matt's sense of humor, ever at the forefront and ready to burst out. He'd

been the master of the non sequitur, among other things.
And his puns!

Jax had a more somber mood. As if he had delved
into some very dark places. But no, that couldn't be quite
right, because Matt had delved into those same places
when he'd been deployed.

She sighed and decided she'd better drop the comparison game. Different men, differently attractive. Different
natures, different personalities.

But she'd loved Matt.

After they ate, she went to the sink to clean up and was
suddenly speared by sorrow. *Matt.* For all she'd begun
to collect the good memories of him and the grief struck
less often, it still surged at times. At night she still sometimes cried herself to sleep. She still wished she could
share this remodeling with him. Wished they could be
building their dreams together.

Seldom, however, did grief pierce her like this, freezing her in place, filling her eyes with stinging tears,
demanding its due. She gripped the edge of the sink,
wishing she could shake free of her sorrow, at least
briefly. She wasn't alone. Not a good time to break down.
That was for her private moments.

But her chest tightened until she could barely breathe.
Her throat hurt as if a wire wrapped tightly around it.
The tears didn't spill but hung from her eyelashes until
all she could see was a blur.

A gentle arm wrapped around her shoulders. Another
slipped around her waist and turned her until Jax surrounded her in a warm embrace.

"It's okay," he murmured. "Just let it happen."

And it did. Wrenching sobs escaped her, the tears
spilled in hot streams down her face and onto his shirt.
His steely strength supported her, but softened enough

to welcome her. Her fingers gripped his shirt, hanging on for dear life.

It seemed impossible that she would ever escape this wrenching, clawing feeling. That her insides would unknot and her chest loosen enough to breathe again. That life would ever feel normal again.

But as always, with the passing minutes, grief slowly released its hold. Setting her free. But for what?

Oh, God, she couldn't afford to think that way.

Sniffling away the last of her tears, she tried to step back, but Jax wouldn't let her go.

"Take it easy," he said quietly. "Just give yourself a few more minutes."

She lifted her face, tilting it back so she could dash the remaining tears from her eyes. "I've made you wet."

"I've been wetter."

"I don't usually cry all over people."

"Of course not. You're one hell of a brave, strong woman."

"Not at this minute," she said, her voice cracking from sobbing.

"This is a kind of strength, too. Being able to let it out."

"I've been getting better."

"I've noticed."

He felt so good against her, that hardened body, those strong arms. Suddenly, a spike of fear hit her. What the heck was she doing?

This time when she stepped back, he let her go, his arms dropping to his sides. His expression was grave, however.

"I need to get back to pulling that wall out," she said steadily, grabbing a paper towel and wiping her face. "God, I must look a fright."

"Not possible," he answered. "Let me take care of the lunch dishes and I'll join you in a few minutes."

Letting her flee toward some privacy.

Damn, how did a man like that grow so sensitive?

His childhood, she thought. Something in it had turned him into a total introvert, yet the man he'd become gave the lie to that being his nature.

Now the familiar questions whirled again in her mind as she picked up the sledgehammer and went back to work. What had created the kid he used to be and the man he was now? At the root of that change, there had to be something, a bridge between his past and his present.

She doubted she'd ever know.

On Saturday morning, Lynn's students, Barry, Tom and Will, went to the city basketball courts to play a little pickup. They couldn't do "shirts and skins" in this weather, so they dragged out some athletic wrap and wore neutral wrapped around their upper arms.

It was all going well until some of the gals, watching from the sidelines, said something that Barry didn't miss.

"That Lynn Macy. Who'd have thought?"

Curious, Barry wandered over, wiping sweat from his face with the arm of his blue fleece shirt that was blazoned with the college's white logo. "Hey," he said, sitting nearby and reaching for a bottle of the water the guys always brought with them.

He raised the bottle toward them as if in toast. "At least the water's not warming up in this weather. Next month it'll probably freeze."

The girls all smiled, and one said, "Well, there are indoor courts at the college."

"True, but they smell sweaty."

That sent the ladies off into peals of laughter.

Then one asked, "You live with Lynn Macy, don't you?"

Barry chose apparent disinterest as a better way to find out what was going on. "I *room* there, not live." He didn't question them about why they asked.

"Well, now she's got that guy living there. The Marine."

"He's a roomer, too." And where was this leading? Barry liked Lynn a whole lot, and the way these gals were giggling, he suspected he was going to get angry if he found out what was behind their amusement.

He took a long swig of water, needing the hydration, but wishing it were hot chocolate. Then he looked at the women. "You got a thing for that Marine?"

"Who wouldn't?" one of them sighed.

Their hair almost looked like a rainbow, one blonde, one ginger, one dark. The one with the dark hair sported blue streaks. He kinda liked the ginger hair, though, and she was the one doing almost all the talking. He offered her his best smile. "If you're looking for an introduction," he said, "I'm not sure I can make one. I barely know the guy. Keeps pretty much to himself."

"Except with Lynn Macy," Ginger said, clearly enjoying herself.

Barry wondered how to wade into the matter without making them clam up. He had the strongest feeling he needed to know what they were talking about. And he doubted he was going to like it.

Barry managed to shrug. "He's only been in town a week, planning to leave any day from what I hear."

Blue-streaks just looked amused. Blondie giggled. Ginger sniffed. "Doesn't matter," she said. "That Lynn is a fast one."

Barry's insides coiled tight, but he achieved a friendly but slightly bored tone. "How do you mean?"

"You mean you haven't heard?" Ginger looked amazed.

"Hey, I'm a guy, what can I say?"

That brought knowing grins to three faces. Ginger turned to the two others, then said, "He's living with her. He deserves to know."

Barry looked from one face to another. Question time, he decided. They all now looked as if they could barely contain themselves. "What should I know?"

Ginger couldn't contain the news any longer. "That nearly every time Lynn Macy left town to go visit her *husband* she was actually meeting someone else. Maybe that Marine."

"Huh?" Barry was stunned to his very core. "How do you know that?"

Ginger waved a hand. "Everyone knows. Except you, I guess. Anyway, kinda interesting that guy moved in with her so fast."

Barry couldn't stop himself. "The motel burned down."

"And there are apartments near the college and a couple of other rooming houses. No reason he had to stay with *her*. Or for this long. He could have left right after the wedding."

Oh, my God, Barry thought. Innocent things all tangled up into a story that sounded plausible.

Except he knew Lynn. And he was getting to know that straight-arrow military guy just a bit. What's more, for the love of Pete, Lynn's *mother* was staying there. Talk about a chaperone!

"Well, that's interesting," was all he said. He drained the plastic water bottle and crushed it in his hand before dunking it straight in the recycling bin nearby. He rose, grabbing his sports bag, seeming to forget the girls.

"Guys?" he called to the other players. "I'm headed back. Calc test Monday morning."

They waved to him and he turned, marching straight back to the rooming house. He was sure he couldn't tell Lynn about this. It would only upset her, and that lady had been upset enough since her husband died, as well he should know since this was his second year rooming with her. Anyway, there wasn't a thing she could do about it.

For once in his life, Shakespeare suddenly struck Barry as a smart guy. *Methinks the lady doth protest too much.* Nope, nobody would care what Lynn said about this and might think she was telling an even bigger lie.

Barry clenched his jaw. He needed to find a way to spike this rumor. Fast. But he had no idea in hell how.

Chapter 9

Saturday afternoon, the rental car company pulled up with a new vehicle for Jax. It had taken a while, but the delivery driver apologized, saying something about needing the police report and whatever.

Yeah, they'd held off until they were sure that Jax hadn't started the fire that had totaled their car. Evidently the sheriff had made the decision about Jax. Which meant Jax was free, although he'd have felt better if Dalton had said so himself.

He also wanted to know what they'd learned about the arson. It had struck close enough to home that he felt he deserved something of an after-action report.

Then Brigg's warning flashed through his mind again. Jax shook his head. He hoped any Marine would do a better job than that fire of taking out a target.

Standing on the sidewalk, keys in hand, he looked at that Jeep and realized he could now just drive out of town. Get on with his plan to find a place of his own in Denver before he returned to duty.

But matters had changed. Suddenly, he wasn't in a hurry to begin this new phase of his life. Instead, he wanted to stay right here.

Lynn. She was the reason, of course. Nothing else on his plate seemed quite as important. That was so ridiculous he wanted to shake the feeling out of himself.

What the hell was happening to him? How had he invested so much in such a short time? There wasn't anything to invest in anyway. She was a grieving widow. He was moving on, always moving on, and she was planted here in the garden of her friends and everything familiar.

Besides, he kept a better guard on his heart than this. From his very early years he'd learned not to care too much too easily. His heart wore armor for good reason, and it took one hell of a lot to penetrate that armor.

The closer you let people get, the more likely you were to get hurt. Jax was very careful about who he let close, who he trusted. Only a very few had jumped those hurdles quickly. Lynn seemed to be one of them.

So it was time to pack his duffel and take this car on the road to Denver. Before he could hurt her.

But deep in his soul that fear had taken root. He could hurt Lynn, maybe without even meaning to, but he might. That woman had had enough sorrow in her life and she didn't deserve any more. Or to feel used. Or soiled.

That word brought up a sudden unwelcome memory of his father waving a Bible at him and his mother on Sunday morning. Ranting and yelling and reading verses that petrified a young boy. The Stone family might not be churchgoers, but they had their own private congregation headed by Pastor Samuel Stone, a man who shouted fire and brimstone threats of hell.

To Jax all these years later, it seemed his father had used the Bible to justify himself and his actions. It certainly hadn't been intended to improve his wife and son, both of whom had an intimate acquaintance with the "wages of sin," thanks to Samuel Stone. No, it was the way Samuel had justified himself as moral judge, jury and executioner.

Even though Jax had eventually learned that his father's Bible readings had been selective to the extreme, the knowledge hadn't erased all of the effects.

What had he hoped to find in this town anyway? Absolution for the sins he'd apparently committed as a child? Well, if his father had condemned him to hell—and he had when Jackson finally stood up to him—then Jax had gone to hell all right: to war.

Jax returned to the present, a chill like wet leaves on his shoulders. The past? The present? If Briggs were to be believed, he might be stalked. Maybe he should spend more time thinking about that. Apply a little strategic thinking to the possible tactics of the person who wanted him dead.

If that person did. It *could* all be coincidence.

But some battle-hardened sense deep within wouldn't let him accept that. He scanned the rooftops once again, made sure the Jeep was locked, then returned to the house. If Lynn was still banging and prying, she could use help.

At least that was something he could do that would matter.

But Lynn had showered while he was taking care of paperwork on the new car, and now sat in the kitchen, wrapped in a green robe, wearing fuzzy slippers, with a towel wrapped around her head. She had her hands wrapped around a mug and the room was redolent with coffee.

"Fresh," she said, pointing at the pot.

"Thanks." Jax helped himself, wishing that chill on his shoulders would vanish. Every time he'd felt it before, it had boded no good. "Finished working for the day?"

"There are times," she said wryly, "when the body says *that's enough*, and I've learned to listen."

"Always a good decision." He sat across from her, studying her lovely face. A beautiful woman in a gentle way. "As you know I now have wheels. I wonder if Gage Dalton isn't as interested in me hanging around town. He hasn't said."

He thought he saw her start, then still, but it was so brief he couldn't be sure. After a moment, she lifted her mug to her lips.

"Good news for you."

"Possibly."

Her green gaze trailed to him. "Why wouldn't it be good? Nobody likes to feel they've lost their freedom for any reason."

"Well, that part's okay." Except he'd begun to like the excuse that kept him in this house. He'd stopped chafing within two days. "Where's Nancy?"

"My mom's always been something of a gadabout. I wonder she can sit still long enough to hold a job, even a part-time one."

Jax laughed. "You seemed to have inherited the gene. She's out all the time entertaining herself, and you spend all your time in here pursuing your remodeling."

That drew a smile from Lynn. "You're probably right. Anyway, she called about an hour ago, said she was going to the market. I wonder what meal she's planning."

"I guess we'll find out. I gather she doesn't approve of what your boys are eating."

Lynn wrinkled her nose. "I'm surprised she hasn't hog-tied them and forced broccoli down their throats."

"There are other veggies."

"Sure, if they top a pizza."

Jax grinned. "Do I hear the Freshman Twenty coming?" He referred to the weight gain many students made in college.

Lynn shook her head. "They play too much basketball. Pickup games. This is Barry's second year with me, and occasionally they forget I'm old and talk to me. Really. We've even played Spades a few times, old-fashioned as it is."

He pretended amazement. "You actually have a deck of *real* cards?"

"Several. Sometimes my friends and I get together for a cutthroat game of Hold 'Em."

"Now that I'd like to see. I'm a Seven Card Stud guy."

"Let's give it a try sometime." Then her face shadowed and she looked away.

Jax figured she had just realized there was no point in long-term planning. She understood that clearly enough, which made him feel...what? Disappointment? Relief? Damned if he knew.

Nancy took that opportune moment to open the front door. "Lynn? Jax? Help with the groceries?"

Lynn rolled her eyes as she started to rise. "I wonder if she bought out half the store."

"I'll help her," Jax said. "You just rest. You've earned it."

There *were* a lot of bags, Jax realized as he reached the trunk of Nancy's car. "You planning to feed an army?"

She shook her head. "Lynn is too low on staples. I'll

bet when I'm not here she resorts to frozen meals." She
raised an eyebrow at him. "I'd almost bet all those toaster
waffles don't belong to her roomers."

"I'll get these," Jax said. "You just go inside and get
warm."

Nancy beamed at him. "You're such a nice young
man."

Nancy sailed away, her faux fur coat flapping a bit to
reveal that today her color of choice was that dark pink,
whatever it was called.

Fascinating woman, he thought as he bent to grab
bags. Although not as fascinating as her daughter. However dressed up, Nancy couldn't hold a candle to her
daughter in jeans and work shirts.

Madge was well pleased when the rumor returned to
her. In the way of rumors, it made the circuit more than
once. Nobody remembered where it had begun, but it
got embellished along the way. Her simple supposition,
phrased as a question and dropped in a couple of ears,
had grown into a full-blown tale with convincing details.

Better than she had imagined. Much better. Just let
Lynn try to quash this one. It would be like trying to
shake horse manure from her shoes.

Quite happy with herself, she arranged to meet Luke
at a roadhouse twenty-five miles deep into ranch country,
a place favored by hired hands and ranchers who didn't
have time to drive to town for a few too many beers or
hard liquor.

Wearing a tight hot pink dress, with just enough cleavage on display for when she took off her jacket, she set
out.

Country music played from a jukebox. The barroom
was a mix of scarred old tables, creaky chairs and a floor

covered with peanut shells. Easier to clean up the spills that way. The bar itself was at least a hundred years old, boasting a real brass footrail that occasionally got polished. Food was limited to things that came out of bags and boxes, all of it salty to encourage drinking.

Not a family in sight. Hardly a woman either, which made Madge the cynosure of all eyes. Fine by her. She enjoyed being admired.

She sat at the bar, her purse and jacket on a stool beside her, and waited for Luke, ordering a beer of her own. It wouldn't be long before somebody sashayed over to offer to buy her a drink, so she hoped Luke wasn't too late. In the ordinary way, she'd have gladly taken the offer of that drink, but not tonight. She didn't want anything to interfere with her talking to Luke.

He showed up maybe ten minutes later, just about the time one of those rangy cowboys, one who hadn't been able to take his eyes off her, appeared to be about to get up. Luke slid onto the stool beside her and smiled.

Man, Madge thought, he had that boyish appeal all sewed up. And she'd trust him about as far as a coiled rattler.

She waited until his beer arrived, then gave him her biggest, most flirtatious smile. Not that she wanted to flirt with him, but she could match his con man smile. "So you heard the rumor I started? It was brilliant, especially the way it took off."

"Genius." He nodded. "Pure genius."

Madge preened. "I'm good."

His blue eyes drifted to her cleavage, then rose again to her face. "Lynn will never shake that."

"And when Jackson Stone hears that she cheated on her husband, he's not going to want to touch her. Maybe he'll even get upset."

"And you'll be a friendly shoulder for him to cry on."

"That's the plan."

Luke shook his head a little. "Come on, Madge, we've known Jackson since he was a kid. He's not one to cry on a shoulder. Maybe less now than ever."

She bristled. "How would you know? He's not the same guy."

"No, now he's hard."

She frowned, tapping her fingernails on the bar, annoyed, but afraid Luke might be right.

Luke soothed her. "Whether he wants a shoulder or not, he won't want Lynn after this rumor gets to him. And you just be there, all pretty and nice like you are."

Well, looks and pretended sweetness had caught her a few husbands, but those marriages hadn't lasted any longer than it took for her patience to wear off. God, guys could be such saps. If they wanted a cook and a maid, they needed to look at someone else.

Luke spoke again. "Now we need to get that rumor into Stone's ear. The problem is I don't think people around here know him well enough to share the grapevine with him."

"It'll get to him because someone will feel they need to warn him that Lynn's a cheater."

Luke turned his frosty beer bottle around a couple of times before lifting it and drinking half of it. "You might be right."

"Of course I'm right," she retorted waspishly. "I told you I could get this whole thing going and you didn't believe me."

"I underestimated you."

That smoothed her ruffled feathers. She raised a finger for another beer, wishing this roadhouse could make something as simple as a daiquiri. Oh, well, she could make one for herself when she got home.

"Now," she said, turning to Luke. "What are *you* going to do?"

"Why, my dear, I'm going to get Stone into some trouble."

"How in the hell are you going to do that?"

"You heard why he's been hanging around, haven't you?"

She shook her head as her curiosity spiked.

"The motel was arson."

"I know that," Madge said impatiently. "So?"

"The sheriff asked him to stay in town. Like he was under suspicion."

Madge shook her head violently. "That's gonna help how?"

"Well," he said quietly, "he was staying at the motel when the fire broke out."

Her eyes widened and she drew a sharp breath. "You're not gonna burn down that house!"

"No, but a little fire will do. Just a little one. Like he's a firebug. How do you think that'll make Lynn feel about him?"

Madge took a long time to think about it, maybe because the daiquiris she'd had at home plus the beer was starting to slow her head down.

Then a grin spread across her face. "I'm not the only genius, Luke."

"Reckon not," he replied, raising his bottle to her and winking. "Reckon not."

Terri Albright's frustration was growing rapidly. Several times a day she had to remind herself that she was on a mission, and missions often required patience.

But this was outside of enough. Hands tied because this town was too small, and that damn Stone seemed disinclined to head for the wide-open spaces. Must be that woman he was staying with. He must be preoccupied with her.

Great. Just great.

Whatever she did, it was going to have to be fast and permanent. Something that would give her just enough time to get the hell out.

The problem was that she hadn't yet seen an opportunity. Shooting was out of the question while he was in town. That would draw immediate attention, and as tight as this little burg was, someone would be able to point out where the shot had come from. Could she get out of town fast enough after that?

She had good reason to doubt it. And she'd stand out as the stranger. Might as well wear a neon sign. Two bottles of spray purple dye sat on the ground beside her. She was thinking they'd make her look more like a young girl, but she hadn't decided to use them unless she needed to be seen.

She had a seven-inch KA-BAR sheathed on her belt and figured that would have to be her tool if Stone didn't leave soon for Denver. She'd find him soon enough in a big city like that, even if she had to wait until he returned to duty. Because once he showed up there, his privacy would be shot.

But what was killing her now was that she couldn't do a damn thing. Stuck in the mud. Hoping she could take care of Stone because her leave was ticking away. She'd have to return to duty, Stone would be headed for Denver and once she was back on duty, she wouldn't be able to reach him until her next opportunity to take leave.

Rolling over in her sleeping bag, staring up at a sky

that looked as if handfuls of diamonds had been strewn across it, she ignored the cold. She had to find a way. Even here.

Problem was, her role in uniform had never included making plans. She just followed orders. Others made the plans. Her brother Ted would have been better at figuring this out. More experience.

That chafed her sometimes. She was always the little sister, and then the junior rank. Regardless, those petty resentments weren't going to stop her from avenging him.

In the distance, she heard a wolf's mournful howl, soon joined by the harmonizing voices of the pack.

Terri wished she could howl along with them.

Lynn's pantry was full now with "staples." Canned goods, jarred goods, dry goods, even stuff in a set of canisters Nancy had bought.

"Mom," Lynn said, "I'm never going to use all that."

"If you *ever* decide to cook for yourself, you don't want to be out of some little thing that you absolutely must have."

Lynn eyed her with amusement. "Seriously."

"I know what I'm talking about."

Lynn wasn't going to argue a truth that her mother believed.

Dinner was late as a result. Night had settled over the world as she served up a beef roast along with mashed potatoes, gravy and asparagus. Lynn loved asparagus.

Jax had agreed to join them, but Lynn was beginning to feel as if he were family and ought to come without an invitation.

Still, Nancy insisted on inviting him, this time by assuring him that she and Lynn couldn't eat all that food and she didn't want to start filling the refrigerator with leftovers. "If we keep that up, the boys won't have any room."

Hah, thought Lynn. They didn't use a whole lot of that space. In fact, they lately hadn't even been making their toaster pastries in the morning. Maybe because Nancy occupied the kitchen like a broody hen?

She also had no idea how long Nancy intended to visit. Her mother hadn't mentioned and it would be rude to ask, a rudeness that Nancy wouldn't overlook.

Still, the boys had kitchen privileges in this house and Nancy had thoughtlessly taken over. But it wasn't as if there was a living room to sit in.

Dang it all, Lynn thought.

Over dinner, Lynn decided to take one bull by the horns. "Mom?"

"Yes?"

Jax continued eating, clearly removing himself from this conversation.

"In the mornings, why don't you take your tea into your room and watch those morning shows you always loved."

"Why would I want to do that? I don't watch them anymore anyway. The news is just too awful. Did you know my therapist told me to stop watching it because there was nothing I could do about most of it? He said it only depressed me and made me feel helpless."

"Your *therapist*?" That floored Lynn.

"Didn't I tell you? The nicest woman. I've been feeling a tad depressed. Not seriously, mind you, but I have. She's a wonderful help. Anyway, no news."

"There must be something…"

"The weather?" Nancy asked drily. "Lynn, what's going on?"

Lynn put her fork down, sighing. She felt that Jax was

paying attention, though he revealed it in no way. He simply scooped up another mouthful of mashed potatoes.

"It's my boys," Lynn said after a moment. "They haven't said a word, but I've noticed they don't pop into the kitchen anymore for their breakfasts."

"Because of me?" Nancy sounded incensed.

"Probably," Lynn said frankly. "Not because of anything you're doing, but likely because you're an older woman. You know how kids are. Uncomfortable with older adults."

"Well, really!"

"They have kitchen privileges, Mom. Can you take your tea and a book or whatever, and give them time to pop in and eat?"

"I could cook for them," Nancy suggested.

"I'm sure that would make them even more uncomfortable, Mom."

"So those boys come before me. I'll try not to get in their way. And I'll consider myself confined to my room." Nancy rose and threw her napkin on the table, then walked out.

"That went well," Lynn muttered to no one in particular. Although "no one" was sitting at the table.

"It appears that fences will need mending," Jax remarked quietly.

"Obviously," Lynn answered. "Obviously. But those boys don't deserve to feel unwelcome down here. I don't want that."

"I don't think she's exactly making them unwelcome."

"No, but she's always in here except when she's out to see friends. They must feel like they're trespassing now."

"Why don't you talk to them?" Jax suggested as he finished his potatoes. "Tell them they're welcome whether Nancy's in here or not. Just like before."

Lynn put her chin in her hand and nodded. "I should. Thanks. I just didn't want to put them on the spot." She sighed again. "So I put my mother on the spot. Great job, Lynn."

She ruminated for a minute, wondering how she could have handled this better. It was even more difficult because she didn't know how long Nancy was staying. She couldn't go to her boys and tell them it would only be another week.

If only she had another habitable room down here besides the kitchen. But she didn't, and now her mom was feeling confined to quarters. Sadness filled her. She hated the idea that she'd hurt Nancy. Much as they could ruffle each other's feathers, she loved her mom.

Finally, she spoke. "I wish I had more room down here."

"But you're in the middle of renovations."

"True." Lynn felt her mouth quirk. "I suppose I should be glad I didn't get started on *her* room. I don't know what I'd have done. Especially since she can't climb stairs."

But now she had a mess of a different kind to clean up. Oh, boy.

Upstairs, as the evening deepened, Barry, Will and Tom gathered in Barry's room at his invitation.

On Barry's desk—an old table, really—sat two extra large monitors, a high-powered computer and all a guy could need for online role-playing games, one of their passions. It was hard sometimes to keep his mind on schoolwork, but he was determined.

Several opened bags of chips sat on a smaller table along with soft drinks in their cans. Tom and Will busily munched while Barry related what he'd heard that morning.

The munching slowed, then stopped.

Will was the first to react. "You gotta be kidding me! *Lynn?*"

"That's what they're saying."

"Sheesh," said Tom, who was going prematurely bald. He'd started shaving his head just a month ago. The girls seemed to like it.

"I have a stronger word," Will offered.

Barry snickered. "Have at it. We've all used it."

But none of them did.

For a while, they were silent, but slowly Tom started chomping chips again, almost violently. "Damn," he said forcefully, a few crumbs dribbling onto his sweatshirt. "That's…that's…"

Barry filled it in. "Awful. Terrible. I can't think of enough words."

"Well, hell," Will muttered. "Can you believe people?"

"Oh, they've really woven this one into a good story."

Tom shook his head. "I can't believe it. How could anyone?"

"Juices up their lives, I guess," Barry said. "Little enough happens around here. Why not have a good scandal?"

"There's nothing good about this one," Tom growled. "How could anyone believe she had a thing going with Jax before, when her husband was still alive? Is that why he took over two years to get here? And why did he book into that motel anyway, if that's true."

"And just look at the two of them," Barry agreed. "They're a bit skittish around each other. Careful. I've seen how they gaze at each other a couple of times, but you can tell it hasn't gone beyond looks. They don't have that kind of…whatever. There's nothing there. Yet."

"What would be wrong with it if there was?" Will demanded. "Doesn't she deserve some happiness?"

"I've heard her crying up there sometimes at night," Barry offered. "It's quiet, but I hear it. She's not over her husband. She cries less than last year, but it's still happened a couple of times."

Silence fell again, except that it was punctuated by guzzling soda and the occasional rustle of chip bags. Will reached over and pulled another can from the cooler bag they used up here. Lynn was nice about letting them stash cold packs in her fridge.

"I don't like going in the kitchen with her mom there," Tom remarked. "She always wants to talk. I bet she thinks she's being nice, but she always gets around to stupid questions like what am I majoring in and what do I want to do and am I going to a four-year school from here. It's like I'm a little kid again."

"Yeah. What do you want to grow up to be?" Barry snickered again.

A few minutes later, Will asked, "Do you think that snake in the mailbox was part of this?"

Barry shrugged. "I don't know when the gossip started. Could've been a prank, not a message."

"Nasty prank," was Tom's opinion. "I can't imagine how she felt when she opened that box and saw that snake. I'd be shocked, and I'm not afraid of snakes."

"Except the poisonous kind," Tom said knowingly.

"I have a brain. Unlike some people."

Barry thought the two of them were about to get into a pillow fight, so he spoke quickly. "We gotta find a way to help Lynn."

Two pairs of eyes met his. Then Will as
important question.

"How can we do that?"

Lynn headed for her mother's bedroom a short time
later. Time to mend fences somehow, although Nancy
could remain in high dudgeon for a long time.

Except she feared that this time she hadn't made her
mother angry, but instead had hurt her. She never wanted
to do that. They might prickle each other, get tart, or indulge in small arguments, but this was different.

This time she'd told her mother to make herself scarce.
Never mind that that hadn't been her intention. The road
to hell and all that.

She knocked on Nancy's door. When her mother didn't
answer, Lynn entered anyway. Her mom sat stiffly in the
upholstered chair beside the bed.

"I'll leave in the morning," Nancy said, an edge in
her voice.

"Mom, no! That's not at all what I meant!" She closed
the door behind her.

"Well, I'm obviously discommoding your roomers."

"Not that much I just noticed they were behaving differently and I felt bad about it."

Nancy finally looked at her. "Maybe I should pay rent.
It would make me equal."

"Oh, God." Lynn sat on the edge of the bed and stared
at the woman she'd loved her entire life. Her heart began
to ache. "I went about this all wrong. I didn't mean to
make you feel this way. I should have spoken to the boys."

"Water over the dam," was Nancy's only response.

Lynn sat quietly, wondering what she could do. "I was
wrong. I apologize. Try to forget what I said."

Nancy sniffed.

ose in Lynn, born in a bottomless
by all the stresses in her life now
d to cope with a million things all
she was through coping.
e got enough on my plate, Mom. I
handle one more damn thing. You
cept my apology. I can't worry about
this, too!"

Then she stormed from the room and had to stop herself from slamming the door.

She fled from it all to her attic aerie where nothing
could touch her. Nothing. Her private hermitage where
she left the world behind.

She was unaware that Jax, standing in his bedroom
door, saw her run. Unaware that his face darkened and
his hands clenched.

Later, after having done countless push-ups, sit-ups,
knee bends, twists and whatever else he could fit into that
small room, Jax washed up in the empty group bathroom.

Then he cleaned the tub and sink. The boys weren't
bad about it, but sometimes the spit and polish in him
took over. Satisfied not even a drop of toothpaste remained on the sink or floor, that everything gleamed as
much as such old fixtures could, he headed downstairs.

Nancy was in the kitchen, sipping tea. At least she'd
emerged from her self-imposed isolation. He suspected
she'd taken her anger out on Lynn, which was why Lynn
had vanished to her apartment.

Other than giving her a brief acknowledgment, he
started making coffee. He wasn't happy with Nancy just
then. Not when she'd clearly upset Lynn that much.

Nancy spoke just as he turned from the pot and tried to
decide whether to sit at the table or take a mug upstairs.

"I acted badly," Nancy said. "I acted like a child, going to my room to pout."

He leaned back against the counter, folding his arms. "I'm not the one who needs to hear that."

"But I can't climb those damn stairs to tell her."

"Then it'll have to wait, I guess."

"Could you…"

Jax shook his head. "This is between the two of you, and I'm not getting in the middle. Anyway, she needs to hear that from you, not me."

Nancy sighed and sipped tea. "I guess you're right." Then, "I suppose it's Lynn's turn to pout in her room."

"I very much doubt she's pouting."

"Then what's she doing, hiding away?"

This really wasn't his place, but he poured some coffee, then sat at the table. "I don't know Lynn very well."

Nancy looked at him. "I feel like I hardly know her myself anymore."

"What she's been through…well, it changes a person. Forever. She's been to hell and isn't quite all the way back. She's working on it, though."

"That's why she's keeping so busy on this house. Hiding."

Jax shook his head. "It may have started that way, but that's not it anymore. She loves what she's doing. She's doing it for *herself.* But it's a big job and, apart from the pleasure and sense of achievement she gets, she's got a lot of worries about it. Puzzle pieces to be balanced against money and time and priority. Every day has her head whirling about this project. I'm surprised she's not wiped out, honestly. It's a hell of a lot for one person to take on solo. But she's doing a great job of it."

"So maybe she's up there collapsed," Nancy remarked.

"Or just out of steam. Needing a break. I mean, not

only is she handling massive renovations, but she has a houseful of people. The boys, me."

"And me," Nancy added.

"Bursting at the seams," he agreed. "Give her some time. She's not a woman to take anything lying down. She'll get back on her feet soon."

At two in the morning, Terri Albright looked up at the house where Jax was staying now. She'd heard he was already under suspicion for her little arson. What if she added to that suspicion? Except they'd probably arrest him and she wouldn't be able to get at him at all.

She ground her teeth, frustrated beyond words while wondering when she'd hear that third juror had keeled over. Too long. It had been too long since she'd left the poison in his stash of soft drinks.

She also didn't have an endless amount of time for leave. She'd have to report or go AWOL, which wouldn't help anything at all.

Hatred filled her, scorching her insides and never quitting. She didn't want to put off getting this Stone guy, although she supposed she could. Go back and get that last juror first.

But with each move, she made it more likely that the current investigation would grow broader and more intense. Making everything more difficult.

No, better to take care of this guy here. In a place where he should be hard to find so it might not be linked to the others. She'd had to access protected personnel information to find out this much.

So it might appear unrelated if she killed him here. It might look like there'd been a fight and he'd gotten the worst of it. As little as she knew about people around here, she knew there were some heavy drinkers and brawlers, especially out at the roadhouses.

If she could lure him to one of those… Or maybe she could get him somewhere else and dispose of him there.

Yeah, that was a possibility.

At last feeling she might be getting a handle on this problem, she turned and slunk away into the shadows.

Ted was going to be so proud of her when she finished. She knew he would.

Chapter 10

Sunday morning dawned with storms. Heavy rumbles of thunder rolled across the city and surrounding ranches. The last leaves were torn from trees, leaving only slender-needled evergreens alone.

By 10:00 a.m. it looked as if winter's breath was finally blowing across the land. The world had turned gray and stark.

So far, Jax hadn't seen Lynn and supposed that she and her mother hadn't made up yet.

Dang! Those two women were close. Even he could see that. But he didn't think that Nancy was considering all that Lynn had been through.

She'd certainly been through a lot, but she'd picked herself up and had taken on a huge task with evident skill and with a heavy dose of determination. He admired her more with each passing day.

And wanted her more.

The car keys he now possessed sat on the small battered dresser, taunting him with his original plans, taunting him with his unwillingness to leave this town he'd hated so much in his youth.

He'd attended schools here, always feeling like a kid outside the window of a candy store, a place he lacked the coinage to enter.

Always the outsider, with the ugliness in his home holding him prisoner. A prisoner of silence because he didn't want anyone to know what was happening. He was ashamed, and even more ashamed on his mother's behalf. She guarded the secret of their painful life as tightly as he did, and he sure as hell hadn't wanted her to get into any more trouble with Samuel.

Although trouble waited around every corner for her. And for him, too. A shameful existence, the shame compounded by Samuel's hellfire sermons directed at making both of them feel like sinners.

And at school he'd seen kids who didn't have problems like his. At least none that showed. The others knew how to exit the prisons of silence, if they were there. Knew how to reach out and make friends with kids.

All he'd had was Adam. Thank God for Adam. He had never known if Adam had suspected the state of Jax's homelife, but his friendship had been steadfast. His military career had proven Adam's quality time and again.

For Jax the military had been an escape. At first anyway. Then as he settled into the Marines, he'd discovered a world that matched his needs and a sense of mission that made him feel whole again. Pride had been discovered, as well as his ability to deal with the worst of situations. A whole new way of looking at himself and the world.

He sighed, looking at those keys, and wondered when Lynn and her mother would sort out all of this. He could understand both sides of this problem. Lynn, probably feeling overwhelmed, had tried to make one little thing right.

Instead, she'd apparently gone about it the wrong way. But Nancy's response had been wrong, too. Instead of going to her room in a huff, she should have discussed the problem in more depth.

Even during his short time as a roomer here, he'd felt the reluctance of the students to barge into a kitchen that was almost always occupied. Maybe he himself was adding to their hesitancy.

But after all his years dealing with young people their age, he understood it. He recognized it. Young people on the cusp of becoming adults were often intimidated by the older adults they'd been taught to respect and to keep quiet around.

None of that kept them from antics or hijinks typical of their age. Not until they understood the seriousness of what was required of them, the knowledge of the importance of their duties. Only then did they begin to slip into the shoes of confident, capable adults.

Regardless, there had to have been a better way to deal with the situation. Maybe this time Lynn had misjudged her mother.

Jax certainly had. He'd thought Nancy feisty enough to withstand such a suggestion. Maybe there were several reasons she was getting therapy.

He shook his head, wondering why he was maundering his way through all of this. Was he bored or something? Or was he being drawn into all this drama? There seemed to be enough of it to go around.

All his new clothes needed a trip through Lynn's washer, so he donned his cammo, belted it and headed downstairs, thinking that he ought to head for Maude's diner to get breakfast. Maybe bring back breakfast to the house.

Except he had no idea whether the two women would emerge from their separate corners to eat.

This would have been amusing had he not come to care so much for Lynn's feelings.

As he emerged from his room, he heard the three young men talking in one of the other bedrooms. Making up his mind, he knocked on the door.

Barry opened it after a short pause. "Hey," he said.

"Hey," Jax replied. "Listen, I'm thinking of going to Maude's to pick up breakfast. Any of you interested?"

"In going to Maude's?" Barry asked.

"Either that, or I'll bring back for everyone."

Barry lifted his brows. "You have any idea how much we can eat?"

Jax answered wryly. "You better believe it. I command units full of guys your age."

That made Barry grin.

"So give me your orders or tag along. My treat, your choice."

The boys decided not to tag along. Calculus test in the morning. Jax was looking forward to taking his new car out for a spin and planned to double all their orders for fried potatoes, flapjacks and more, and even some lattes.

Step in the right direction, he thought.

Neither Lynn nor Nancy were in sight as he passed the kitchen, but he decided to bring breakfast home for them anyway. If they didn't want to eat, the boys would probably scarf theirs down as well.

And he was damn well going to make sure *all* of them ate in the kitchen. Make a point.

He arrived at Maude's before the after-church crowd had taken over, and while Mavis raised her brows at the

size of his order, she and her mother set to work immediately. By the time Jax left, he had six bags full of food
and two trays of lattes.

It might be enough. He almost laughed aloud.

Back at the house, he discovered Lynn in the kitchen.
She looked worn-out. *Bad night*, he guessed. And no
sign of Nancy.

Lynn's weary eyes widened as he brought in the bags
and set them on the table.

"What?" she asked.

"We're having a family breakfast. The *whole* family,
including Nancy. I gotta bring in the coffee, then ring the
breakfast bell. Will you set the table for six?"

And damned if Nancy was going to beg off.

Ten minutes later he had the entire group around the
table. The benefit of being accustomed to taking command. He put a certain tone in his voice, which he used
as necessary, that no one argued with, not even Nancy.

Maude and Mavis had packed the insulated containers with family-sized portions, rather than individual,
when he'd said he was feeding six, three of them college age. Easy.

He opened those containers now and placed them
along the table with serving spoons.

It was a *lot* of food. Both Nancy and Lynn appeared
astonished, but the boys just grinned. Good eats for all
and plenty of it.

At first there was little conversation, but Jax waited
patiently for someone to start the ball rolling after they'd
all filled their plates. He'd done enough, brought them
all together, and now he had to let one of them take the
next step.

Will, with his red hair and freckles, spoke first. "This is great, Jax. Thanks!"

A chorus of agreement passed around the table. Still not enough to kick that conversational ball across the field.

"So what do you do, Jax?" Barry asked. "Apart from the obvious."

Jax smiled faintly. "Now that the war's wound down, I'm going to be in charge of our recruiting operations in Denver."

"Is that a step down?" Tom wanted to know.

"It's an honor, actually. Don't you know I'm the perfect representative of the Corps?"

That elicited some laughter from the boys, but as they quieted Barry said, "You're not kidding, are you?"

"No, I'm not. It really is an honor. I'll be one of the public faces of the Marines. Walk carefully, behave above reproach, etc. Plus, I'll wear the blues all the time."

Tom grinned. "I bet women love that."

"I don't exactly mind it myself, although cammo is more comfortable."

The conversation lagged for a bit, then Nancy said, "I want you young men to know that I didn't mean you to feel you had to stay out of the kitchen when I'm here. You have kitchen privileges, and rightly so. I guess I was getting in the way."

The three students hastened to assure her she had not, even though it had become patently obvious that they'd been avoiding the room.

"We just didn't want to intrude on you," Tom said.

"Well, you won't," Nancy replied firmly. "Not at all. You may have to sidestep occasionally if I'm doing something, but we'll all manage."

Lynn looked at her mother, a smile dawning. "Thanks, Mom."

"It's only right."

The conversation continued more easily then, the students talking about their courses, their majors, and even some of their hopes for the future. Meanwhile they demolished the flapjacks and potatoes, along with the remaining scrambled eggs.

Nancy joined the conversation. "I've always thought that the saddest part of this town is how little real opportunity it offers to young people. It's bleeding the youth away from here."

"There's plenty of life here, Mrs. West," Barry protested. "I'll be coming back after nursing school. I like it here that much."

"Good for you," Lynn said. "We need more nurses."

"*Everywhere* needs more nurses," Barry replied. "Lousy wages and miserable hours. But it's important work."

"Without enough respect," Lynn remarked.

After breakfast, the three boys kicked into high speed. Will said, "Just sit here and enjoy coffee while we clean up. Oh, wait, you like tea, don't you, Mrs. West?"

"Call me Nancy, please. Just put the electric kettle on if you don't mind. I can make my own tea." She smiled warmly.

Jax sat back to finish his own latte and watched the young men. And this, he thought, ought to ease at least one tension around here.

Lynn was astonished how much one breakfast together had achieved. Jax had been right—a *family* meal. She only wondered why she hadn't thought of it herself.

But then, she wasn't one to organize other people's

lives. She gave her roomers all the freedom young adults deserved and didn't want to encroach or make them feel obligated.

But Jax had taken care of it, maybe because he was just a roomer, too. One of them. And maybe because he knew how to corral people and get them in line, turn them into a friendly group.

Whatever it was, some of her tension eased out of her. But this entire experience hadn't dimmed her attraction to Jax one bit. It had enhanced it. Another kind of tension.

The desire to feel his hands on her naked skin, to feel his mouth and tongue finding their way around her every curve and hollow, had made it hard to sleep last night.

Guilt and yearning had warred within her, along with her upset with Nancy. It had been a long night of arguing with herself. A very long night.

She knew she hadn't any reason to feel guilty. Matt was no longer with her, and she believed he wouldn't want her to remain alone. But feelings didn't yield to logic, and her feelings for Jax were growing stronger by the day even as her guilt persisted.

Damn, she really *liked* Jax. That was what made it so hard to resist his pull on her. Desire meant nothing without something more, at least for her.

But last night, in the privacy of her own thoughts, guilt aside, she had fantasized about making love with Jax. She didn't know what kind of lover he might be, but that didn't matter. It was her own fantasy, after all.

Her body had begun to respond as she imagined him kissing her, holding her against that hard body of his. Imagined him slowly undressing her and baring her to his gaze.

Felt his touches and caresses, all gentle as the smoky haze of passion enveloped them.

Then with a snap, she came out of the fantasy and faced reality again.

Damn, sometimes it was almost too much to bear.

This would be another day off, she decided. She needed to recover, although from what she didn't know.

The kitchen had been completely cleaned and the students had headed back to their studies. Nancy sat at the table with a fresh cup of tea. Lynn sat beside her, the two of them murmuring away last night's rupture.

Jax was just deciding he needed to leave them alone when his cell phone rang. Lynn immediately looked at him.

Jax answered the unspoken question. "In the military, you can't go anywhere without leaving a contact information behind." He smiled to reassure her, then headed for the cold front porch as he answered.

The biting wind snatched at him with icy teeth. Cold tendrils crawled through his short hair. His cheeks started to stiffen almost immediately.

It was Sunday, yet Hugh Briggs was calling from his home.

"What's up?" he asked Briggs with the merest preamble.

"Another juror has died. Looks like poison, but they're not sure yet. Keep on your toes, Jax. This'll heat up the investigation, but you can't count on that."

"I know." Any thought that there wasn't a real threat was gone now. Any notion that no one would be able to find him here vanished on winter's breath. He'd been on alert, but maybe not high enough.

Briggs waited for his further response.

So much to consider now. "Maybe I should get along to Denver. I don't want anyone here to be at risk."

"So far these deaths have been carefully pinpointed. No one else has been hurt."

"Doesn't mean it can't happen." Jax ran his hand over his head. "Okay, it's time for me to start seriously thinking. Time to somehow become proactive."

"I don't know how," Briggs answered. "But you're the tactician."

"Right now I'm rooming with a houseful of people. That should give me some time."

Briggs answered after a few beats. "Yeah, it should. These other guys were living alone. It's not as easy to get to you."

"Maybe not. Thanks for the warning, Hugh."

"What else are friends for? Watch your six, man."

"You watch yours, too, Hugh. Don't forget you were the prosecutor."

Jax disconnected and slipped his phone into his breast pocket. *Watch his six?* Right then he felt as if a full three-sixty-five might not be enough. Behind him was a houseful of people. Was he putting them at risk? How could anyone hope to take him out in a town this small without doing something so obvious that the killer might not be able to escape?

He'd want to get away, that was certain. There was still another juror besides Jax. And Hugh.

All the others had been at the same station. Hugh would be an easier target than Jax.

Might be easiest for this lunatic to kill the others first. The assassin only needed to wait for Jax to return to duty, even if it would be in Denver. And easier to escape in a large city.

The other juror was probably next.

Not that that made Jax feel one whit better.

He swore, considered packing up right then, and walked back into the house.

To see Lynn sitting alone in the kitchen. She looked as if she'd had a really rough night.

And she mattered a hell of a lot more than he did. He was essentially sure that the others in this house weren't at risk, but he should go anyway to add that last sliver of safety.

Only he couldn't leave her. Something stronger than his own survival had gripped him.

As the day meandered on, Lynn left the living room alone and sat on a folding chair in the dining room. Papers were spread out in front of her on the table she'd built with sawhorses and plywood. The room had become purely a work space, with tool chests lining one wall and bigger tools, like the circular saw and trowels, on top of them. Stacked drywall leaned against another wall along with a couple of buckets of joint compound and rolls of drywall tape. Not to mention a pretty large bucket of nails for the job.

Everything she needed for the moment.

She studied her lists of supplies for future projects and a sketch of what she wanted to do with the upstairs bath. Trying to figure out costs and quantities. Tapping a pen against her teeth from time to time.

Lost in safe thoughts. Thinking it was a shame that Adam was away having a good time on his honeymoon. A selfish thought, but he'd always been willing to help her with the large, heavy sheets of drywall. One person alone couldn't do the job on such large walls.

Not that she needed to do any more drywalling just yet.

She was trying to avoid thoughts of Jax. He'd come

back inside from his phone call, his face expressionless, but still he had struck her as disturbed.

And the way he had looked at her. As if he were making a decision of some kind. As if she existed on the far side of a rushing river he couldn't hope to cross.

That wasn't true at all, but she didn't know what she could do about it. Nor was she even sure she should. Matt sometimes seemed to hover around her, a warm presence. But if he was, he could see everything. More guilt.

Rain began to fall outside, tapping gently on the porch roof, a muffled sound from here. It would be stronger in her attic and she'd always enjoyed the sound. With possible snow flurries later in the afternoon, her electric fireplace sounded really cozy.

Maybe she should just quit pretending. Maybe she should invite Jax to join her upstairs. TV, music, whatever. He might like some quiet escape, too. His bedroom wasn't exactly a great hangout.

"Lynn?"

She turned her head and saw Jax standing in the doorway.

"Busy?" he asked.

"Pretending to be. It's kind of a lazy Sunday afternoon, I guess. Anyway, I'm not on any clock but my own."

"You have a demanding clock from what I've seen around here. Your mother went to take a nap."

"She surprised me this morning." Then Lynn straightened and almost before she knew it, she said, "How'd you like to come upstairs? I have a big-screen TV and it's rumored there's some football on."

A smile flickered over his face. "An invitation I can't refuse."

"I didn't think so." Her spirits began to lift.

"Need me to bring anything up?"

"My huge secret is that I have game food up there. And coffee, beer and soda. In fact, I've got plenty of food up there. Just bring yourself."

"I certainly will."

Leaving all her plans and her lists as they were, she headed for her attic, wishing she'd worn something nicer than her usual work clothes. Of course, Jax was wearing his. Hah!

As she walked down the second-floor hall, she heard the boys talking together in Barry's room. A funny way to study for calculus, but what did she know?

She felt a flicker of suspicion when she realized they were talking far more quietly than usual. That snake? No, not these boys. Not *her* boys. They weren't in there conspiring. Even if they sounded like it.

The attic was just what she needed on this gray day. Warm light from lamps reflected off gleaming wood. The big-screen TV she rarely watched hung over her electric fireplace, and she clicked it on, then ran through the guide to find the games.

"Pro or college?" she asked Jax as he stood nearby.

"Is there any soccer? I've seen enough young men get hurt that I don't appreciate football anymore."

She looked at him with surprise, then got it. "Those long-term concussion effects?"

He nodded. "And more."

She scrolled down a few more channels, then found the soccer. "UEFA Champions League or Bundesliga?"

"Champions," he answered.

She clicked it on, then passed him the remote. "Surf all you want. Take a seat. Beer? Something else?"

She brought him a beer and a soda for herself, then

sat in the other chair, putting her feet up on one of the ottomans. Maybe this setting was *too* cozy. "I need to get some recliners. Seriously. That dang TV is hard to watch from here."

"But not from the bed."

Everything seemed to still. The voices of the soccer commentators fell into the background. Their eyes locked and Lynn felt there wasn't any air left in the room.

Then Jax looked away, releasing her. "We used to play soccer a lot when we were overseas. Touch football didn't interest the locals much."

She looked at the can of diet soda in her hand, then popped the top, releasing the sound of fizz. "Why should you care what interested the locals?"

"We weren't there to make enemies, Lynn. Far from it. Get up a good soccer game and plenty of young locals wanted to join in. Make friends. Get to know each other."

She tried not to look at him for fear the room would become airless again. For fear the heat that had begun to fill her would worsen into a blaze. "I had no idea."

"It sure as hell wasn't meant to be a war of conquest. Alexander the Great was the last man to ever conquer any part of that land and we didn't try. A war against an insurgency. Against extremists. A war for freedom."

She nodded, interested in whatever he chose to say about it. About anything.

"Our reasons didn't matter when things heated up," he said after a few moments. "But enough of that."

Given his on-the-ground perspective, she could understand why he didn't want to talk about it. Matt never had, either. Some things were kept in a locked box, safe from the knowledge of the uninitiated. She'd seen some of the effects of that war on Adam. She hoped Jax didn't experience the same fallout. Not everyone did, Adam had told her.

The game on TV was moving fast. The ball hardly ever held still and those men were running back and forth at top speed.

Jax spoke. "A dive? Really? The other player didn't even touch him."

Evidently, the official agreed. No penalty.

Lynn pretended to watch with interest, but the truth was her gaze kept wandering from the screen to Jax. She could have simply stared at him for hours, drinking him in.

Oh, man, she had it bad. Once again she forced her attention to the screen.

A soccer game, however, had nothing on Jax. Her situation was growing more precarious with each passing minute. She shouldn't have invited him up here. He could have entertained himself.

And now she feared her haven would always remind her of him.

He turned his head toward her as the game drew to a close. "Lady, if you keep looking at me like that, I won't be responsible for the consequences."

"What?" she asked on a sharp intake of breath. She was horrified to have been so transparent.

He smiled, an almost lazy expression. "You're not alone. And this is not wise. Not now. So I'll take myself downstairs and try to forget I want you like hell."

He rose, took his bottle to her sink and rinsed it before dropping it in the trash. He gave her another smile as he headed for the stairs. "See you later."

Oh, God. Lynn pressed her hands to her hot cheeks. It had been a gentle but embarrassing letdown.

I want you like hell.
Oh, man. Oh, man oh man oh man.

One floor below, the three students still filled Barry's room. They all had their laptops and were, indeed, trying to study for the calculus exam. Mostly.

"Why the hell did I sign up for this course?" Tom asked the world at large.

"Beats me," Will answered. "So you go to Ag school and then back to the family ranch? Are you going to teach integrals to the cattle?"

Tom joined the laughter. "We got some smart steers out there on the range."

"Smart enough to stay away from you," Will snickered.

"I hope so. Some of them still have their horns."

Barry stood up. "Break time. I'm gonna run down to the kitchen and grab some sodas."

Will and Tom, left by themselves, closed their laptops. Will spoke. "We're not getting any good ideas about Lynn."

"Nope," Tom answered. "And I don't see what we could do to change the gossip. That's the problem."

Tom reached for some chips, dumped a handful into his plastic bowl, then passed the bag to Will, who took a double handful.

Barry returned with soda and handed the cans around. "So?" he asked as he sat on the edge of his bed.

The other two shook their heads. "No new ideas."

"We gotta do something. This ain't right."

The sound of crunching chips filled the room.

"That was some breakfast this morning," Will remarked.

Barry cocked a brow. "Did you feel rounded up?"

The other two snorted.

Tom asked, "What else do you expect from a Master Gunnery Sergeant? You wanna argue with him?" Then he added, "That's a mouthful of a title, isn't it?"

After a few more minutes, Barry started talking again. "It seems like gossip has a life of its own, right?"

Nods.

"And it soaks up new bits as it goes around. Like that game of telephone."

"Right," Tom answered.

"So how about we put a few more tidbits out there?"

"Like what?" Will asked.

"Well, if a military man gets involved with another military man's wife, there's some kind of charge. Maybe even the end of a career. Jax isn't stupid."

Tom and Will forgot the corn chips.

"You sure about that?" Will asked Barry.

"Positive. Remember my cousin Jim, the one in the Army? He told me about it once, how a colonel got into all kinds of trouble by sleeping with a sergeant's wife."

"Oops," said Tom.

"It's totally against the rules."

"Plus," said Will, raising a finger for attention, "say that Jax and Lynn were having a serious affair while Matt was still alive. Then why would it take two years for Jax to get here? Seems like he'd show up sooner than this."

"There's another thing we could plant as soon as we have the chance," Tom offered. "Put it about that this rumor was started by someone with a serious grudge against Lynn."

The other two looked at him.

"Isn't that obvious?" Will asked.

"I'm not sure people are thinking about it. They've

just got a juicy story to enjoy. And by the time it got to Barry here, it even made sense."

"So who has the grudge?" Will wanted to know.

Barry stood up. "Luke Macy and Madge Kearney."

"Madge?" Tom said. "Why the hell Madge?"

"Didn't you hear?" Will asked. "She made a little scene at Maude's with Jax. Just a little thing, but people noticed, then brushed it aside. After they'd shared it, of course. Evidently she's had a thing for him since high school."

"My, my, my," murmured Barry, imitating his favorite TV detective. Then he set his can of soda aside, saying, "Calculus, guys. That exam is still tomorrow morning."

Two groans answered him.

Luke and Madge rendezvoused again at a different roadhouse, this one farther from town. Neither of them wanted to appear to be an item for two reasons. First, they weren't. Second, they didn't want to be linked in any way to the mess they were busy creating.

"That rumor has sure taken hold," Luke said over a beer. "It's gotten even bigger."

"Yeah, but what about your part of this?" Madge wished she'd brought an insulated bottle of daiquiris. She settled for a shot of bourbon, which she hated.

"I told you, a fire."

"What in the hell good will that do? And why burn down the house you want so much?"

"At least Lynn wouldn't own it. Anyway, my thinking is, if there's a second fire where Stone is staying, it might get him tossed in jail."

Madge's head lifted as she considered. "Yeah," she said quietly. "Yeah. That might be good."

"Anyway, it won't be a big fire," Luke continued,

draining his beer and signaling for another. "Just a small one."

"What makes you think that'll make Lynn give up?"

"Well, if it doesn't, there are stronger persuasions. I'll bet she doesn't have a will."

Madge's eyes widened, then a slow grin spread across her face as a delicious shiver ran through her. "Oh, I like that."

"Thought you would."

Madge's smile grew almost dreamy. "Him in jail and her...well, whatever." She didn't want to say the words.

After a few minutes, sick of the bourbon in front of her, she announced, "Before you do anything, I want another crack at Jax."

"Soon, then," Luke answered. "Because I can't wait forever."

"And *I* can't get him if he's in jail."

FREE BOOKS GIVEAWAY

2 FREE SUSPENSE BOOKS!

2 FREE SUSPENSEFUL ROMANCE BOOKS!

GET UP TO FOUR FREE BOOKS & TWO FREE GIFTS WORTH OVER $20!

We pay for everything!

See Details Inside

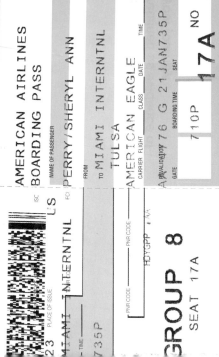

AMERICAN AIRLINES
BOARDING PASS

NAME OF PASSENGER
PERRY/SHERYL ANN

FROM
TO MIAMI INTERNTNL
TULSA

AMERICAN EAGLE
CARRIER FLIGHT CLASS DATE TIME
A PREVALIDATION 76 G 21 JAN 735P

GATE BOARDING TIME SEAT
710P 17A

17A NO

GROUP
8

ISC
LS

FOI

PLACE OF ISSUE
23

TIME
735P

MIAMI INTERNTNL

PNR CODE AA
HJVGPP

GROUP 8

SEAT 17A

****

7834699529 5

EB ¡MIA

PASSENGER AND BAGGAGE CHECK IN

ISSUED BY

AMERICAN AIRLINES

NAME OF PASSENGER (NOT TRANSFERABLE)

FROM PERRY/SHERYL ANN

TO MIAMI INTERNTNL

TULSA

ENDORSEMENTS/RESTRICTIONS

CARR AA

FLIGHT 4776

CLASS G

DATE 21JAN

FARE BASIS

* *

BOARDING PASS

BOARDING ENDS 15 MINUTES

BEFORE DEPARTURE

MAIN

ISS AGENT ID. 21JAN

3 001

it today to receive up to **4 FREE BOOKS** and **FREE GIFTS** guaranteed!

▲ If offer card is missing write to: Harlequin Reader Service, P.O. Box 1341, Buffalo, NY 14240-8531 or visit www.ReaderService.com ▲

BUSINESS REPLY MAIL
FIRST-CLASS MAIL   PERMIT NO. 717   BUFFALO, NY

POSTAGE WILL BE PAID BY ADDRESSEE

HARLEQUIN READER SERVICE
PO BOX 1341
BUFFALO NY 14240-8571

NO POSTAGE
NECESSARY
IF MAILED
IN THE
UNITED STATES

Chapter 11

In the morning, Jax walked briskly to the Sheriff's Office, needing to stretch his legs rather than drive. His laundry was in the dryer at Lynn's, but the camos he was wearing again were also in desperate need of a wash. Later today. Lynn was generous with her machines.

Thanks to the motel fire, he didn't even have his regulation parka. Couldn't be out of uniform, though. Even though he shouldn't be wearing his camos while he was here and not traveling on business. Oh, well. Who was going to gig him?

A minor shakeup in his otherwise orderly world.

The gray sky overhead still promised snow or sleet, but yesterday's predicted flurries had never arrived.

By the time he entered the warmth of the Sheriff's Office, his earlobes were burning from the cold. The dispatcher, of indeterminate age with a smoke-roughened voice, sent him straight back to Dalton's office.

Dalton nodded him inside and waved him to a chair.

"What's up?" Dalton asked.

"The fire," Jax answered promptly. "What happened and am I still under suspicion?"

Gage Dalton lifted one eyebrow, probably the only one he still could, since the other side of his face was badly scarred by fire. "I never said you were under suspicion."

Jax nearly snorted. "What else does it mean when I'm asked not to leave town? When you find me a place to room an hour after I meet you?"

A crooked smile crept across Dalton's face. "I didn't want any moving parts of the puzzle to slip away. There were a few others I asked to hang around. Truckers. They were *not* happy."

"I bet not. So?"

"So." Dalton leaned forward, picked up a pencil, and rapped the eraser end on his nearly buried desk. "I'm limited in what I can tell you."

"Understood."

"It was arson, definitely. A lousy arson. A man with your experience would know how to do a better job. A much better job."

Jax favored him with a short nod. "That place still went up like tinder."

"It *was* tinder. The fire marshal isn't saying much in detail yet. She has a lot more work to do. Suffice it to say she thinks a nuisance turned into a much bigger fire than intended. And resulted in an unintended homicide."

"I can see that. But it's a danger in setting any fire in an occupied structure."

"And a danger to those who have to put it out regardless. We've got two firemen with contact burns. Nothing major, though, and they're carrying on as if it's nothing."

Gage would certainly know that burns weren't *nothing*. So did Jax.

"Anyway," Gage said, changing the subject. "How are you making out at Lynn's? No desire to escape her mother and her roomers?"

"Lynn's a gracious landlord. Her mother is a trip, and her roomers are all nice guys. No complaints at all. Thanks for the referral." More than thanks, actually. Despite everything, he was enjoying himself more than he probably should have.

Except for this tug and pull of his attraction to Lynn. In a way it was uncomfortable. In a way it was a constant, good surprise. Years ago he'd decided to have only casual relationships with women. Women who knew the score. Anything deeper might cause a lot of pain if it didn't work. God knew, it never did.

Lynn was different. Honest, earnest, delightful. The fact that she'd already done the military wife thing meant she knew *that* score. Maybe she hadn't minded it. Maybe she had.

But given that she'd paid the ultimate price of it when Matt was killed, he seriously doubted she'd want to take that chance again. There was never a guarantee that he'd finish out his career in a safe job like Denver. Never. Security was sure as hell one thing he couldn't offer a woman.

Especially with an assassin on his tail.

Ridiculous to waste his time even thinking about it. But Lynn made it impossible to ignore.

Annoyed with himself, he stopped at Freitag's Mercantile to get a warmer jacket than the one he'd purchased only a few days ago. The weather was changing faster than he'd expected. Besides, he hadn't planned to linger this long.

While he was there, he purchased a large insulated bottle, then backtracked and rounded a corner to Maude's diner. It had begun to fill up with the retired crowd. What was it that made older folks gather in places like this for breakfast?

He stopped at the counter and asked Mavis to fill the bottle with lattes. Maybe Lynn would join him.

As he turned away to leave with his coffee and shopping bag, he realized the room had grown silent and everyone was staring at him, differently than the first time he'd come here.

He paused a few seconds, scanning all the curious faces, then left. What the hell had that all been about? He hadn't received that kind of attention before. But he sure as hell couldn't ask them what was going on.

Odd. Useless to speculate. Meaningless since he'd be leaving soon.

Or so he told himself.

Hugh's warnings, however, clung to him. He'd been stalked before in much more dangerous situations, but if someone had their sights on him, he wasn't yet sure what he could do about it.

He needed a clue of some kind. A clue about who was after him. A clue whether he was here. A clue to what he intended.

His current living situation was a kind of protection. This killer didn't seem likely to want to take out a houseful of people. No, his mission required accuracy and secrecy, and Jax doubted it would be a bullet from a roof above. Unless this guy was some kind of fool, or very desperate.

So what then?

* * *

Lynn wanted to make herself scarce, but there was no place to do it. She couldn't play hermit in her attic—that would seem too obvious. If she tried to work, she wouldn't be in isolation.

She listened to the forced air heat rumble to life and thought yet again that she needed a more powerful heater or blower or something. Enough to push sufficient hot air up to the attic vents beyond the trickle she currently received.

But that would be a professional job, just like most of the plumbing and all of the wiring. Expensive. She could probably afford it, but still had so many things left to repair and replace, she wasn't certain she ought to do it yet.

But with another winter moving in fast, she couldn't help but think about it.

When Jax returned, she was almost afraid to look at him.

He dropped a bag outside—she heard the rustle—then appeared in the kitchen carrying a large insulated bottle.

"Lattes," he said. "Want some?"

How could she refuse, even if she felt an urge to run. She'd revealed so much yesterday, she was uncomfortable with herself, with him.

"Where's Nancy?" he asked.

"She's in her room, I think."

Without a word, he headed down the hall and rapped on Nancy's door. Lynn heard her answer.

"Coffee klatch," Jax said. "Join us?"

"Well, for some tea…" Nancy answered on a light laugh.

"Great. I'll start the kettle for you."

A buffer, Lynn thought. He was creating a buffer. She didn't know whether to be more relieved or embarrassed.

Maybe just as interesting was the way her mother had kept out of sight this morning. Perhaps Nancy hadn't recovered from yesterday's hurt yet.

Lynn sighed. How had everything become so jumbled?

Jax brought Nancy her teacup, saucer and box of tea bags. While the water boiled, he got two mugs and filled them from the insulated bottle, placing them on the table.

"There's more, Lynn, so enjoy."

He poured Nancy's hot water for her, then sat. "It's cold out there," he remarked. "Lynn? When I clear my clothes out of your dryer, would you mind if I wash my camos? They're on the edge of becoming ripe."

She had to chuckle. "I wouldn't know. You still smell of cold air. So you went to Maude's?"

"And Freitag's to get a parka. I didn't expect to be here long enough for the weather to turn like this. And to the sheriff's."

Lynn darted a look at him. "Everything okay?"

He nodded. "For me at least. No solution on the arson." Then he added drily, "*I*, however, would obviously know how to set a better fire."

Lynn nearly spewed coffee. "Oh, God," she said, reaching for a napkin from the stack in the middle of the table, then she started laughing.

"Exactly," Jax answered, smiling. "I thought that motel went up pretty good, but apparently the fire marshal doesn't think it was intended to. So some random firebug."

Nancy, dipping her tea bag in and out of the hot water, looked disturbed. "A firebug. They're dangerous."

"I agree," Jax replied. "Very."

Lynn relaxed at last. "I guess that takes you off the local speculation loop."

"I'm not so sure. When I can walk into a diner and make everyone fall silent, then find them staring at me, I must be suspected of something."

She looked at him. "But of what?"

He shrugged a shoulder. "What's the point of worrying about it? It was just strange."

"I should say so," Nancy said tartly. "And rude besides. Well, I haven't heard a word about you from my friends, except some remarks about what a fine man you've grown into."

"They need to know me better," Jax answered her. "I'm not flawless."

"Who is?" Lynn asked, thinking of her own plethora of flaws. Such as mooning over a guy who was bent on leaving and finally had to tell her this wasn't the right time. How humiliating. She couldn't remember having done such a ridiculous thing since high school.

Maybe you never grew up.

"Anyway," Jax continued, "I stopped by Freitag's to get a parka. I didn't expect the weather to change so fast and it got me thinking it might not be as mild in Denver as I'd planned on."

"It might not," Lynn told him. "Weather reports a big cold front is pushing in. Something about the polar current dropping down early this season." The weather. She was reduced to talking about the weather?

Nancy flashed her a look that said she needed to do better than that. She probably did or become the most boring conversationalist on earth.

Jax's phone chimed and he fished it out of his shirt pocket to read a text. "Adam," he said, sounding surprised. "He says he and Jazz are having a wonderful time in Cancún and wants to know if I've had enough of the cold yet. Right!"

He tapped a response, then tucked the phone away. "That's great news."

"I really like Adam," Lynn volunteered. "He's nice, and he's the most helpful neighbor imaginable. Have you met his dog, Sheba?"

"Just briefly the night before the wedding."

"She's a prize, too. I guess she and Jazz's niece, Iris, are the best of friends, so I imagine Iris is glad to be dog-sitting."

"I barely got to meet Lily, either. Just dinner the night before. She's new around here?"

Lynn nodded. "Maybe six years. She wanted to raise Iris in a safer place. With a firebug, maybe we're not."

Nancy tsked. "This place is like any other, just not on such a massive scale. I used to hear the old sheriff, Nate Tate, muttering about how this county was going to hell in a handbasket."

Lynn swallowed her coffee quickly as a laugh tried to overtake her. "Really?"

"Really. Conard County doesn't have to be huge to have problems."

"True. There seem to have been a few lately." She looked at Jax and realized he'd gone very still, his gaze distant. "Jax?"

He seemed to shake himself. "I'm sure there were always things happening, but most of them never reached the public eye."

Such as? Lynn wondered, but didn't feel comfortable asking. She sensed that in some ways, Jax was locked up tighter than a drum. And again she wondered what had made him that way.

On his way back from the miserable, endless and, in ways, terrifying exam, Barry had a brainstorm. He diverted his route and trudged his way over to Edith Jasper's house.

Miss Jasper had been a fixture in the school system for years, and even though Barry hadn't been old enough to take any of her English classes, everyone knew about her and some even joked that she'd die in that classroom using her pointer on the blackboard. She was famous, though, for getting chalk all over her hands, then putting them on her hips, leaving streaks on her skirts. Or forgetting she held the eraser and tapping it to her side.

A figure of humor although one of respect.

Everyone knew Edith Jasper in a new way now, as the elderly woman who walked a harlequin Great Dane around town. The dog was nearly as big as Miss Jasper, but so well-behaved he never tugged on the old woman.

Even at the grand old age of twenty, Barry was still nervous about approaching a teacher. With trepidation, he knocked on her door.

The elderly woman, with a crown of white hair and wearing a baggy sweater, answered with her dog in the background. Barry didn't expect her to recognize him, but she did.

"Why, Barry Hutchins!" she exclaimed. "To what do I owe this honor?"

Barry managed a smile, despite the rat-a-tat of his heart. Was he doing the right thing? "I wanted to talk to you, Miss Jasper."

"Well, come in, then. Bring yourself out of the cold. I was about to make tea. Join me?"

Barry hated tea. "No, thank you," he answered as he stepped inside. The house definitely smelled like dog, and said dog merely gave him a sappy grin before lying down.

"Well, I believe you won't refuse one of the scones

I made this morning. From all my years of reading, I started to fancy the idea of a British high tea. It has replaced my supper." She waved to a chair that looked almost as old as she did. "Do sit down while I bring you a plate."

"Thank you, ma'am."

Despite the warm greeting, Barry felt like a trespasser here, and sat on the very edge of the chair. The next thing he knew, Edith Jasper handed him a napkin and a small plate with three scones on it. A few moments later she returned with her tea.

"Now, what can I do for you?" she asked.

"Well, it's kind of hard to explain."

Edith Jasper nodded. "Many things in life are. Start where you like and we'll sort it out."

Barry looked at the scones, a great way to stall, and besides, he didn't want to be rude. He bit into one. "These are wonderful!"

Miss Jasper smiled. "I've gotten pretty good at it. So what's troubling you, young man?"

Barry wiped his mouth with the napkin as his mother had taught him. "It's about Lynn Macy."

Edith frowned. "Has she come into some trouble?"

"Not exactly. But someone started a nasty rumor about her. I'm sure she hasn't heard it yet, but I was hoping you could help me stop it somehow before she does. You know everyone in town."

"The downside of having taught so many of them." Edith's eyes twinkled briefly. "What's the rumor?"

Barry hesitated, then jumped in. "That she was having an affair somewhere else when she said she was visiting her husband, Matt."

The corners of Edith's mouth turned down in a clear frown. "Now, who could be so cruel?"

"I don't know for sure. But then the rumor got worse."

Her brows, what was left of them, rose. "What could be worse?"

"That she was having an affair with Jackson Stone."

"Oh, now..." Edith fell silent for a minute. "That's quite beyond enough. Who could believe that claptrap?"

"I don't know if everyone believes it, but nearly everyone is talking about it."

Edith set her cup and saucer on the side table, beneath a fringed lamp that struggled to add a warm glow to the gray day. "I see. Bunch of fools. If that were true, then Jackson Stone would have arrived here long ago."

Having found a like mind, Barry's mood lightened. "That's what I think. Just that alone should make people question the story."

"People aren't logical, and even less so as winter begins to confine them indoors. Lacking sufficient entertainment, they make their own. Or lose their minds. Who knows, but it'll grow worse as the snow begins flying."

Barry nodded. "I need to find a way to stop it, but who's going to listen to me? I'm just a kid."

Edith's eyes sparkled. "Not a kid. A young man. Apparently with a good head on his shoulders. Let me think for a few minutes. More scones?"

Barry looked down at his plate and realized he'd devoured all three. "I don't want to eat your supper."

"There's no chance of that," Edith answered. "When I bake, I bake more than enough. Saves time for reading, walking Bailey and having friends over from time to time. I'm always ready for a drop-in."

She disappeared into her kitchen with his plate. Barry waited with a dry mouth, wondering if she'd be able to help, wishing he'd accepted the tea.

When she returned, she resumed her seat. "I suppose I could use my authority as teacher of so many of those people. Shame them into being quiet, shame them into feeling cruel. But that might take a while, and you're right, we don't want this claptrap getting back to Lynn."

Barry shook his head. "I'm worried about that. Me and the other students at Lynn's, we're all worried about that."

"The other students and I," she corrected him absently. Clearly, she was thinking.

Barry ate another scone. Well, two, while he waited.

At last Edith stirred. "Do you have any idea who might have started this malicious gossip?"

"Guesses," Barry answered, barely remembering to swallow the scone before he spoke. "Luke Macy. Madge Kearney. We can't think of anyone else with a grudge. I guess there might be some, though."

"Madge Kearney?"

"She made a play for Jackson Stone at the wedding, then again at Maude's when he and Lynn were there for lunch. People noticed, but it wasn't juicy, I guess. They moved on."

"Moved on, indeed. To a *real* scandal." Now Edith tapped her fingers lightly on the arm of her chair.

Barry put his empty plate on the side table so she wouldn't offer him more scones. He felt guilty about pigging out on them.

Edith spoke eventually. "I taught Madge and Jackson. They were both in my senior English class. Luke, too, a few years behind them."

Barry nodded. "I guess, from the gossip, Madge feels she and Jax were an item back then."

Again Edith's brow rose. "Not a bit of it. Not even remotely. If Jackson knew she was on the same planet, he showed it in no way. Nor, frankly, did she in him. I guess that Marine uniform is a drawing card."

Barry had to grin. "Why wouldn't it be?"

Edith eyed him. "I always thought the other services could learn from that uniform. Regardless, this *is* a problem. Lynn doesn't deserve to have her reputation trashed."

"No," Barry agreed. "She's the nicest person. And she's working so hard on that house."

"Resurrecting a dinosaur," Edith said drily. "I was in there a few times when Matt's father was still alive. He'd let it go to rack and ruin. I hope to get a tour when she's finished."

"She ought to be proud to show it off."

But Edith had resumed thinking. "Madge Kearney. Now there's one whose reputation isn't the best. As for Luke Macy…someone should have taken him to task years ago. It's no wonder that Andy Macy left the house to Matt. Luke was, in the truest sense, a wastrel. Drinking. Fast women. Maybe some gambling. Spending whatever money that came into his hands as if it were water. He'd have lost any share in that house long ago."

"I didn't know."

Edith looked at him. "If anyone should be the subject of gossip, it's those two. Although perhaps they were, in years past. How would I know these things? I don't have my ear to every keyhole in town."

The image made Barry grin.

"But as to the present problem…" Edith sighed. "I don't want to slander anyone by claiming he or she planted this rumor. It's malicious. Terribly malicious. In any event, it very likely grew over the course of the telling. That makes many people responsible. Well, those who repeat it are responsible regardless."

Barry waited hopefully, even as he felt his hopes were being dashed. If no one could point a finger, then what?

Edith nodded slowly. "Very well, young man. Let me think about this. I doubt it will get much uglier in the next day or so, but we need to find a way to kill it. You keep thinking. I'll keep thinking. And perhaps I'll speak to some trustworthy friends."

Did she have any other kind? Barry wondered as he stepped again into the stinging cold.

And that damn calculus test. The other two guys had needed to run to following classes, but they'd be back soon and he could hardly wait to hear their moans and groans.

And if *they* had any ideas.

It wasn't easy for Luke to hold back at Madge's request. He wanted nothing more than to scare Lynn, and while he was at it, he had to get rid of that Marine, who might prove to be too protective.

Why was Jax hanging around anyway? It was bound to make Madge madder than a hornet, wondering if he was developing a thing for Lynn.

Even Luke had the sense to see that angry as he was with Lynn, she was plenty desirable. She'd never returned that feeling, though, and he was enraged with her for being a constant thorn in his side.

Still, his ideas for how to deal with this didn't seem likely to achieve his goal. But as he'd said to Madge, he knew *other* ways to get rid of that infuriating sister-in-law of his. A perfect solution, as long as he could carry it off without coming under suspicion. No easy task in a town this size, especially when he had a motive.

He kicked a rock in the graveled parking lot of yet another roadhouse, wanting to drink himself into oblivion. Maybe he should. Forget it all for a while.

It had been consuming him for too long, and sometimes he needed a break. But that house was rightfully his, and the fury never entirely subsided.

Matt should have at least willed it to him. It was Luke's by birthright, after all. And Lynn? She could have made a new life elsewhere with all that insurance money.

He laughed bitterly when he thought of Madge's rumor taking on a life of its own. That might be enough to drive Lynn out of town. Maybe.

But Madge wasn't going to give up on that Stone guy. Not as long as he was here, and that had become his problem, too.

Why had he ever teamed up with her?

Of course, if he could frame Madge for whatever he did to Lynn...

He liked that idea. He liked it a whole lot. Whistling now, he headed inside for a few draft beers. He still had enough money for that.

The flurries started to thicken by midmorning. Lynn took herself to the grocery to acquire some simple fare that would feed at least three people, and maybe the boys as well. That "family" breakfast had worked very well, and while kids that age might think they could survive on fast food and fat, they occasionally needed a dreaded vegetable or two.

For a fact, they *could* get decent food at the college cafeteria, but she guessed spending money on a balanced meal wasn't as attractive as spending money on hamburgers and pizza.

Maybe she should make her own pizza sometime. Better than that chain pizzeria on the edge of town, and Matt had always loved her pizza. But how many would she have to make for the crowd? She'd bet each of those boys could eat an entire pie.

The idea of making all the dough overwhelmed her. Which was kind of ridiculous, considering how much effort she spent on the house. On the other hand, she wasn't fond of bread dough. Such a mess with flour all over everything. She preferred plaster dust. A small laugh escaped her.

She scrapped the pizza idea before she reached the store. Beef stew, a great cold weather meal. Lots and lots of beef stew with some fresh French bread. She'd even sneak in a bunch of vegetables.

As she was about to enter the store, she ran into Madge Kearney. "Hello, Madge," she said, intending to pass by.

But Madge wasn't going to allow it. "Where's Jax?"

"I'm not sure." Which was true.

"Setting your cap for him?"

Lynn blinked. "No. Why would I?"

"Then why don't you let me see him?"

"You can always knock on the door."

"As if you'd tell him I'm there."

Lynn frowned, anger stirring in her. "What are you accusing me of? Keeping him prisoner? As if."

"He's mine," Madge said, glaring. "You keep your hands off him."

Lynn had had enough. "Listen, Madge, if he's yours he can find you. He's an adult and I'm sure he's found his way across more difficult terrain than this town. Maybe he doesn't *want* to find you."

"How dare you!"

"How dare I tell you that you're acting like a fool for

all the world to see? Give it up, Madge. He's his own man and I don't want to hear another thing about this!"

Then she brushed by, ignoring whatever came out of Madge next. Dang! Even a trip to the grocery had become fraught.

Terri Albright was beginning to fear that she might lose it. She had one goal and one goal only, and it seemed to be slipping further away. Denver would come, she promised herself. Soon enough. Besides, waiting might cool down any heat behind her over the other deaths.

Still, as snow flurries started to swirl in the air around her remote camp, she wondered if she shouldn't just go on ahead to Denver. Damn weather. Even with the best sleeping bag she'd been able to find on her way out here, the nights were awful.

A small fire kept her fingers from freezing, but it wasn't enough. The coffee from the tin pot was the worst she had ever tasted, some kind of dried stuff. Food came out of a can, not very warm, or a packet of something dried. Water was another pain. She had to trudge a mile or more to reach a stream.

The cramps in her belly were a warning, too. Maybe she shouldn't have drunk any of that water before boiling it. She'd forgotten just once, and she hadn't brought any purification tablets with her.

From a desk job to this. Gloomily, she considered how ill prepared she was for this particular stage of her mission.

Denver sounded better by the hour. At least she'd be able to get a motel room.

Not here, however. A bitter laugh escaped her. The fire she'd set at the motel had put paid to that.

What the hell was Stone doing, hanging around for so

long in that houseful of people making it more difficult for her to reach him? Getting it on with his landlady?

Oh, damn it all to hell, she thought as she tossed a few more twigs on the paltry fire.

And damn Jackson Stone. Oh, how she was going to enjoy killing him.

Chapter 12

The next afternoon, the flurries had grown to more than occasional whirling flakes. Beef stew simmered in a huge pot on the stove, filling the house with its delicious aroma.

Lynn sat at the kitchen table studiously ignoring her work area. Somehow she'd lost her momentum, and assured herself it would return. It always did.

But another thought began to plague her. Had she imagined some people at the grocery giving her sidelong looks?

She must have. In this town where she'd lived most of her life, the only time she had received looks like that was after Matt died. As if people didn't know how to approach her.

An odd thing about grief. Most people avoided it like the plague. It made them feel uneasy, maybe helpless. Maybe it reminded them of the icy breath of death whispering through their lives. That no one was immortal.

Everyone had to live with that eventually, some sooner than others. Or maybe folks just didn't want to be reminded of their own losses.

Whatever, the glances troubled her in retrospect. While she'd been in the store, she'd been too preoccupied to think about it. Now that she could, it proved to be a puzzle.

Whatever, she thought, dismissing it. There were no secrets in this town so eventually she'd find out, unless it had been her own imagination.

She heard her boys burst through the front door, laughing and talking together. She called out immediately.

"Fellows?"

A pause in the conversation, then all three came to the kitchen.

"Something wrong, Lynn?" Tom asked.

"Not a thing, except I expect you guys for dinner tonight. Beef stew. Hot, tasty and too much for the rest of us to eat by ourselves. You better come." She smiled as she said it.

Three grinning faces answered her. "You bet," Will answered. "Home-cooked. Yum."

Then they headed for the stairs, gabbing once again.

Each year she grew fond of her students, this year most especially Barry because he'd stayed here last year, too. She was going to miss him when he moved on to nursing school.

Tom, of course, would head back to the family ranch—unless something diverted him along the way. No, he'd be back to join his brothers and dad in managing a huge spread. Tom seemed by turns to be happy about it, then not quite so happy. She suspected that might have something to do with the ups and downs of life at home.

Her mother had vanished early this morning to join a

friend on a trip to Casper. Expected back by dinnertime. As for Jax, she wondered where he'd gone.

None of her business, of course, but he'd been out for hours and hadn't taken his car with him. As cold as it had grown, she'd wondered where he'd gone to ground.

Madge's place? Lynn could have snorted coffee. Jax couldn't have made it any plainer that he felt not the least interested in that woman.

I want you like hell.

That had sounded almost like a promise, and it hadn't been directed at Madge.

Hot desire began to zing through her. Yeah, she was getting it bad, and today she didn't mind at all.

Wrapped in a pleasant haze of need, she closed her eyes and listened to the stew slowly bubble.

Jax could no longer persuade himself that the assassin would leave him alone in this small town. While he was at the rooming house, yes. But out here on the streets? There were a lot of ways that didn't involve bullets to kill someone. He knew quite a few himself.

The senselessness of all this didn't ease his mind any. Someone had a hell of a grudge, and while it wouldn't change Albright's situation at all, this could only be a very angry man. Angry beyond any common sense.

He had set out on a scouting mission, looking for anything that didn't seem right, looking for someone out of place. Someone too interested in him. Checking all the remote byways in the town, including alleys.

All the while he felt a tingling between his shoulder blades, a sense that something might strike him at any moment. He knew the feeling well. It had saved him more than once.

But it also didn't necessarily mean a thing. It would

sure help if he didn't keep getting sideways looks from people he hardly knew, if ever he had. What the hell was bringing this kind of attention to him? Not that it was a lot, but it was enough to set his teeth on edge.

Unfortunately, after hours of pacing the streets, alert and scanning all the time, he concluded that he wasn't going to find a thing today. Not one damn thing.

This was a problem he wanted to take by the horns. Not let it ride as it seemed determined to do, despite making himself one big target today.

Unsatisfied, but unable to do any more unless something changed, he headed back to Lynn's house in snow flurries that were beginning to feel like the inside of a snow globe.

He was cold. It wasn't that he couldn't handle it or wasn't accustomed to it after the temperate climate of Afghanistan, but a couple of hot cups of coffee sounded really good. A luxury, one he was consistently grateful for. Like a hot shower.

Inside, the house was warm, and he shed his jacket, hanging it on one of a row of hooks near the front door. The aroma of wonderful food reached him. Since he didn't see Lynn working in the dining or living rooms, he headed for the kitchen.

She was sitting at the table, looking thoughtful and a little lost.

When she saw him, she smiled faintly. "How is it possible to feel alone in a house that's so full of nice people?"

Her words tugged his heart, but he didn't know how to answer her. He wished he had some wise or comforting words to offer.

"The coffee's getting old," she said with a wave of her hand. "Make more if you want."

He wanted and set about stacking the drip coffee maker for a fresh pot. "How are you doing?" he asked.

"I'm moody for no good reason."

He imagined she had any number of reasons, but didn't want to share them. He looked up as he heard a thud from upstairs.

"The boys are home," she said. "As if you can't tell. By the way, I'm making beef stew and everyone is invited."

"Sounds good, especially on a day like this." He rubbed his earlobes, warming them. "Thanks for the invite. You're sure I'm not imposing?"

"Of course I'm sure. I'm running a rooming house, not a hotel. If I didn't want the company for dinner, I'd have only cooked enough for Mom and me."

The coffee had finished and he asked Lynn if she wanted some.

"No thanks. I drank so much today that I ought to be jangling."

He sat across from her, studying her, seeing a very different side of the bright, driven, usually cheerful woman he'd come to know. "Where's Nancy?"

"Off to a shopping expedition in Casper. Man, how that woman shops."

"Must make her feel good."

Lynn rested her chin in her hand. "I guess. How was your day?"

"Wasted." But he didn't tell her why. "I'm used to being physically active. Walking around is relaxing." Not today, however, although his legs felt pleasantly stretched. "You're not working today?"

"I guess I need a break. Even the usual planning that's always rolling around in my head has fallen silent. But that's okay. I enjoyed making the stew. It's the kind of thing you wouldn't make for just yourself."

"If you did, you'd have to eat it for a week." He was glad to see Lynn perk up a bit as she smiled.

"I like stew, but not that much. I should probably put some in the freezer out in the mudroom and start cooking in advance to avoid the daily attempt to come up with something just for myself. Seems like too much trouble, though."

"The winter could do all the work for you."

She finally laughed, easing his concern for her. "I've used the porch that way a couple of times."

He drank his coffee, swallowing the heat gratefully. In no time at all, he was up for a second cup. Then he asked baldly, "Did something happen, Lynn?"

She looked up immediately. "No. Why?"

"Because while I've known you only a short time, you seem to be pretty upbeat. You don't look like it now."

She shook her head. "This happens from time to time. It'll pass. Probably at dinner tonight with everyone all around talking and, of course, praising my wonderful stew."

He chuckled. "I'm sure it's wonderful. I can smell it."

"There's no old shoe leather in it, that's for sure."

But then the faintly forlorn expression returned, and he thought he heard a faint sigh.

Damn, she was tugging at his heartstrings. He ached for her, a sensation he didn't often experience.

Helpless in a way he didn't like, he rose and rounded the table so he could sit beside her.

Then he wrapped an arm around her shoulders, offering the only comfort he could.

He was astonished when she turned toward him and leaned into him. His heart skipped a beat, then he wrapped his other arm around her, holding her snugly as if he could keep her troubles at bay.

He knew he couldn't offer her much beyond this, but his mind rambled over his idea of not being able to provide security. No, he couldn't. But if anyone knew life didn't offer any security, it was Lynn. The person she had most loved had been torn from her. It must feel so senseless.

With one hand, he rubbed her back gently, hoping it helped to remind her she wasn't alone. At least not right now.

Then she tilted her head back, looking straight at him. That did it.

Lynn wasn't certain what she was doing, and she was past caring. When she tilted her head back to gaze at this remarkable man, one who was so gentle despite his calling in life, she knew she needed much more than a hug, much more than his hand stroking her back. Her entire body cried out for more. For the gift he could give her.

His head lowered. She knew what was coming and she didn't try to evade him. He hesitated just a moment, then she felt his warm mouth settle over hers, questing softly for her response.

God, he tasted and smelled good. Fresh air. Coffee.

Needy, she raised her arms and hugged him back, pressing into him as well as she could, given their awkward position on the bench. It didn't matter. The closeness mattered. The heat mattered. The *man* mattered.

Parting her lips, she invited him in. He accepted the invitation, and their tongues danced together, stoking the fire even more. A kiss, a wonderful kiss from a man who knew how to do it. The world spun away, no longer part of this private universe they were creating.

Just as she felt she needed to breathe, he raised his

head, then began to trail butterfly kisses over her cheeks, to her earlobe, his heated breath sending a delighted shiver through her.

Now she wasn't hugging him, she was clinging to him, feeling his every hard muscle, loving his strength. Wanting to drag him upstairs to her attic and keep him there for hours on end.

Delightful fantasies skimmed through her mind, images of the two of them by firelight, away from everyone and everything. The scent of lovemaking commingling with the blaze in their bodies in the slightly chilly air that would keep them beneath the blankets. Laughter coming later. Private laughter, laughter to be shared only by the two of them.

The pulsing between her thighs, faint before, grew as strong as a bass drumbeat. Yes, they needed to go upstairs. Now.

Now.

Just as she made the decision, just as his lips started trailing along her neck, she heard the front door open and the rapid tattoo of feet on the stairs.

She jumped back like a startled deer. Jax still gave her a sleepy smile, but turned away, reaching across the table for his mug.

Lynn started to feel like a deflated balloon.

"Lynn?" her mother's voice called from the hallway.

"Lynn," called Barry from the stairs.

She saw Jax grin. "Oh, Lynn?"

And she started to laugh. A laugh that felt so good, reaching to every dusty part of her soul.

Nancy entered the kitchen, carrying several shopping bags. "I found the greatest outfit for you."

"Oh, God," Lynn groaned.

Barry peeked in. "You said dinner tonight, right? What time? I need to run to Freitag's. I found a hole in the sole of my running shoes."

"Six," she answered promptly.

"Thanks. Man, that smells good!" Then he was gone.

That left Nancy and her bags, which she placed on the end of the table. "You don't have to groan until you see it!" she announced sternly. "I think I'm getting the measure of your tastes. Or should I call them non-tastes."

"Oh, Mom…"

Nancy looked at Jax. "She'd be beautiful in anything, including those work clothes."

"She absolutely would," Jax agreed. A smile danced around his dark eyes.

"What is this?" Lynn asked. "A gang-up?"

"Well, you know," Nancy replied, "sometimes you have to go somewhere besides the lumberyard and hardware store. That stew smells good, by the way."

"Thanks," Lynn answered, dreading the moment the bags opened.

"I know you like denim," Nancy said with an exaggerated sigh. "But it *does* come in different shapes than jeans."

Nancy reached into the bags and pulled out a neatly folded set of denim. "See?" she asked triumphantly.

She shook out the fabric and displayed a denim pencil skirt with a cute embroidered jacket. "Now, you can't possibly object to this."

Nor did Lynn. She felt her mouth open in amazement.

"I knew she'd like it," Nancy told Jax. "There they were, on a rack, practically labeled with her name. In fact, they shouted at me. So did a couple of shells to go beneath the jacket."

Then Nancy began to refold the items into the bags. "You can try them on in your hermitage, but I want you to do that at the very least."

Lynn nodded, still astonished. "Mom…"

"Don't thank me." Nancy smiled. "Just try them on. If you don't like them, I can donate them to someone who will. I'll put these bags near the foot of the stairs. I mean it about trying these on."

"Wow," said Lynn, watching her mother take the bags out. "Wow."

"I guess she tried really hard," Jax remarked.

"Evidently so." Lynn smiled then, feeling a whole lot better than she had earlier. She felt wrapped in love.

But she didn't dare glance at Jax. They had come so close. Now the moment was broken, possibly never to return.

Dinner was as boisterous an affair as Lynn had hoped. Once again the young men cleaned up, leaving the kitchen spotless.

It would have been a good time to retire to a living room with coffee, except there was no living room. Not down here, and she was damned if she was going to head up to her attic with Jax, not with Nancy here. Boy, wouldn't Nancy make a field day of that.

Thus the three of them sat at the refectory table over cocoa. But of course, Nancy couldn't leave well enough alone.

"You really need to get this remodeling done, Lynn. Or hire someone so it will go faster. It's ridiculous to sit around this table all the time. We ought to be able to go into the living room."

At last, Lynn glanced at Jax. A smile danced around

his eyes, creasing the corners, but he didn't let it reach his mouth. She was glad *he* was so amused by Nancy.

"I like doing the work," Lynn said for the umpteenth time. "And I'm sorry your room isn't comfortable enough."

Nancy raised her brows. "I didn't say that. Regardless, three people can't gather in my bedroom."

"And you can't climb the stairs to the attic where we *could* all gather. So here we are, like it or not. I need the dining room for a work space or I'd spend a bunch of time in an unheated garage that needs repairing as much as any other place. The living room has to be done for obvious reasons, and that's first on my current agenda."

Nancy sighed. "I know, I really do know. It's just that I worry about you. You can't even entertain, the way this house is now."

"My friends are familiar with the kitchen. Which is on my list after the upstairs bath. You won't have to endure this ugly avocado green forever."

Nancy tutted. "It *is* ugly and so out of fashion. But it *does* work after all. You made a wonderful stew for dinner in this room. And we seated six for dinner. Back to the old days, I guess."

Lynn was surprised. "Old days?"

"You couldn't possibly remember, but once upon a time, families ate in the kitchen along with hired help if there was any. Living rooms were reserved for Sundays and guests. Dining rooms? Well, if people had one, they were reserved, too, for holidays and perhaps Sunday dinners. The front-facing parts of the house, I guess you could say. And all the furniture was well protected. Meant to last more than a lifetime." Nancy shook her head. "Try to find that quality of furniture anymore."

"It would be hard," Jax agreed. "At least at a reasonable price."

Nancy tilted her head in acknowledgment. "Well," she said, rising to carry her cup to the sink, "I guess I'm worn-out from all that shopping. I'll go to bed now if you don't mind."

"Sleep well, Mom," Lynn said.

"Oh, I will. A couple of ibuprofens for these knees and I'll be out like a light. Good night, Jax."

"Good night, Nancy."

Which left the two of them alone once more in the kitchen.

Right back to where they'd been before Nancy had come home. Sort of.

Then Jax rose and reached for cups. "Why don't you head on up and relax? Maybe try on those clothes," he suggested. "I'll take care of these mugs and the saucepan."

"Thank you," she answered, but her feet felt leaden as she left the room.

Frankly, she didn't want to go alone. She wanted to feel his arms around her. His lips lightly tracing her face and neck. She wanted to feel that rush of desire again.

But it was not to be.

Instead, she steeled herself to try on the outfit her mother had given her. When at last she stood trying to see as best she could in her bathroom mirror, she decided she liked it. But where would she ever wear it?

Still in the kitchen, Jax stood looking over the top of the café curtain at the night. He considered going out into the darkness to do another recon, then dismissed the idea. Not tonight, because he might have been obvious during his walk today. But at night the world provided a different view of dangers, of hiding places, of the shadows that could deceive.

Tomorrow night, he decided.

He just wished he'd been able to walk up those stairs with Lynn. Desire clamped his loins like a vise, aching and throbbing.

But it didn't take long for him to remind himself of all the reasons to avoid a deeper involvement.

There were sure as hell plenty of them.

Outside during the wee hours, in the cold night, Terri Albright watched the rooming house, puzzling whether she could somehow take advantage of the situation as it stood. So far, no idea had occurred to her. How long was she going to have to wait, damn it? She had a limited amount of time because she was on leave and would have to return to duty, giving her no further chance to get at the guy.

Sure as hell Stone didn't appear to be in any hurry to head on to Denver. He'd have to leave soon, she promised herself, but the promise did nothing to ease her impatience.

God, this situation sucked!

Then she saw a dark figure approach the house slowly, looking around, mainly at the house.

What was he up to? His own game of vengeance? Against who? The woman who owned the place? At last he walked away.

For once her impatience eased. Maybe she needed to take some time to watch this guy, especially at night. Most especially at night. He might turn out to be a useful tool.

Nodding to herself, she slipped deeper into the darkness, making up her mind to use that purple hair spray.

A dog barked behind a fence, then fell silent after she passed. No one even looked out a window.

Terri loved dogs and wondered what kind of owner would leave that pooch out in this cold. None of her business, she reminded herself, as if she could do anything about it. She had more important matters to engage her.

Chapter 13

Two days later, a phone call at 6:00 a.m. startled Barry Hutchins from sleep. Nobody called at this hour and he was annoyed.

"What?" he nearly snapped into his cell phone.

"Edith Jasper, young man."

At once Barry sat up, rubbing the sleep from his eyes.

Edith continued. "I realize that at your age anything before 9:00 a.m. is uncivilized, but for someone my age sleeping until six is a major achievement. When are you done with classes today?"

"Three," he answered groggily.

"Then get yourself over here for tea directly after. I'll expect you by three-thirty. I want you to meet some of my friends."

"Yes, ma'am," Barry answered, stifling a yawn. "I'll be there."

Then he wondered if he'd dreamed the call. He gave

in to the yawn. No, it had happened. So off to the Jasper house this afternoon. A few of her scones sounded really good, whatever else was going on.

"I scoped out the house," Luke told Madge later that morning. Once again country music played in the background. This roadhouse opened early, not wanting to miss even the smallest business.

This time Madge got her daiquiris from a brilliant bartender who knew how to do something besides pull a beer or pour a shot—and disregarded the early hour. Luke was initially glad to see her drinking what she wanted instead of complaining about beer.

She didn't wait for Luke to explain what he meant. "Can you believe that damn Lynn Macy all but told me to stay away from Jackson Stone? What right does she have to say anything about it?"

"Good question," Luke said soothingly. "About the house…"

But Madge interrupted him again. "God, this is maddening. I saw him walking around town the day before yesterday. I wanted to talk to him, but that awful Edith Jasper got in my way. This town could do without her. Busybody."

Luke stared at her as she drained her daiquiri and signaled the bartender for another. Odd how he'd never noticed she was a lush. Not likely she'd ever be attractive to Jackson Stone if he noticed her drinking. The guy appeared to be a straight arrow. Damn him. But at least Madge's interest in him had led to her starting a useful rumor.

"Lynn needs this rumor to get back to her." With that, he finally gained Madge's attention.

"Why?"

"Because it will hurt her."

Madge smiled sourly. "You really want to hurt her, don't you."

"Believe it. That house is half mine—I don't care what the court said—and she's a bitch to not share it with me."

"I agree," she said, apparently not wanting to get into this whole house thing again. "But it's like nobody wants her to know about the rumor. Which is amazing in this town."

"I could tell her. Keep you out of it. Be all sympathetic. Maybe she'll even throw Stone out on his ear to let everyone know he wasn't her lover."

Madge pondered that. "I dunno," she said finally, draining her second daiquiri. "Where's he gonna go? I need time to reach him."

Luke sighed. "I don't have all the time in the world, Madge."

She scowled at him. "You've waited this long for that damn property. You can wait a week or two longer."

One thing Luke knew for sure. He wanted Lynn to suffer for her unkindness to him. Wanted her to pay. If she felt like she couldn't lift her head around here, that would be a start. Maybe she'd even decide she had to get rid of the house. Maybe. Then maybe she'd think about Luke and his position. Maybe she'd stop being so self-centered.

"I'll tell her," Luke said finally. "She won't throw Stone out. It'd be too obvious."

Madge regarded him dubiously and ordered her third drink. "Okay," she groused finally, "but you better be right about this. And honestly, I want to hurt that woman."

Well, at least they were together on this one point. Luke sighed and ordered a second beer himself.

And Madge moved on to her fourth drink.

"You'd better not drive," Luke said.

"I hold my liquor better than that."

"Lots of experience?" he suggested. She scowled at him. "Better watch it," he cautioned, "or the bartender will cut you off."

She waved her hand. "I'll just go somewhere else."

Luke began to wish he'd never teamed up with her. Constant objections, and all that drinking, which probably made her as porous as a sieve when it came to secrets.

He decided not to tell her about his idea. About how Lynn lived in her attic. He could arrange an accident up there easily enough.

Yeah, better not let Madge know or she'd drain a bunch of daiquiris and brag about it to the whole world, satisfying her ego by letting everyone know that *she* knew the truth.

"I'll talk to her," Luke said. "Soon. So find a way to get Stone's attention fast."

Meanwhile, Jackson Stone was having a very difficult time reining himself in when it came to Lynn. She'd become a constant torment in her own way.

Like the rounded contours of her butt when she bent over her worktable. By the way her breasts lifted the front of one of her long-sleeve shirts. He supposed he should be grateful she didn't pull on any snugger tops.

Then there was her pretty face, those soft lips he'd only begun to discover. His hands itched to touch her intimately.

Not to be. Not when he needed to find an assassin first. Not when he was heading to Denver soon. Not while he was still wearing a uniform. Military uniforms probably put her off these days. Small wonder.

He'd noted all the photos of Matt Macy upstairs, too. She probably wasn't completely over him. He understood that. There were things in his own life that he wasn't completely over, too.

But damn, the way she had turned into his embrace, the way she had hugged him back, the way she had lifted her face for a kiss. All of that haunted him, kept rousing his desire.

Aw, hell.

Lynn seemed to be avoiding the work in the living room, so he wandered into the dining room, where she was poring over some drawings.

"Give up on the living room?" he asked lightly.

She turned to smile at him without straightening. Her forearms rested on the table, one hand holding a pencil. And her heart-shaped butt was raised like an invitation.

He drew a deep breath and steadied himself.

"No, I didn't quit. It's just that it struck me since I had the roof replaced there's not going to be any more water damage. So I can take a few days to concentrate on something else."

Now she straightened. "Question?"

"Sure."

"You've been using the second-floor bath. Should I leave the tub and add a shower? Or remove the tub?"

He tilted his head thoughtfully. "I'm a shower man myself, but don't women like a long soak in the tub?"

She shrugged. "I suppose some do. I don't. The water gets cold too fast, for one thing. The other is that after sitting in my own dirt and all the soap in a tub, I still want a shower to get clean."

He laughed. "But that tub you have must be worth a fortune."

"Maybe. Cast iron, claw-foot. With a jury-rigged shower. Although if I put a separate shower in..."

She trailed off, looking down at her drawing. "It would fit even with the tub. Nah. I'd better keep the tub, too."

"How come?"

She smiled faintly. "I presume people prefer to bathe small children in one."

"I didn't think of that."

"I almost didn't, either."

He then asked a personal question, treading where he might not be welcome. "Did you and Matt want children?"

She nodded and sighed. "Yeah. Two. It never happened, obviously. Never the right time for one reason or another. I guess in the end that's good. It would be hard to raise two children alone."

He paused, then tried to leaven the moment. "Why do I think Nancy would move in to help?"

That drew a bright laugh from her. "You're right. I wonder if the two of us would survive it."

"You two get along pretty well. You're just both opinionated."

"To say the least. What about you? Do you think of kids?"

"Once in a great while, but as you say, the time…or the person, isn't right." Nor did he have the least idea how to be a good father, a worry that often troubled him.

Then he decided he needed to share some of his past with her. It would probably appall her and push her away. Which would save him, too.

"Got some time to talk? Privately?"

She nodded.

"Nancy?"

"She's out with friends again. But let's go up to my attic. No one will disturb us there."

He wondered what the hell he was about to do. He

never shared his childhood with anyone. The humiliation still hadn't completely faded away.

Nor had the sense that he should have done something much earlier than when he turned sixteen. The feeling that he should have killed the SOB to protect his mother. Guilt plagued him as much as shame.

Upstairs in her charming apartment, seated before her fireplace, its cheery flames causing shadows and orange light to dance around the space, he sought a way to begin. Speaking about this was such unknown territory that he wasn't sure how or where to begin.

"This would be a good time for a shot of whiskey," he remarked when they were seated with the coffee she made. He was glad of the space the individual chairs put between them. Made it harder for him to look directly at her, too. He wasn't sure he wanted to read her reactions.

"I'm sorry. Teetotaling house. Well, mostly, except for the beer up here. Do you want one?"

"No need to apologize. It would just be Dutch courage anyway."

She took a few minutes to make coffee in a small pot before saying, "I guess this isn't good."

He shook his head. "I've never told anyone else."

"It's safe with me."

He wouldn't be here if he'd thought otherwise. But where to begin? Samuel, of course. His fiery sermons that had left his wife and son feeling like sinful slugs destined for hell.

"My father," he began slowly, "was emotionally and physically abusive." He heard Lynn draw a sharp breath.

"Oh, God," she murmured.

"Yeah. I realize it happens to a lot of people. It also leaves an indelible mark. Anyway, I grew up with his Bible-thumping daily rants about how my mother and I were heading to hell if we didn't stop sinning. In my earlier years I didn't know what sins were, or which ones I was committing, but his description of hell terrified me."

He sipped coffee to wet a suddenly dry mouth. "I grew up believing I stood on the edge of a fiery abyss. Trying to behave in a way that wouldn't take me there, although I never knew what those sins were."

"That's awful beyond words," Lynn said quietly.

"It seemed natural to me at the time." He shrugged. "There was Adam, of course. We had good times together, but we never, ever, talked about what was going on at home. I was too ashamed. Maybe part of me assumed it was that way in every house. As I grew older, I knew it wasn't. I heard other kids talk."

"So you grew even more ashamed."

He didn't answer, but sat silently staring into the flames on the fireplace. He remembered how terrified he'd been of putting logs on the woodstove as a youngster, seeing those flames and embers as the gateway to hell.

"It was a secret," he said presently. "A family secret, and huge penalties were threatened if I talked outside the house."

He rubbed his eyes. "Anyway, I'm not sure how old I was when I woke up one night and came down the stairs to find my father beating my mother. Badly. I hadn't known, despite her bruises. She always explained them away and I finally quit asking. I guess she was trying to protect me."

"Probably," Lynn said quietly.

"After I saw that happen, I was no longer spared the physical punishment for every imagined sin or misdeed. I became terrified. And even though the thought crossed my mind, I didn't dare tell anyone else. I wasn't worried about myself so much, but I was terrified about what he'd have done to my mother."

He didn't look at Lynn. He didn't want to see her revulsion or, worse, her disappointment in him.

"Mom was never allowed out of the house, except once in a while when Adam's mother came over and brought him along. The bastard left her face alone, mostly. Same with me. I guess he didn't want anyone to see the bruises when I went to school."

"Oh, God," she breathed.

Jax shifted on his chair, facing perhaps the worst part of all. "It wasn't until I was sixteen that I...took it on. Stood up to him. I punched him out good. Really good. Threatened to kill him if he laid another hand on Mom. I must have had some kind of look in my eyes, because it stopped. It just stopped."

He sighed. "Too late. The damage was done. I should have killed him long before that. I'm sorry I didn't. Ashamed that I didn't do something sooner."

Then he fell silent, staring into the flames of hell.

Lynn ached for him, ached so hard that it hurt. With each breath the band around her chest grew tighter. Now she knew why he'd been such an introvert in school. Shame had kept him silent and withdrawn until it had become a way of life.

Thinking of all the hatred and pain he'd endured, all the suffering, facing it all alone without a living soul to turn to. Maybe even afraid to pray,

But to which god? she wondered. The god of vengeance or the god of love that he probably couldn't have imagined or believed in.

"Oh, Jax," she whispered.

"I survived," he said after a bit. "I survived and found

out that Samuel's view was absolutely wrong. I found a different world, a better one in many ways. Well, except for war. There I walked into the very hell that Samuel had ranted about. But it was different because *men* make war."

She could understand that, glad only that he had made a distinction between men and God.

"Anyway, when you asked about kids, I thought about all of this. I wouldn't know how to be a good father. Not after Samuel."

Lynn hesitated, then offered, "It might be simpler than you think. Just don't do anything your father might have done."

At last he looked at her, his face stony. Then, slowly, he smiled faintly. "I guess that's one road map."

Barry arrived at Miss Jasper's house just before three-thirty. He'd heard she was a stickler for promptness and he didn't want to irritate her.

She welcomed him into a house redolent of delicious baking and his mouth immediately began to water. "Your house smells wonderful, Miss Jasper."

Her elderly face crinkled in a smile. "I imagine you can't smell Bailey right now."

Barry laughed. "Absolutely not."

"Well, come in, come in. We're having a bit of a meeting in the living room, thanks to you. Just find a seat and I'll bring tea. Full tea, plenty of those baked goods."

Barry went to the living room on the left and froze on the threshold. What was he doing *here*?

He recognized Judge Wayne Carter and his father, lawyer Earl Carter. Reverend Molly Canton of Good Shepherd Church. Librarian Emma Dalton who was married to the sheriff. Sarah Ironheart, who'd been a deputy here forever. A high-powered group.

A young college student was bound to feel intimidated.

But Miss Emma, as everyone called her, waved him to a seat beside her. "Don't be nervous, Barry. But since you brought this to our attention, you should be part of discussing solutions."

"Thank you, Miss Emma."

He had little to say except *thank you*, as Edith Jasper passed around plates and told everyone to help themselves to the pastries on one of those tall stands of stacked plates. Barry couldn't pass on the cinnamon buns, sticky or not.

Earl Carter, in his rumpled tweeds, began the conversation. A plump man in his sixties, he wore a gray comb-over proudly. "Unfortunately, we can't make a claim of slander against anyone, especially since we can't pinpoint the person who started this."

His son, the judge, spoke. He wore his usual jeans and cowboy boots with a blue flannel shirt. Barry had heard that he even wore those clothes under his judicial robe. "It wouldn't matter. The embroidery that's probably been added while this story has made the rounds would make it impossible to find the responsible parties anyway."

Reverend Molly Canton joined in. Her face was invitingly warm, her hair a rich chestnut streaked with gray. She wore her favored black skirt and a clerical shirt with collar. A dark gray sweater wrapped her. "I rarely give a fiery sermon, but I know how, and I'll give one. There's Saint Paul, of course. He *did* have something to say about gossip. Then there's the commandment *You shall not bear false witness against your neighbor*. Harmless rumors are one thing. Malicious gossip is entirely another."

"Malicious gossip can ruin lives," Sarah Ironheart agreed, neat in her deputy's uniform. "We've *got* to spike this one."

"Countergossip?" suggested Edith.

"Can you make it juicy enough?" wondered Sarah.

"That's the problem," agreed Miss Emma. "The entire problem. We need to move the town on to a new harmless scandal of some kind. I swear this is the spiciest rumor to ever spread around this county. No wonder it's on so many tongues."

Barry listened, then had an idea of his own. "I kinda know the girls who mentioned it to me. Well, I could identify them again anyway, I guess. And I could tell them they're totally wrong about Lynn. I mean, if Jax had been her lover all those times her husband was out of town, why would it take him over two years to get here? And why is he sleeping on a different floor of the house in his own room?"

He reached for another roll. "Besides, that house is almost never empty. If the guys suspected anything, they'd talk about it. As it is, they're upset by the gossip."

"That's a good argument," Edith said. "But will it spread far enough?" She looked at Barry.

"I can get the guys to help spread it. And our other friends. The thing is, don't most people feel important if they know a different story? One that really makes sense?"

Sarah Ironheart nodded. "It's true. People *do* like to know more than others. They won't be able to resist spreading it."

Barry felt pretty good then. He was the recipient of a lot of smiles and nods. He also felt better about having allies besides the other roomers. That deserved another cinnamon roll.

"All right," said Edith, apparently the chairwoman of this gathering. "We'll spread the truth as a counter-measure. It may take a while for it to get very far, but once the ball is rolling, it should start rolling faster. And Molly will give a splendid sermon on Sunday." She shook her head slightly. "In my experience, most people would rather be nice than ugly, so that will help. I just hope we can stop this before it gets back to Lynn."

Barry hoped so, too. Lynn was far too nice to be treated this way.

But he had a feeling this was going to be like Sisyphus trying to roll that boulder uphill.

As Jax finished his second beer, emerging steadily from the past, he looked closely at Lynn. Beneath the layer of her sympathy for him, he saw heat building in her gaze. She wanted him. God.

He'd have been only too happy to oblige, but the mem-ory of being stalked by an assassin reared up and silenced other thoughts. God, to drag Lynn into that. However remotely. She didn't deserve a large loss in her life. Not another one.

But the urge to move toward her steadily grew, until it had become nearly overwhelming.

Abruptly, she stirred. "Oh, dang. I can hear clatter-ing up through the heating duct. Mom must be cooking. I need to go help." She gave him a wan smile. "You can stay up here, if you want."

Given how raw he'd been feeling such a short time ago, the invitation tempted him. But he shook his head. "Time to face the world again."

She rose. "I thought you were doing that."

He rose to follow her down the stairs, hoping the boys

wouldn't see him emerge from the attic. Wouldn't that set their tongues wagging.

Nancy had indeed begun cooking dinner. She smiled as Lynn and Jax joined her. "Steaks," she said. "I found some excellent ones from the butcher. Expensive, I know, but it's a treat. I have one each for the boys, too. I hope they like baked potatoes and broccoli."

Group dinners were going to become a tradition here, Lynn thought with mild amusement. Except for the fact that she wouldn't be able to keep it up once Nancy returned home. If Nancy ever did.

"You have that nice cast-iron grill to cook them on, too," Nancy continued. "I'm assuming, since it fits over two burners, that the whole thing heats well?"

"If you let it preheat long enough. I also have a smaller one if you need to add it."

"Good. We'll see."

Nancy nodded, then began to rub butter on the potatoes, wrapping each in a separate piece of foil. When she at last put them in the oven, she announced she was making tea and wondered if they'd like coffee. She didn't wait for an answer. "Of course you will." She set about making it, while heating water for herself.

"I like this induction boiler," she announced. "I wish you had an induction stove. So efficient and easy to clean."

Lynn watched her mother, wondering why she was being so chatty about dinner. It was almost as if she were distracting herself. But from what?

Nancy at last joined them at the table, hot beverages all around. Jax remained silent, watching alertly. Evidently, he too felt something was going on.

At last satisfied, Nancy put her tea bag on a nearby saucer. Then she sighed.

"Mom? What's going on?"

"It shows?" Nancy shook her head. "I didn't want to tell you this."

"What's that? You've never kept secrets from me before."

Nancy looked down. "Because I've never had an embarrassing one before. I lost my job."

Lynn drew a sharp breath in shock. "But…but why?"

"Downsizing. Isn't that what they always call it? The legal business has fallen off because of the economy. Part-timers go first."

"Damn it," Lynn said. "Damn, that's awful! But then why are you buying steaks?"

Nancy shrugged. "Because, unlike your father, I know how to save money. Plus the firm cashed out my 401K. I still have time to decide whether to roll it over. Anyway, I'm financially set for years yet, especially since I've stopped paying rent on my apartment."

Lynn's jaw dropped. "You've given that up, too?"

Now Nancy grimaced. "It was financially wise."

Lynn braced herself, guessing what was coming. "Mom?"

Nancy averted her face. When she spoke, her voice sounded muffled, thick with embarrassment or sorrow. "Will you rent me a room? That one in the back that I'm using?"

Oh, God, Lynn thought. Her mother fussing around all the time? She loved Nancy, but this? Full-time? "Of course I will," she said, feeling bad about her reaction, knowing full well she'd never, under any circumstances, leave her mother homeless. Hell, she'd share her attic if

Nancy could climb those stairs. "But no rent. You're my mom."

Nancy shook her head, sounding as if she sniffled a bit. "No, you're entitled to that. And I'd feel better about it, too." Then she shook herself. "Maybe it won't be for too long. I'll try to find my own place."

"Mom, don't even think about it. We'll manage."

Nancy at last offered her a watery smile. "I'm so ashamed. Humiliated to have to ask."

"God," Lynn said, "don't be. Things like this happen to a lot of folks. But you've got to stop buying steak for six people."

Nancy sniffled once, then gave a small laugh. "I promise." She looked at Jax. "I hope I didn't embarrass you, spilling all this in front of you."

"No, Nancy. I'm a lot harder to embarrass than this." Surprising Lynn, he reached across the table to cover Nancy's hand with his. Lynn was touched by the gesture.

Nancy drew a deep breath. "Earl Carter asked me for a date just yesterday. I suppose I should be happy about that. I haven't lost all my attractiveness."

"No, you haven't," Lynn protested. But her mind still ran over all the changes this would mean. "Well, as long as you can stand me stirring up dust and making a lot of noise, it'll be okay. And don't forget I'll get around to your bedroom eventually."

"I don't object," Nancy said. "I actually admire what you're doing. You'd never guess how much I wanted to remodel that house we lived in when you were young. Your dad never had two dimes to rub together, though, and I doubt I could have done the work myself. Even if I could have afforded the supplies. Anyway, I just worry about *your* finances, not to mention your safety."

"I've been doing this for a while," Lynn reminded

her. "I'm careful. And Matt left me very well-set. Although," she added, trying to tease her mother, "when I get finished here, I may do some remodeling in other houses as a job."

"Oh, goodness!" Nancy answered. "Are you serious?"

Lynn had certainly thought about it. With all the skills she was learning and all the pleasure she took in the work, why not? But she merely smiled. Now Nancy would have something else to nag her about. *That* thought didn't exactly make her happy, but she didn't truly mind.

Her life had just majorly changed. Not good. But maybe not so bad either.

Later that increasingly cold night, Luke stood on the sidewalk looking at the house that should have been his. The bitterness never left him, gnawing away at his brain, at his gut. Sometimes it was so strong that he thought it would kill him.

He wished he'd never teamed up with Madge. Her rumor idea had been good, but it was only temporary. Sooner or later, the rumor mill would move on to something more interesting. Whether it did or didn't, though, he was sure it wasn't going to harm Lynn in any way. People knew her well—she'd grown up here. Her character would not yield to this kind of smear, not for long anyway.

But his concern about Madge extended far beyond her reluctance to do anything that might interfere with her ability to stalk that Stone guy. It was interfering with his own desires.

Worse, she was a lush. One big lush, and with four or five daiquiris in her, who knew what she would say? Would she repeat his unwise threat that there were other ways to get rid of Lynn?

Man, he should have kept that to himself, instead of trying to play the big, tough guy. Once again he'd shot his mouth off when he shouldn't have. He'd always done that too often, and despite being aware of it, he kept right on doing it, mainly because in the heat of the moment he couldn't zip his lips.

Now, on top of everything else, he had to worry about Madge.

Standing there, looking at his house, trying to figure out a decent plan, he kept coming back to a fire. A small one that wouldn't do too much damage but that might frighten Lynn.

Or better yet, might make her accept his help with some repairs. He had to be careful, however. His desire for that house had blown up big-time when he'd sued her. Everyone knew about it.

Maybe he hadn't been wrong when he'd suggested killing her. He wasn't sure he could do it, but damn, he wanted to.

Unfortunately, Madge knew all about it. Because he'd shot off his mouth.

Damn it all to hell. He might have to silence Madge as well. Or maybe silence Madge first so no direct line could be drawn between him and anything that happened to Lynn.

But first he needed people to see him as the sympathetic brother-in-law. The one who would put aside his grievances to help Lynn.

That would be a good thing. If he could ever get the bitch to stop slamming the door in his face.

His thoughts returned to the idea of a small fire. Yeah, maybe that was it after all. And damn Madge and her stupid idea that the Stone guy would ever want her. Only a blind fool would want that woman.

* * *

Crouched behind a bush on the far side of the street, Terri Albright watched Luke Macy study the house. In her rare ventures to the bar, where if anyone asked, she could claim to be checking out the college, she'd heard about the lawsuit. About how he'd lost.

Her instincts said Luke was planning something. Maybe she could use him as a means of getting close to Jackson Stone.

Because Stone sure as hell didn't appear to be in a hurry to move on. No, he was settling in like a bug in a rug.

She swore silently. She had to get close enough to shove her KA-BAR into him. Or slash his throat. It shouldn't be this difficult. It shouldn't.

But it was.

She squatted there, wondering if there was some way to use Luke Macy as her tool. There had to be. After all, the guy was still apparently bitter about the house. Why else would he be standing there staring at it in the middle of the night?

She began to consider ways to get close to Luke, to manipulate him. To make him do something to get Stone alone. Just for long enough. Soon enough.

Ideas began to fester inside her.

Chapter 14

In the morning, winter's cold breath blew through the streets, tearing the very last brown leaves from the trees. Gray, skeletal fingers reached toward a dark sky filled with heavy, drooping clouds. There'd been no more flurries, but the skies augured blizzards to come.

Halloween was right around the corner. Lynn didn't indulge in the increasingly popular decorations, but she asked her mother to go to the store for a ton of Halloween candy and a pumpkin.

Nancy brightened. "I can make pumpkin pie!"

Lynn smiled. "You do make the best piecrust."

"I tried to teach you," Nancy replied, ever the one to get in even the smallest of digs. "But you never liked any kind of cooking."

It was true, Lynn admitted to herself. She really didn't. Never had, never would. For her it was a necessity, unless an infrequent urge struck her.

She heard the rapid clomp of three boys racing down the stairs, one of them calling out, "See you later!"

Before she could answer, she heard the front door close behind them. Nancy was already pulling on her coat, undoubtedly with visions of a shopping expedition in her mind. Boy, did that woman love to shop, even at the grocery.

Jax had gone out earlier, saying something about a run.

Which left Lynn at sixes and sevens. She ought to be working, but the desire to do so had recently fled. She supposed it must have to do with all the recent changes and trying to adapt to them.

For some reason, with Halloween looming that weekend, she started to think about the upcoming holidays. Thanksgiving, Christmas, New Year. The boys would go home to their families, Jax would be off to his new posting and she and her mother would rattle around in this big old house.

So she started making a guest list of her friends, then asked herself what she was doing. This house wasn't ready for any kind of entertaining.

In past years, friends had asked her to join them when she was alone, but she always felt like an intruder amidst all those happy families. An outsider, even among good friends.

Odd. But then, she was odd.

Smiling wryly at herself, she looked around the kitchen, imagining how it would look repainted, resurfaced, with new appliances and a smaller table. Her mother was right about getting an induction stove. She truly liked her gas range, but one of those ceramic tops would be a whole lot easier to clean.

A Christmas tree, she decided. She hadn't put one up

in quite a while, in fact not unless Matt would be home. When he wasn't, the sight of it never cheered her.

But now she had her mom here, and maybe the boys would enjoy it, too, before they skedaddled for the holidays. Maybe she and Nancy could wrap some empty boxes to put under it for some cheer. But man, wouldn't it look odd in that torn-up living room?

She laughed at herself, feeling a tad better. Holidays were always a tough time for her since her marriage, and tougher now that Matt was gone.

So she generally skipped them.

Perhaps not this year. Soon she should be able to find live poinsettias, too, to put around downstairs. Somewhere.

Okay, maybe lights to string up outside. Twinkling colors. She bet her boys would be glad to help her hang them. They were such good guys.

And green garlands with red bows along the porch railing.

Satisfied with her mental image, she tried to return her thoughts to work. They didn't want to go there. Not at all.

Too many changes too fast. Especially Nancy. Her mom was certainly going to change the dynamics around here. Lynn wondered how much she would still claim charge of. Her work, obviously, but what about the rest?

Only time would tell.

Gads!

Her mother returned surprisingly soon with several grocery bags. "The dentists around here are going to love me," she announced cheerfully.

She emptied the bags on the trestle table and Lynn was amazed. Bags of miniature candy bars, packets of M&M's. Gummies individually wrapped in small bags.

"Wow!" Lynn said.

"And these," Nancy announced, showing her a stack of decorated brown bags.

"You're going to bag them?" Lynn had never bothered.

"Oh, yes," Nancy said, pleased. "I'll do all the work, but it will make the children feel special."

"I know it will."

A knock at the front door dragged Lynn's attention away. "Be right back."

Lynn opened the door and found herself facing Luke Macy. God, no. Couldn't this guy take no for an answer?

"Hey, Lynn," he said with his smarmy smile. Then he frowned. "There's something I think you should know about. It's important."

"What? You're leaving town?"

He feigned sadness. "Seriously? No, there's a lot of gossip about you right now. I'm telling people it's not true, but…" He shrugged.

"So now you're my gallant defender?" She couldn't keep the sarcasm out of her voice. Nor did she invite him in from the cold, even though keeping the door open was freezing her.

"Hey, there's a difference between going for what's mine than letting you be slandered!"

"Slander?" She shook her head. "I suppose it all begins with you."

"Hardly." He put his hand to his heart. "I swear I didn't have anything to do with it. But they're saying you cheated on Matt all those times you claimed you were visiting him. And that you cheated on him with Stone."

Lynn felt as if he'd slapped her face. She wanted to slap his. Her breath stuck in her throat.

"That's a vicious lie," Nancy said sharply from behind her. "Vicious and malicious, and it's not one bit true. You get out of here, Luke Macy. Don't ever come back!"

He turned and walked away, shaking his head.

Lynn stood frozen and Nancy had to close the door. Which she did with a bang. "Nobody would believe that tripe about you."

"But what if they do?" Sudden tears began to stream down Lynn's face. "Oh, Mom…"

Nancy gathered her close and stroked her hair. "It'll be all right, baby. You'll see. Just keep holding your head up."

Lynn spent the next few hours sitting at the refectory table alternating between horror, pain and anger. And doubt. Luke could have made it all up. He was such a snake.

But she also doubted he *had* invented it. Was he bright enough to create a rumor that fit together so neatly? Or to be believed when everyone around here had his measure?

Someone smarter would have had to start it. But who?

Nancy put several miniature chocolate bars in front of her. "Chocolate always helps. Sorry I don't have a pint of ice cream. It's so soothing to sit and eat the whole thing with a spoon."

Lynn tried to smile but failed. She hurt too much.

"You'll see. People will come to their senses."

If it suited them, Lynn thought. But only if it suited them.

When Jax returned, his heightened senses alerted him to a change in the house. He hooked his jacket on a peg and went to the kitchen, finding Nancy and Lynn sitting at the table, Lynn looking sad enough to nearly break his heart.

He looked at Nancy. "What happened?"

Nancy snorted. "Dear old snake-in-the-grass Luke

Macy came running by with an ugly bit of gossip about Lynn that he just couldn't wait to share."

Jax spied a nearly full coffeepot and poured himself some before joining the two women at the table. "What is it?"

Nancy answered. "Did you know you were having an affair with Lynn before Matt died?"

Jax's head jerked in shock. "Seriously?"

"So Luke said. It seems that every time Lynn left town to visit Matt, she was actually visiting you."

Rage rushed through Jax. "Really. During all those times I was probably on the other side of the planet. Besides, Lynn wouldn't dream of such a thing."

"Well, someone's cruel enough to deserve a piking."

Jax fell silent, unable to think of any way to stop the rumor. Except one. "I'll leave in the morning. Head on to Denver."

"Don't you dare," Nancy said sharply. "Don't give in to this. Besides, you don't want to inadvertently support the rumor right about the time you might have heard it. Leaving to protect Lynn. No, you stay right here. And I'll talk to all my friends, making it clear that not only is the rumor not true, but it's vicious and only a vicious person could have started it. They're not the kind to believe such a story anyway or they wouldn't be my friends."

Jax fell silent for a minute or more. "Madge Kearney caught up with me as I was cooling down after my run. I feel like an elk in that woman's sights. Could she be malicious enough to start this kind of talk?"

"It's possible," Nancy answered. "Anything's possible, but how drawing you into it would make it easier for her to lasso you I can't imagine. Or maybe someone added that bit later."

Lynn spoke, her voice a bit unsteady. "Does it matter who started it? What am I gonna do? Sue?" Then she rose and went up to the safety and security of her attic apartment.

A short while later, Nancy prodded Jax. "Go on up to her. I would, except those stairs would cripple me. She doesn't need to be up there brooding by herself. God knows that girl has had all the brooding and sorrow she needs for a lifetime."

Jax nodded, agreeing. He didn't feel perfectly comfortable about invading Lynn's private space without an invitation, but Nancy was right. Lynn didn't need to be alone with this.

Before he left the kitchen, Nancy pressed a small bag into his hand. "Offer her this box of chocolates. I was saving it for her for later, but this seems like a good time. I'll take care of dinner, so she doesn't need to think about that."

"Thanks, Nancy."

She shrugged. "Unless I miss my guess, you have strong shoulders. Strong enough for her to cry on if she needs to." Her face darkened.

"I swear if I find out who started this…"

"Wait," she said. "Just a moment."

He heard her walk to her bedroom, then return quickly. She handed him a bottle of wine. "I know I'm not supposed to have this stuff here because of the students, but I keep this in my bedroom where they won't find it."

He smiled and started for the stairs. "I think Lynn will survive."

Jax had strong suspicions about Madge because he couldn't imagine who else might have a reason to start this rumor. But even though he'd grown up here, he was still a stranger and didn't know all that much about people here. He could be wrong.

Regardless, he was getting sick of Madge. He'd have loved to tear into her, but he wasn't the type. He hoped Lynn was, although he'd gathered from Madge's complaining a little while ago that Lynn had already told her to stuff it.

She's keeping me from seeing you.

Yeah, right.

At the door leading to Lynn's stairs, he knocked. He didn't wait for a response, but passed through and marched up those stairs. If there was anything he could do to make Lynn feel better, he was going to do it.

And screw the assassin who was on his tail. He'd given him opportunities and they hadn't been taken, even last night when he'd wandered streets and alleys while the rest of the household slept. The guy couldn't be here, must be waiting for Denver, a much larger city where a killing wouldn't stand out as much.

He *had* seen Luke staring up at the house, though. That man would bear watching.

He found Lynn curled up on her bed under a comforter in the relative dark. There was little enough light from the gray day to pour through the attic windows. He set the wine on the kitchen counter, along with the bag of chocolates, then turned on a few lights and the electric fireplace. The room filled with a warm glow.

He sat on the bed beside her and began to gently rub her shoulder through the comforter. He thought he felt a shiver run through her.

"It's too much, isn't it?" he said quietly. "Too much happening, a lot of it not so good. Although I must say your mom is a gem. Irritating, but a gem nonetheless."

He thought he heard a watery chuckle, then slowly, her damp face emerged from beneath the covers.

"I'm overreacting," she said shakily.

"I don't think so. Now you're going to feel uncomfortable every time you leave this house. That's not right."

She didn't deny it. Her eyes closed and she drew an unsteady breath. "No one who knows me will believe it."

"Nope. Not a one." He didn't mention those who didn't know her well, the ones who were doing the talking.

"But someone's talking. A lot of someones." She pushed herself up, wiping at her face. "I've dealt with worse. Like after Matt died. It wasn't only the grief, it was the folks who avoided me, like I had the plague or something."

"Probably because they didn't know what to say. Maybe because they didn't want to bury you in condolences that wouldn't help at all."

"They don't, do they? In fact, they feel empty. Automatic."

"Heartfelt, I'm sure. But I know what you're saying. They just don't matter at such a time, except maybe from a very few people."

He wanted to hug her, but wasn't sure she was ready to be touched. "Listen, your mom sent up some chocolates and wine for you."

She sat up straighter. "Wine? She knows the house rules."

"She's human and stashes it in her bedroom. Where no one will open it without her knowing, if they even find it."

She rolled her eyes, sniffling. "That's my mom. I promised the college I wouldn't have any spirits in the house. Well, except for my beer up here. And you're right, the boys never come up here. It'd be a dead giveaway if they took some of those bottles."

He chuckled. "None of them strikes me as the type to want to get into that kind of trouble. And while I've been here, none of them have come home smelling like beer or acting like they've had too much to drink."

"That's true," she admitted. "The college tries to make sure I don't get any troublemakers."

"There you go. Want a glass of wine? Or would you prefer chocolates?"

At last the smallest smile dawned on her face. "You don't have to babysit me, Jax."

"It may surprise you, but I *want* to be here with you. This isn't babysitting." Far from it. Wrong time, but her mere presence was fanning the flames of hunger in him.

After a moment, she threw back the comforter and padded over to the small counter where he'd left the bottle and the bag.

"A screw-top chardonnay," she remarked.

"What? You expect her to deal with a cork in that room?"

At last she laughed. "I was joking. I'm not some kind of wine snob."

"Good, because I don't know a damn thing about it. My education was deprived in some areas."

She sent him a sideways look. "This isn't an important one. Would you like a glass? No goblets up here."

"A glass would be perfect."

She poured for them both and handed him a glass. "I love chardonnay," she told him. "I guess Mom's tastes are similar."

They sat before the fire, feet up on hassocks. Jax felt pleasantly warm, and the soft glow of lamps held the unpleasant day at bay.

"Why," Lynn asked, "do you think Luke came to tell me about the rumor?"

Jax shrugged. "He's the guy who sued you. I get the feeling he'll do anything to make you miserable."

"Yeah, probably." She shook her head. "Sometimes I think he's a bit unhinged."

"He's obviously nasty."

"He started that lawsuit only a couple of weeks after Matt was buried. I'll never forget how I felt when the papers were served. Thank God for Earl Carter. He stepped in and told me he'd take care of everything. He pretty much did, but it didn't make me feel any better."

Jax sipped his wine, deciding he liked it. "How could it? I'd have hated Luke."

"I think I still do."

And none of this was helping her get away from her sad, grim thoughts, which was what he'd come up here to do.

Then at the same instant, they looked at each other.

The heat of desire broke its bonds.

Jax rose slowly, never taking his eyes from her, everything else forgotten.

Lynn too rose, facing him. "Jax?" she whispered.

"I don't think I can stop," he answered, his voice low. "Tell me to go now."

She gave a jerky shake of her head. "I've been wanting you almost since I saw you. I'm as bad as Madge."

"You couldn't possibly be. Besides, I feel the same about you, and don't mention that woman to me. She's infuriating and a liar. You're not. You're lovely, admirable and, oh, God, so beautiful."

"Me?"

"You need to look in a mirror." He stepped toward her,

slowly closing the space between them. "Even in your work clothes. I can't stop staring at you. Do you know you have the most attractive tush?"

She gasped, then a laugh spilled out of her. "Don't make me laugh. It'll ruin the mood."

He reached her and pulled her into his arms. "Laughter *is* part of the mood. Laugh away, you won't stop me."

She drew a sharp breath and her eyes grew hazy and heavy lidded. "I don't want to stop you. Don't stop, Jax. Please don't stop."

As if he could. Pressing his mouth to hers, he once again tasted the honeyed space, drawing his tongue along her lips, feeling a shiver course through her. From there, temptation led him down the side of her throat, feeling silken skin with his lips and tongue.

"You smell so good," he murmured huskily.

"So do you," she whispered.

But he also detected the scent of rising passion just beginning. The scent itself was nearly maddening. Soon it would perfume the entire room.

His fingers plucked at the buttons on her shirt, opening them, eager to bare her to his gaze. His body engorged almost painfully, not wanting to wait. Too bad.

Then he felt her reach for the hem of his sweatshirt, sliding her hands beneath, touching him, touching his heated skin, fingers dancing in a way that drove him even higher if that was possible. Light touches, growing bolder.

He stripped the shirt from her at last, revealing a plain white cotton bra. He dealt with it with a simple twist of his fingers and then she fell free.

Reaching out, he cradled her breasts. "So perfect," he murmured, brushing his thumbs over her hardening nipples.

"Jax, please," she moaned. "Please!"

Reluctantly, he released her long enough to rip his sweatshirt over his head, to unzip his jeans and kick them away. Then he knelt before her, kissing her just beneath her ribs, then over her belly as he pulled away her jeans and undies.

Kissing her at last at the apex of her thighs.

She trembled and he felt her on the verge of collapse. He rose to his feet and lifted her easily across his arms, carrying her to the bed.

She lay there naked, looking up at him with a drowsy smile, surely the most gorgeous woman he'd ever seen. A firm body from hard work, delicate feet with high arches. The stuff of his dreams.

Lynn, aching though she was, stared at the man who stood over her. Perfect in every respect, muscled for endurance, not for show. Hard, even around his waist, a surprising washboard belly. She hadn't guessed...

Not a spare ounce of weight on him. Not one. And as she took in his arousal, her every nerve cried out for the pressure of his body on hers, for him to fill her until she cried out.

But instead of giving her what she wanted right then, he bent over her, stroking her gently, igniting zings of electricity everywhere he caressed her.

Reaching out, she wanted to touch him as he touched her, wanted to memorize all of him with her hands until he was imprinted forever on her memory. Longing to savor every moment while still growing impatient for fulfillment.

When at last he lay down beside her, she was burning like a torch. The press of skin on skin filled her with pleasure. He radiated heat that wrapped around her, seeming to make her safe, safe enough to throw caution to the wind.

Then he took her around the waist and lifted her until she straddled him, his hardness pressed to her softer petals.

"Ride me," he said gutturally, lifting her by the hips and lowering her gently until he filled her. She threw back her head as tender tissue stretched to receive him. So good.

Then she leaned forward, hands on his broad shoulders, rocking slowly. Groans escaped them both.

She rode him to the stars, then at the same moment she shattered into a shower of sparks, he joined her.

Later they rested beneath the covers in gentle embrace. Her head rested in the hollow of his shoulder, her arm stretched across his chest. One of her legs lay across his.

His arms wrapped around her, holding her close. The air around them held the perfume of their lovemaking but Lynn could still inhale his particular scent. The scent of man. The clinging scent of the outdoors. A wisp of soap.

The taste of wine as she raised her head briefly to kiss him.

When he spoke, it was a single word. "Wow."

"Double wow," she replied, feeling as if she could purr like a contented cat.

He laughed quietly, giving her a squeeze.

Lynn could have lain there nearly forever, enjoying this closeness, hoping for another experience like the one they had just had. She was, she realized, going to hate it when this man returned to duty.

But Jax's mind had begun to stray. He'd been lax about this assassin. What if he was pulling Lynn into danger beside him?

The idea of leaving her had been difficult for some time, but now he hated the thought.

But the danger. Oh, man, the danger. He ought to pull on his clothes right now and leave her safely in her world while he dragged himself away from it.

But now that might seriously wound her.

Soon, he promised himself, but not right this instant.

A few minutes later, his cell phone rang. He stiffened immediately.

"Do you have to answer?" she asked drowsily.

"Yeah." He tried to lighten his tone. "A Marine is never off duty, even while on leave."

She sighed, but didn't protest when he rose to tug the damn thing out of his jeans on the floor. Then he closed himself in her small bathroom.

Damn, it was Briggs again, but the call had already ended. He returned it immediately.

"Stone," he said.

"News," Briggs answered. "The investigative team suspects Albright's sister, Terri Albright. A Marine. She's on leave right now."

Jax swore. "Well, that might explain a lot. I've been on the lookout for a man."

"That would be the first thought, given the violence. Nobody's sure yet, but the circle is closing."

A woman, Jax thought after he disconnected. A woman. He knew women in the Corps, efficient and deadly. Good fighters. Certain stereotypes lingered, he thought with disgust. Including in him. He never would have thought this assassin could be a woman. But why not, given what he had seen of women in battle?

He wore his own blinders.

Damn it to hell. He'd been looking at the wrong people. He could have let Terri Albright walk up to him in broad daylight and shove a knife under his ribs.

Stupid. Stupid, stupid, stupid.

Madge was on her fourth daiquiri in the middle of the afternoon. Luke sat across the table at the roadhouse, fuming. God, he should never have hooked up with her.

"I put a snake in her mailbox," Madge said, her voice slightly slurred.

"Why the hell did you do that?"

"I wanted to scare her. But Stone was there and got to play the hero. I didn't expect that."

"What good would scaring her do?"

"Make me feel better," Madge answered. "Plus, I wanted her to wonder if somebody was out to get her."

"Guess that didn't work."

Madge shrugged. "The rumor is working better."

"Yeah? Well, I told her about it and all I got was a door slammed in my face. What's more, there's push-back now."

Madge looked at him. "Pushback?"

"Seems some people aren't going to let it continue. They're making it die down already."

"Hell," said Madge and waved to the bartender for another drink. "Doesn't matter. You'll think of something." She gave him a sloppy grin. "It's your turn now."

Like kids playing a game. Only this was no game. Luke eyed Madge with disgust. How had she ever gotten married so many times? He guessed some guys hadn't been able to see anything but her ample breasts and generous cleavage.

Instead of bringing another daiquiri, the bartender came over holding a cup. "Sorry, Miss, but I'm cutting you off. Too much, too fast."

"You can't do that!" Madge's voice rose.

"I can. Next drink is coffee." He put a full mug on the table in front of her.

"This is an insult!"

The bartender shrugged and walked away.

Luke struggled to suppress a grin.

"I'll just go somewhere else," she announced loudly. "You treat a lady like this? This bar sucks."

Luke watched her yank her jacket on and storm toward the door. Her unsteadiness was visible. He hoped, savagely, that she'd wrap her car around a tree. Or a signpost. At this point he didn't care if she died or spent the rest of her life in a wheelchair.

Then he returned to thoughts about how to get even with Lynn. Damn her to hell. Would it have been so hard for her to just *share* with him? He was entitled.

He was sipping his way through his second draft beer when an attractive young woman with nearly black hair streaked with purple walked through the door. She was wearing jeans and a jacket, but that did nothing to detract from her. She wandered up to the bar, unzipping her jacket to display a nice rack beneath a tight turtleneck.

Luke waited a minute, saw men look, but none moved toward her. She sat on an empty stool, no one nearby. Then Luke approached the bar. "Buy you a drink?" he asked with his most winning smile.

She looked at him from dark eyes, hesitating. He liked that hesitation. Not a bar rat. Then slowly, she smiled. "Sure, why not?"

Before long he learned her name was Terri and that she was scoping out the area with an eye to attending the community college. A very open young girl, not in the least trying to keep secrets from a stranger. Naive. Oh, yeah!

After a bit, feeling he'd created a trustworthy impression and some decent rapport, he offered to show her around, waxing eloquent about his knowledge of the area. Even offering to introduce her to some other students who could talk with her about the college.

She seemed so appreciative. Well, she might be an amusement to distract him while he plotted. He sure needed something to use to put a brief hold on his fury. It was starting to wear him out.

Terri smiled at him, looking as if he were the best thing since sliced bread.

That was fine by him. And it appeared he was done with Madge. Even better.

"I needed to meet someone like you," she said quietly, and let him buy her another beer.

Chapter 15

A woman. Jax was still mad at himself. Stereotyping. Damn, he ought to know better. But kicking his own butt wasn't going to improve anything. Now he had a better idea what to watch for. Just be glad that Hugh Briggs had given him the heads-up. Maybe Briggs had suspected that Jax would fall for an assumption. Maybe Briggs had initially fallen for it, too.

Not that it made Jax feel any better about himself.

When he looked at Lynn, he was reminded of all the amazing things a woman could do if she put her mind to it. How could he have ignored that fact, even though it was about someone else?

But self-castigation wasn't going to get him anywhere.

Nancy invited him to join her and Lynn for dinner. The woman was still working on her matchmaking. He'd have been amused if the truth weren't getting so close to Nancy's wish.

When he looked at Lynn now, all he could see was her gentle face, all he could do was remember that wonderful time they'd shared just this afternoon. A time he wanted to repeat soon, but instead he had to figure out how to deal with a killer. One who might not care if someone else got in the way.

But in the process of stepping back, he might wound Lynn, who wouldn't expect a distance between them now. Nor should she.

God, the horns of this dilemma had pierced him to the core.

After a savory dinner of roast pork and stuffing, after he had helped clean up, he announced he needed to go out for a walk.

"Gotta keep those muscles stretched," he said. Lynn appeared disappointed, maybe even a little hurt. But why should she? At this time of evening, she couldn't expect them to trot upstairs. Not with Nancy still up and very much aware, judging by the faint smugness on her face, of what might be happening.

The three students blew in along with the frigid air, carrying pizza boxes that had to be stone-cold by now, considering the pizzeria was on the edge of town.

Jax shrugged inwardly. What kid didn't like cold pizza, as long as it hadn't sprouted icicles?

So once again he trod the night-darkened streets of Conard City. Tonight, for some reason, the streetlights, turning into lanterns as he approached the downtown area, didn't seem to be driving back the shadows very well. In fact, they added to them.

At night, though, he could see the increased number of hiding places, especially in the alleys. But what made him think this woman would hide? The best strategy of all would be for her to appear in the open, as if she belonged here.

Early holiday shopping had begun, drawing many residents out on this cold evening. Freitag's was bright with light and full of people. The little toy store he'd never seen as a child also contained quite a few people. The bakery was open, catering to shoppers who might need a warm drink or a hot bowl of soup.

Inside it, he saw about a dozen people at tables. At one table he spied Luke Macy with a black-haired young woman with outrageous purple stripes in her hair. She was smiling and he was laughing.

Damn, Jax hated that man. But there he was, catting around as apparently he always had. Her expression suggested she was fascinated. He hoped she figured out that jerk before she got hurt.

But nothing seemed out of place. Not one thing. No one acted suspiciously. No one looked at him oddly or too intently. No battle-honed instinct warned him.

Damn, he just ought to get on to Denver, promising Lynn he'd return soon. He'd be able to. Recruiting had fallen off markedly after a twenty-year war. A generational war, some called it, because sons and daughters had followed their fathers and mothers right into it.

Because many young people couldn't remember a time without a war.

Besides, the number of recruits sought by the military had fallen off, too.

Starting to feel grumpy, seriously annoyed with himself, he slowly walked back to Lynn's place.

Denver, he thought again. It would be easiest to kill him in the bigger, more anonymous crowds. They would provide the best cover. The best escape routes. His death could easily be passed off as an unfortunate mugging.

A return to Denver would be the best way to protect Lynn from the ugliness that stalked him. And he was far more worried about Lynn than himself.

Lynn shared a cup of tea with her mother after Jax left. Tea and sympathy, she thought, though she wasn't asking for the sympathy.

She had other things on her mind, things she didn't want to share with Nancy.

She didn't know whether to be disappointed or worried that Jax had left for a walk. She'd felt the tension in him since that phone call and wondered if he'd been called back to duty. That had happened once with Matt, when his unit received orders to depart. He'd had to race back to join them.

It could happen.

But what if he was regretting their lovemaking? What if he considered it just a fling he needed to escape? She hadn't gotten that feeling, not the way they had hugged and laughed afterward. Not the way he had squeezed her with a tight hug before he dressed. He hadn't acted like a man who wanted to get away.

But what if he'd been disappointed in her? What if he'd wanted something she hadn't provided? What if she was a lousy lover? Matt had never complained about any such thing, but Matt had loved her. Jax did not.

She looked down into her teacup while Nancy talked about a card game she had planned for the next evening with her friends. She resisted the urge to press her hands to her warm cheeks. God, what if her mother saw her blush?

Suddenly a word that Nancy spoke caught her attention. "Did you say *poker*?"

"What's wrong with that?" Nancy asked her. "You think we should play Old Maid?"

Unhappy or not, Lynn had to laugh at that. "Just tell me you're not gambling for real."

Nancy shrugged. "None of us is wealthy enough to play for real money. Chips only, dear. Give me some credit."

Lynn answered drily. "As long as it's not a credit on my bank."

It was Nancy's turn to laugh. "What a thought!"

"I never know what you might do, Mom."

"Good. I wouldn't want to be too predictable."

But Nancy was in so many ways. She loved to shop. She loved to gather with her friends. She loved to needle her daughter. Lynn hadn't gathered with her friends in a few weeks now. She missed them.

But not as much as she was missing Jax, and he'd only been gone for a few hours. Not long at all. Dang, was she going to feel truly awful when he left to return to duty.

She ought to be worrying about that. Instead she worried about the tension she'd sensed in him since that phone call.

Jax turned around and returned to the bakery instead of heading straight back to Lynn's place. Melinda still had some baked goods left for her evening crowd, so he bought some cheese Danish for the women back at the house.

While he stood paying, he felt a niggle at the back of his neck. He was being stared at.

He turned quickly but saw no one looking at him. He scanned the room again as he left with his white bag of delights, but everyone appeared involved in their own conversations.

Heading down the streets, he was reluctant to dismiss that feeling. Even animals knew when they were being watched, and war honed that instinct in humans.

But wherever the feeling had come from, it was gone as he walked away from the bakery. Casual interest on someone's part? Maybe. But whatever had caused it, given that an assassin was after him, he took it as a warning.

And a reminder to get out of this small town as quickly as he could unless he discovered a valid clue. But first he had to find a way to ease himself away from Lynn. A way that wouldn't leave her feeling wronged or used.

Damn it all to hell. He should never have given in to his desire for her. Should never have put her in the position to feel wounded.

Maybe it was time for a brain transplant.

Luke enjoyed himself hugely with Terri. She hung on his every word, laughed at even his worst jokes, and the expression in her dark eyes... Well, he figured she was seriously drawn to him.

Over the last couple of years, he'd forgotten how good it could feel to win a woman's undivided attention.

After they'd filled themselves with the bakery's delights, Luke suggested Mahoney's bar, right around the corner.

Terri looked hesitant. Luke liked that in her. Not at all easy. A little hard-to-get only made the chase better.

But at last she nodded. "I can't stay too late," she told him. "I'm staying with a friend out on one of the ranches. I don't want her to worry."

"I'd even be glad to take you home."

She shook her head. "I have my own car. But thanks."

Well, strike one. No hanky-panky in the back seat of his car. Maybe tomorrow night.

Mahoney's was crowded. It always was. The jukebox played, voices grew louder as the alcohol flowed, but Luke didn't mind. The noise would make a cocoon for them to talk without being overheard. Although why he should worry about being overheard he didn't know. Or didn't think about.

After a couple of beers, while Terri sipped slowly on her first one, he found himself talking. About the house, about Lynn, about his anger and frustration.

He had found a sympathetic audience, so he didn't hold back. He went so far as to say he wanted to get even with Lynn.

Terri was all sympathy. "I wish I could help," she said when he finished his rant.

"Maybe you can," he said heedlessly forgetting that some things were better kept to himself.

"Just let me know," she replied with the sweetest smile.

Luke was pleased. She understood why he was so angry, and she wanted to help him in some way. Good. He might have found a better ally than Madge.

By the time they parted, they'd made a date for the next afternoon. His head swimming with desire and beer, Luke ambled home. He felt as if he were walking on air.

Terri returned to her miserable camp about a mile out of town, beneath trees that lined the side of a dirt road. Almost nobody drove along there, she'd found, so her small camp stove wouldn't be noticed, especially since she'd pulled back farther into the woods.

But it was getting outrageously cold and she was outrageously tired of instant coffee. At least it was hot. She warmed her hands over the propane burner, then put the small pot on to boil water. Her gloves didn't feel thick enough, her hands lost the flame's heat too quickly.

Meeting Luke Macy had worked out better than she had hoped when she saw him standing in front of that house. Now she had the entrée she'd needed in the one-horse town. Potential college student, friend of Luke Macy. She didn't have to lurk any longer.

The more important thing was now she could walk around town on the arm of that lousy con artist who presented himself as the Big Man-about-town. She'd have to giggle like a disgusting infatuated kid. People would look and hardly notice, including that hateful Stone. She'd have cover to get close to him, but her time was getting short. Too short.

She might just have to kill Stone *and* his new girl-friend. Both of them. Leaving a bigger trail than she wanted to.

When at last she crawled into her sleeping bag, using her jacket for a pillow, she stared up into the night, indulging dark thoughts of her own, thoughts darker than the midnight above.

Figure it out, she told herself. *You're smart enough.*

Chapter 16

When Jax returned to Lynn's place with his bag of pastries, Lynn had vanished and only Nancy sat in the kitchen, drinking her inevitable tea. He placed the white bag on the table, saying, "Danish for you two." Then he looked around. "Lynn?"

"She went up to her hermitage. Why don't you go on up?" she added suggestively.

This time, Jax was far from amused. "That's enough, Nancy. I wasn't invited."

For an instant she appeared taken aback. "I was only thinking about her being alone. She hasn't been too happy of late. Anyway, I wish to hell she'd get a house phone or something so I could call her and tell her you brought home these nice Danish. She loves them."

Well, Jax allowed, Lynn had seemed a little down. And she was only going to get more down when he had to tell her a lie, that he'd been called early to Denver. He never lied.

God, how was he going to manage that? If it felt like his skin was being ripped off, how would she feel? Not that bad, he hoped. He hoped like hell he hadn't taken this too far for her sake.

But he couldn't tell her the truth. He couldn't make her worry about him. She'd had enough of that with Matt.

He made coffee to drive away the chill and plopped down at the table with Nancy. She got a plate and put the Danish on it. They both looked at it, but neither reached for any.

"Melinda makes the best Danish," she remarked.

"I haven't had any before."

Inanities, both of them acutely aware of Lynn upstairs. Hiding? Fearing what he might say? Trying to pretend it didn't matter?

Or kissing him off first, to spare herself humiliation.

After a while, Nancy made herself some more tea. Eventually she spoke.

"I know Lynn finds me irritating," she said. "She's grown up and I'm still acting like her mother."

"You *are* her mother."

She shook her head. "I don't quite mean it that way. We clash a lot, mostly because I keep wanting things to be different for her and she doesn't want the same things. I need to learn to bite my tongue. I doubt I ever will."

"She loves you, too."

"I don't doubt it, but she's never tried to tell me how to live or how to dress. She's never been a girlie-girl, if you get what I mean. No interest in clothes or makeup or all that other stuff. A tomboy of sorts. A special person."

"Very special."

Nancy smiled faintly. "She's also very strong, as well

as strongheaded. We've been clashing since she was ten years old over one thing or another. A decent father might have understood better, but she never had that."

Looking down into her cooling tea, she sighed. "I never wanted her to restore this house. An overwhelming task requiring so many skills, but look how well she's done, how much she's had to learn to do all this. I definitely didn't want her to take roomers. I thought of college students as wild, partying young men. Well, look at this group. I was wrong once again."

Jax nodded, listening with interest. Nancy was opening up in a way he never would have suspected. He also thought Lynn needed to hear this more than he did.

He looked up at the ceiling.

Nancy saw his gaze and nodded, as if she understood he was thinking of Lynn upstairs by herself. "She needs the space up there right now. If we're going to live together, I need to learn to give her space. Living apart achieved that for a while, but no more living apart, at least until I can manage a place of my own."

Jax nodded and went to get another cup of coffee before returning to the table.

Nancy sighed again. "She's been so wounded in important ways. Losing her father, losing Matt. Especially Matt. Yet she just keeps plowing ahead. She's remarkable."

"She's got a spine of steel," Jax agreed. Down, but apparently never out for the count. She just kept right on putting her life back together.

He'd known a lot of people who weren't capable of that. He never wanted to be someone who made her rebuild herself all over again. Another good reason to hightail it out of here, before feelings grew too strong.

A little while later they heard Lynn's light footsteps in

the hallway overhead. She appeared just a minute later, her hair damp, her clothes fresh.

"Man," she said as she joined them. "That shower felt good. I hope I left some hot water for the boys."

"They can take cold showers," Nancy said. "Might do them some good."

Lynn grinned. "Now, Mother..." Then she saw the plate on the table. "Ooh, is that Danish?"

"Jax brought it home," Nancy said. "Grab some coffee and dive in. I know you love it."

Jax was so relieved to see Lynn smiling that some of his tension seeped away. For tonight at least. She grabbed a napkin and tucked into a large piece of the Danish.

"Heaven," she said as she slipped a bit into her mouth. "Thanks."

"Speaking with your mouth full?" Nancy teased.

Lynn swallowed. "Not fair, asking me a question when I can't answer."

Jax laughed. "You two make quite a pair."

Sitting there, he realized that the bonds of this small family were strong, and that he'd been invited into the tightly knit group created by mother and daughter. A special place. Something he'd never known, except in the brotherhood of the Corps. And that wasn't the same. Not like this.

"I think I'll get back to work tomorrow before the fundraiser for the motel," Lynn announced. "Well, I've sort of been working, but that's more like daydreaming about later projects. The point is, if I don't get that living room done, nobody will have any place to congregate except in this kitchen. I don't know about you, Mom, but I'm getting awfully tired of it."

"And I'm sick of this ugly green," Nancy remarked

tartly. "If I could, I'd pay someone to come in and blow it up."

Lynn giggled. "That'd ruin all my plans."

Nancy arched a brow. "No, it'd just mean you don't have to do the demolition."

Even Jax laughed at the image, although he felt far from laughing about anything.

"Or," said Nancy, "I could just get a gallon of paint and cover it all up."

"Dang, Mom," Lynn said. "This room would be unusable."

"Well, of course. And then you'd have to get to it sooner."

"Sheesh, organizing my life much?"

Nancy smiled. "Just trying to be helpful."

Nancy went to her room a half hour later, saying she wanted to watch the late-night comedy shows. "I love them. When you get to my age, you don't seem to need as much sleep. Staying up late and getting up early. Sort of like my father used to do."

"While dozing in his chair on and off," Lynn teased.

"Well, yes. And if I doze off, you won't hear me complain."

Feeling suddenly shy, Lynn looked at Jax. In the instant their eyes connected, a powerful electricity surged between them. Jax's eyes blazed. Her own felt heavy lidded. Her heart skittered.

"Upstairs?" he asked quietly.

She nodded and headed that way with him right behind her. As they passed through the second-floor hallway, sounds of a video game emerged from one of the boys' rooms.

Imagining their fun leavened her heart. Then her feet

grew lighter as well. She and Jax took the stairs to her attic like kids at a full run.

By the time she reached the top, she was laughing and he was grinning.

He spoke. "We aren't eager or anything."

"I can't wait," she answered truthfully, breathing more heavily. Familiar with each other now, they stripped before one another's gaze. Lynn enjoyed unwrapping herself all the while watching him do the same, as if he were a Christmas present. Maybe he was, early or not.

A wonderful-looking man. She wouldn't have changed a single thing about him. He drew her to him, pressing their bodies close together.

"You're beautiful," he said, his voice husky.

"I'm too ropy from all that work."

He pulled his head back a bit. "Ropy? You need to look at yourself in a mirror sometime. What you are is gorgeous and perfectly proportioned."

A giggle rose in her. "You're just saying that."

He lifted her from her feet and placed her on the bed. "You're perfect."

He lowered himself beside her and began to run his hands over her. "Perfect," he murmured again.

He sure didn't take long to arouse her, she thought hazily. His hands seemed to be painting her with fire. The kisses he dropped lightly over her neck and breasts made her sizzle. She heard herself call his name.

But he was far from done teasing her. He drew one of her engorged nipples into his mouth, and with each suck he plucked a cord that ran all the way to her center, causing her to throb. She dampened, readying for his possession.

"Jax…"

"I want to take my time," he whispered, "learn every inch of you."

She grabbed his shoulders, pulling hard. "Screw that," she said. "Next time. This time..."

He slid his hand between her legs, rubbing gently. "Easy, easy..."

But she didn't want to wait. Each moment felt as if it were stolen, a gift, one she didn't want to waste. Her body demanded him with the force of the tidal wave he unleashed in her, a wave that rolled over her, then pulled her into a rip current she couldn't escape.

"Jax..."

He gave in to her demand at last, settling himself over her, finding his way inside her.

She gasped with sheer pleasure, feeling that she was somehow coming home, even as his steady movements and his mouth on her breast lashed her higher into the wilds of passion.

For this short time, he belonged to her. He *was* hers.

With a shudder, she exploded into hot embers in his arms. She felt him jerk, then follow her into a place beyond the stars.

Afterward, still damp, they cuddled beneath the comforter, wrapped in each other's arms as if they had melded into one.

Neither spoke, as if they both knew they had been thieves of time, stealing these minutes out of the maw of reality.

A sudden hammering on the downstairs door jerked them out of heaven and dropped them with a thud back into the present.

"Lynn!" yelled Tom. "Lynn, there's a fire!"

Lynn opened her eyes and saw the flicker of firelight in the front attic windows. "Oh, my God…" She was out of the bed like a shot, cramming herself into clothes.

Jax jumped up as if he were on fire himself. He started yanking on his clothes.

Lynn headed down the stairs as fast as she could go, with Jax right behind her.

The boys already clutched Nancy and her jacket and were scuttling her to the back door with them.

Seeing the hot red glow through the front window, Lynn and Jax grabbed their jackets from the hall peg and hurried after them, bursting through the door into the backyard.

"I called the fire department," Will said just as the sound of sirens filled the night air.

"I need to see," Lynn said, heading around the side of the house to the front. She couldn't possibly stand there and just wonder. "I *have* to see!"

"Be careful," Jax said, taking her arm. "Steady. You don't want to break a leg out here."

She didn't care. Was all her love and work going up in smoke? A dream, once shared with Matt, now hers alone, but still a dream to take the old run-down house and make it bright and beautiful once again. Dying in a blaze.

She rounded the corner to the front and saw that her porch roof was on fire. She froze, but Jax pulled her back to the sidewalk across the street.

All she could do was stare. Just stare helplessly.

Flames licked their way along the roof of the front porch, blackening the porch ceiling beneath, trying to leap up the side of the house above it. Her heart began to crumble even as the sirens drew closer. The coda to her life as she'd rebuilt it?

* * *

Jax saw that once her shock began to pass, fury began to tighten her face. He got it. He definitely got it. All he could do was draw her into his arms and hold her as the fire seemed to grow like a ravening beast.

But before it could spread much beyond the porch roof, the fire department arrived and began to douse it with water. A few of the firefighters retrieved Nancy and the boys safely from the backyard and insisted they all move to the far side of the street.

She couldn't take her eyes off the mess, hardly noticing her mother and her roomers.

"My roof," she murmured. "The heat will peel the paint. The gingerbread will have to be scraped and painted again. The new roof... All that work..."

At last she began to cry.

And Jax began to think of vengeance. He thought of Luke. He also knew he couldn't leave Lynn as soon as he'd planned. To hell with whether he got knifed in the back.

Pastor Molly Canton arrived, edging her way through the growing crowd of onlookers. The fire was out, the flames gone, but the firemen still had to pull out their axes and open the roof, open the walls to make sure there were no remaining hot spots. More damage. More destruction.

Molly, dressed haphazardly in jeans, Wellingtons and a bright red parka, approached Lynn and gave her a tight hug. "We've got the church hall set up for you. All of you. You'll be warm tonight, or as many nights as you need."

Her feelings dulled, Lynn barely managed a nod, clinging to Jax's arm. "How could anyone..."

Then she stiffened and straightened. "Boys," she said
to her roomers, "please take my mother to the church."

"What about you?" Barry asked.

"In a bit," she answered tightly. "In a bit."

"They're ready for you," Molly said to the students.
"I'll stay here for now. In case Lynn needs anything."

But all Lynn could do was stare at the destruction. As
if trying to believe it. As if mentally and emotionally trying to grasp the catastrophe.

Jax stood with her, wishing he had more to offer than a
hug. Then he urged her to follow the others to the church.
"You can face it in the morning," he said firmly. "In the
morning light. It's not going away."

Neither was he.

Good Shepherd Church boasted a large basement
hall for gatherings. Old fieldstone walls encased it, covered these days with banners for various organizations.
Guarded by a wooden cross with golden rays surrounding it. Stacked chairs lined the sides, six cots had been
prepared with sheets, pillows and brightly colored quilts.

A group of women had come out of nowhere and had
started making hot soup, coffee and toast. Nancy marched
into the group and joined them in preparing the food.
"Keeping busy," she said. "Before I find someone to kill."

The firefighters had been invited down for hot soup
and coffee. They paraded through in their turnout gear,
jackets hanging open now, helmets gone. The students
each sat on the edge of a cot, looking so out of place, as
if they didn't know what to do.

Lynn couldn't stop pacing. Jax watched her, seething
with an anger he couldn't show. Wanting to wrap her
up in comfort and safety, a safety he couldn't promise.

"I'll fix it," he heard her mutter as she strode by him,

rubbing her upper arms, wrapping herself tightly in them. "I'll fix it all."

It was the same grit that had carried her through the loss of Matt, the remodeling of his family's house and a lawsuit by her brother-in-law. Jax wanted to be there to help with every step of her recovery. But first he had to deal with an assassin. To make her safe from that. To make himself safe enough for her to be around.

Terri Albright was in a hellish mood, burning with anger. Yeah, she'd wanted to give Luke a bit of help with his house problem to keep suckering him along, but she hadn't wanted anything like this. Maybe she should have believed him when he'd said if he couldn't have that damn house then neither could Lynn. A male reaction. The same kind of reaction that made men grow violent over a divorce. But this made the whole situation more dangerous, hanging around a guy who would probably become the primary suspected arsonist.

Damn, she'd planned to go with him to the fundraiser in the afternoon, the one planned to rebuild that outdated motel. She was sick of hearing how it was a landmark. That fleabag?

But she figured that in a crowd, clinging to Luke as if he were God's gift, she'd look innocent enough, much as acting like that sickened her. She was no insecure teenager to hang on a guy the way she pretended to hang on Luke. But he made her part of the local scene. He gave her a chance to watch Stone and possibly separate him from the herd as night fell.

Now this. She had to work it to her advantage somehow. Maybe it would be enough to make Stone move on to Denver, now that he wouldn't have anywhere to stay.

He hadn't been in that house long enough to develop any kind of enduring relationship with the Macy woman.

No reason for him to hang out in this two-bit town that laughably called itself a city.

She still wanted to bash Luke's face in. The guy was a damn fool. He'd done thousands of dollars of damage to a house he wanted to claim as his own. Did he somehow think this fire would make Lynn Macy give up the house? Did he really just want to ruin what he couldn't have? He'd said so, but was he really that twisted?

Well, maybe he was. What did Terri care if she could turn it to her own ends?

Maybe, she thought as the morning began to arrive with a pale gray light, the fire would provide enough of a distraction to keep anyone else from paying attention to Stone's disappearance.

Because she *could* make him disappear. There was a lot of empty land around this town, land where a body could get lost forever.

She pulled her open sleeping bag tighter around her shoulders as she sat staring at the slowly brightening sky. Then she lit her camp stove and boiled water for instant coffee, for hydrating that dried-out crap that some called food.

After this, she was going to have a big, juicy steak. For now, she considered her waning time for this mission, and decided that if Stone didn't leave fast, she *had* to do him here.

And maybe give Luke some payback.

Nobody slept in the church hall that night. Everyone was too wound up. Soup simmered on the stove, the bevy of women who had showed up to cook had taken their departure. The firemen had vanished.

Then came the police, along with Melinda, who owned the bakery. With helpers, she arrived with sweet rolls and breads fresh from her ovens. A few others trickled in, among them Edith Jasper, this time without her dog, Bailey. Earl Carter arrived shortly after her and focused his attention on Nancy West.

Well, that was blossoming, Jax thought. He hoped it would help make Lynn happy despite the night's tragedy.

Sheriff Gage Dalton stepped up to Jax. "It seems fire follows you."

"Unfortunately." He met Gage's dark eyes. "You think it's linked with the motel?"

"We've surely got us an arsonist. And no, I don't think it's you. But this fire doesn't need the fire marshal to tell me it's no accident. Notice anything unusual around the house?"

"Just Luke Macy, and I gather he's not unusual."

Dalton chuckled. "Oh, he's unusual all right. But not just as an annoying visitor to Lynn. So nothing?"

"I've been...watching for something out of place," Jax said reluctantly.

One of Gage's brows lifted. "Trouble on your tail?"

"Maybe so. But it's directed at *me*."

"How bad?"

Jax shrugged. "Nothing I can't handle."

Gage nodded slowly. "If you remember anything, or need my help, let me know."

Jax agreed, then looked around at the other deputies who were taking statements from Nancy and the boys. It didn't require much time. None of the house's residents had been aware of anything until the fire.

As the day outside the basement windows brightened, Lynn came over to Jax, who had paced nearly as much as she had. Anger still burned in him, but for now his concern for her triumphed. One blow too many for this brave young woman?

"I'm going back to the house," she said tautly. "I have to see the damage."

"I'm sure it's extensive." His answer was cautious. Just then her face was so stiff he couldn't read her.

"Oh, I'm sure, too," she answered almost bitterly. "I want to blame Luke, but why would he try to burn down the house he wants?"

Good question, Jax thought. Just as they were approaching the basement stairs, Madge appeared. Her jacket was open, just enough to display her ample cleavage.

She simpered beautifully when she saw Jax. "I guess you'll be needing to find somewhere to stay, Jax. I have an extra bedroom…"

Lynn cut her off. "You're making a fool of yourself, Madge. Leave the man alone."

Then she shouldered past Madge and started climbing. Jax smothered a grin and followed right after her as if Madge didn't exist. He took some small pleasure in the moment.

The walk to the house didn't take very long. A couple of blocks. Lynn ate up the distance, her strides long, maybe driven by fear of what she would find, or perhaps by fury. Or perhaps by a determination to see the full dimension of the destruction she faced.

They came around the corner and Lynn stopped so suddenly that Jax nearly bumped into her. "What?" he asked.

She pointed and breathed, "Oh, my God."

He looked down the street and astonishment flooded him. A small lumber truck filled the street in front of her house, fully loaded. A dumpster occupied her front yard and men on ladders were tearing away the porch roof.

"I can't afford this," she whispered.

He studied the scene and felt an unusual warmth grow in old, cold places inside him. "Somehow I don't think you'll have to."

She looked sharply at him, then continued her march down the street. One of the men supervising from the sidewalk greeted her with a smile from beneath an orange hard hat. Tall and lanky with a weathered face, he wore jeans and a shearling jacket. Worn work boots encased his feet.

"It'll take a few days, Lynn, but we'll get this fixed for you."

"But Len, how do I pay for all this?"

"You don't," he answered with a shake of his head. "You're one of my best customers, to begin with. Then a funny thing happened. A bunch of guys showed up and volunteered. Can't do much about how this is making you feel, but we can fix the property damage."

Jax saw a tear run down Lynn's face. "Oh, Len…"

He waved a hand. "We all know how you feel. Just glad we can help. Now you go back to the church, eat something and stay warm. You'll be surprised by the end of the day."

"I don't know what to say," Lynn said as she and Jazz walked back to Good Shepherd.

"How about that sometimes people can be wonderful?"

"They can, can't they."

"I've seen the worst in people, but I've also seen the best. And the best is pretty amazing." Which was true. When you saw a man give his life to save a buddy… Well, people didn't get much better than that.

* * *

Lynn was still overwhelmed by the time they reached the church basement. Now Maude and her daughter, Mavis, had showed up with plenty of hot food.

"Soup ain't enough." Maude sniffed as she thrust foam containers at the two of them. "Now sit down and get something warm inside you."

Chairs had been stacked along one wall, ready for meetings, and the boys had pulled a few off the stacks. Nancy sat on one of them, conversing with Barry.

She looked up at Lynn. "It'll be okay," she offered quietly.

Lynn swallowed hard. "Apparently so. Len Danvers is already out there with a crew, ripping out the mess. How did your knees survive the excitement?"

Nancy smiled. "These boys of yours practically carried me all the way here. Remarkable young men."

All three looked uncomfortable at the praise.

"You *are* remarkable," Lynn told them. "All of you. And thanks for the warning last night."

"Lucky we were still playing video games," Tom answered. He elbowed Will. "Except this sleepyhead kept dozing off."

"Did not."

"No, you just lost a thousand points without clicking a button," Barry retorted. He and Tom both snickered, while Will looked embarrassed.

"Eat," Maude demanded, hands on her ample hips. "All of you. I didn't carry all this damn food over here to have it ignored."

"Yes, ma'am," Barry answered meekly.

Maude snorted. "You won't sell me that attitude, boy."

Barry clearly tried to smother a grin.

Nancy had opened her box and picked delicately at the

mound of home fries. "How are you going to pay Len for the work?" she asked bluntly, heedless of who might hear.

"Apparently I don't have to." Amazement touched Lynn's face once again.

Nancy nodded with satisfaction. "That's the kind of neighbors I remember. I guess this town hasn't changed all that much in nearly twenty years."

Lynn nodded, reaching at last for the omelet in her box. "I have a lot of good neighbors. It's overwhelming."

She had finished half her omelet when Luke Macy showed up. Lynn felt Jax stiffen beside her and heard her mother mutter something.

"Lynn," he called from across the basement, hurrying toward her. "I just heard. My God!" He dragged another chair over so he could sit facing her. "I am so sorry!"

"Sorry for what?" she snapped. "That *your* house is damaged?"

"No, no," he said hastily, reaching for her hands. She jerked them back and would have spilled the remains of her breakfast if Jax hadn't snapped out a hand to grab the container and pull it away.

"Lynn, please," Luke said, looking wounded. "I just wanted to offer my sympathy. I want to help with the repairs."

Lynn had had enough. "Leave me alone, Luke Macy. And if you ever set foot in my yard again, you'll be trespassing. Do I make myself clear?"

"But Lynn..."

Edith Jasper, who'd been over at the food table talking with Maude, spoke up loudly. "You, Luke. Yes, I'm talking to you. When a lady tells you to get lost, you'd better get lost. You wouldn't know anything about that ugly rumor that started running around last week, would you? Because it's got your fingerprints all over it."

"I never—"

"You heard the lady," Jax said, rising, towering over Luke. His voice was steely, his posture subtly threatening.

Luke looked up at him and decided to skedaddle. Without another word, he strode away and up the stairs.

"I can't believe the nerve!" Nancy exclaimed.

"Me neither," Tom said. "Don't you worry, Lynn. We see him in the yard, we'll send him on his way, won't we, guys?"

The other two nodded.

"What's the rest of this rumor?" Lynn asked quietly. Another problem, another thing to worry about.

"Pay it no mind," Edith Jasper said. "We're taking care of it. Aren't we, Maude?"

"Damn straight," said the heavyset woman. "Sorry, I got to get back to my diner. I'll be back with lunch, just before the fundraiser for the La-Z-Rest. What's this town coming to?"

With a shake of her head, she pulled on her coat and departed with her daughter, Mavis, on her heels.

Terri Albright wanted to throttle Luke Macy. Right on the spot and damn the witnesses. They were meeting in Mahoney's bar and she'd insisted on a back booth. They were supposed to be acting like lovebirds, but at that moment she could barely control her face.

"What do you mean you're not taking me to the fundraiser?" she asked quietly.

Luke looked startled. "What do you care about a stupid fundraiser?"

She struggled to smile adoringly. "You said you'd help me meet people. There'll be lots of people there."

"None I want to see."

She leaned forward, trying to appear girlish and disappointed. She hoped he couldn't read murder anywhere in her expression. "You promised," she pouted.

"We can do other things."

"I don't want to do other things. Just for a little while. Please?" Now she was wheedling and hated the sound of her own voice.

He signaled for another beer. "Okay, what the hell. But I want you to spend the night."

More fury rose in her. This sleaze expected her to pay with her body for a small favor? He was lucky his beer didn't wind up in his face.

"We'll see," she said coyly, glad she didn't have to try to blush. As if she could.

"There's no *we'll see* about it," he said flatly. "You're playing me."

That was so close to the truth that Terri was astonished. The fool actually had enough sense to realize that? She couldn't afford to lose him yet. Her mind swiftly calculated her next move.

She summoned a hurt expression. "I am not," she answered. "How could you even think that of me? Maybe I don't want to go with you *anywhere* now."

That took him aback. "I didn't mean… Oh, okay. We'll go to this damn thing. No strings. But not for long."

"Thank you," she cooed.

And wished for a hot shower to wash him off.

Chapter 17

After the lads and Jax had folded up the cots and leaned them against the wall and had helped open the lengths of folding tables that nearly filled the basement, the fundraiser began.

First came the men and women bearing delectable cakes, pies and cookies for sale. A ton of food. There were even crafts, hand-stitched quilts, knitted sweaters and scarves, and some very pretty handmade jewelry. Beautifully embroidered linens took up a large space on one table. Pastor Canton had offered a door prize of fifty dollars.

Local businesses had leaped in to help as well, making every kind of donation from winter clothing to groceries.

In fact, the long tables were loaded with donations, all proceeds to go to rebuilding the motel and helping its hapless owners.

Quite a well-organized little do, Jax thought. He was

surprised by the number of people who turned up, people more than willing to purchase a glass of hot cider on a cold day, glad to pay for a ticket for a free meal, or to purchase so many of the other donated goods.

Purses and wallets opened easily among people he was sure didn't have much extra money to spare. All for a good cause.

Like Len Danvers busy working on Lynn's porch.

Jax hadn't noticed anything like this when he'd lived here as a kid. In his isolation, it had all passed by him, escaping his awareness.

God, he'd been bent.

Lynn's mood appeared to have improved, although he couldn't tell if it was a front. If it was, she was doing a great job of it, constantly moving and smiling and helping where she could.

Then Luke Macy arrived with that girl on his arm, the one with the black bob and purple streaks. That hair was memorable. He watched with interest as Luke guided her around the tables, as she cooed over things and managed to get him to buy her a few trinkets from the woman selling handmade jewelry.

It seemed to Jax that Luke withdrew his wallet reluctantly. Tightwad.

But as the couple left after only a short visit, he noted something in the woman's movements.

It niggled at him. Something upright in her posture when she escaped Luke's arm for a minute. Something in the way she moved. Uneasiness prickled him even as he reminded himself he'd probably seen her before around town.

He couldn't escape the feeling there was something more.

But damn it all if he knew what it was.

* * *

As if by magic, all the donations disappeared in around four hours and the raffle prize was awarded. Quite a few folks lingered for a while, chatting as they drank coffee or cider, some even eating their recent purchases. Molly Canton moved among them, smiling pleasantly, thanking them all for coming.

Eventually, though, the inevitable cleanup began. Some people remained behind to help. Lynn, the students and Jax pitched in as well. Edith supervised, declaring that her age made her well suited to management. A lot of laughs answered her as good-humored people worked.

Then the basement became a shelter again. Tables gone except for two with chairs around them. Cots once again ready to hold refugees such as Lynn and Nancy.

"It went well," Lynn remarked to Jax as at last they sat at one of those tables with fresh coffee and a large walnut coffee cake between them. "Unfortunately, I don't know how much it will help the Blent family, the ones who own the motel."

He blew gently on his coffee, then sipped. "Every bit helps. Even if they had insurance, there are still the deductibles."

"I didn't think of that." She sighed, pushing a stray auburn lock behind her ear. "I suppose now I'll have to think about deductibles, too. And I guess I'd better call *my* agent. Len's a dear soul, but he shouldn't have to bear that cost alone."

"I think Len's more interested in getting things squared away as fast as possible for you, to allow you to go home again."

She smiled faintly. "He probably is."

Nancy joined them. Someone had even rustled up some tea bags for her. "Isn't this cozy?" she remarked lightly. "A few curtains, a couple of easy chairs, some low lighting instead of that miserable overhead fluorescent tubing? It would be perfect."

Lynn nearly choked on her coffee. "Mom!"

Nancy laughed. "Knew that would get you. It's been an awful day in so many ways, but a good one, too, if you know what I mean. We had hundreds of people go through here this afternoon, and from what Molly says, many more dropped donations in the bucket just inside the church door. It's always nice to see so many people pull together."

"It's a good feeling," Lynn agreed. But inwardly, she was still reeling. Her house was a mess, but that could be repaired one way or the other. It was the fire that bothered her more than anything else. Arson. Who the hell would hate her so much?

The only person she could think of was Luke. But he wanted the house, too. Why would he set a fire?

There was the motel fire, too. Maybe just an arsonist running around town? That was truly scary. Any of her neighbors and friends could become the next targets. And what kind of person got a thrill from setting fires, especially fires that could kill people?

She didn't want to ever know someone like that. But it *could* be someone she knew, even if only distantly.

Through all the riot of emotions that had swarmed through her today, this was the first time she felt the icy trickle of fear.

What next? Who next? Herself again?

Desperate to escape this new anxiety, she rose. "I'm going to look at what Len accomplished today."

Jax stood immediately. "I'm going with you."

She was so grateful for his company and felt weak for wanting it. She could take care of herself. She always had.

But something was different this time.
Malice.

Terri wanted to ditch Luke, wanted badly to *throw* him into a ditch. Everything about him disgusted her, but his utter lack of loyalty, his utter lack of honor—these were intolerable. Luke was a man without purpose except his own gratification.

He was a weak, selfish, childish man who used charm to oil his way through his petty cons. But that charm was only skin-deep. The man inside was a cesspool filled with snakes. And they weren't even deadly snakes. The rub of it was that she'd need him at least a little longer.

But he'd given her what she wanted. Recognized now by any who gave a damn, she was *Luke's new girl*, able to walk around town as freely as anyone. And today's trip to the fundraiser had given her an added bit of intelligence. Stone was joined at the hip with that Macy woman. She doubted she'd be able to separate them long enough to get him alone.

She might have to kill them both. But this time the idea didn't daunt her. Instead, it excited her.

A new plan began to take shape in her head.

Luke was angry with Terri. She'd expected him to pay for her every drink, her every meal and now that ridiculous costume jewelry at the fundraiser.

And that business about wanting to go to the fundraiser to meet people? She'd hardly talked to a soul.

But she *had* clung to his arm and hung on his every word. He was mad that she'd refused to come home with him, but, he reminded himself, her reluctance would make the conquest all the sweeter.

After a third beer, wondering where the hell the girl

had gone, he had soothed himself. Having her hang on him like that, look up at him with adoring eyes for all the world to see...

Well, that swelled his ego pleasantly. He'd never minded when someone had made him feel important, look important.

Because somewhere deep inside, Luke knew he'd never been important.

But he was important now. To Terri. And to Lynn, whether she knew it or not. He was going to enjoy seeing that house burned to the ground. No one would have it then, and destroying all her ridiculous hard work would only make it better.

He wished that damn Marine would leave, though. It would make his life so much simpler.

Lynn and Jax walked toward her house. The evening wind had taken on a sharp bite as daylight began to fail.

Astonishing Lynn, Jax reached for her hand and held it. All she wanted, she realized, was to be back in bed with him in her attic. Under the covers or in front of her electric fireplace, sharing some wine, maybe some cheese. Talking. Getting to know one another better. Finding heaven in each other's arms.

No. It couldn't happen, and not only because of the fire. He wore a uniform. He could be called into danger at any moment, maybe never to return. Going to be a recruiter right now didn't make him safe in the future.

And Matt had taught her the dimensions of real loss.

Seeking to corral her thoughts, she said, "You got that phone call yesterday. Or was it the day before? Everything's running together."

"A hell of a lot has been happening."

"No kidding." She hesitated, plunging in even though

she felt she had no right. "You tensed. You have to go back on duty soon, don't you."

It wasn't a question. Nor did he offer her a denial. "Yes," he said. "It's only to Denver. I'll come back to visit."

To *visit*? Oh, she wanted much more than that, but had no right to ask.

Then, as she sometimes did, she felt Matt with her, a warm presence that occasionally seemed to be watching over her. She felt a glimmer of reassurance. *It will be all right.*

The front of her house was illuminated by floodlights, probably driving the neighbors crazy. Len was there, however, loading up his truck to leave.

"Sorry we can't take the Dumpster away yet," he said to Lynn. "There's still some more demolition to do. We got the building permit and I persuaded the inspector to come out and look this over."

"Thank you," she answered, staring up at the front of her house. A tarp covered the porch roof, sealing out the elements. "Big job," she said quietly.

"Not that big," Len said bracingly. "Some roof joists need replacing, of course all the roofing. A few slats of siding, but the good news is the inspector found no damage inside the house wall. Some of the gingerbread on the porch took it on the chin, though."

"Oh, God."

Len laughed. "I remember your misery at having to paint all that stuff. Trust me, we'll make it as good as new."

Lynn faced him. "Keep good records, Len. Of the damage and of the work you're doing. I'll get on the insurance company tomorrow."

Len touched the brim of his hard hat. "Photos, photos and more photos. I think I've taken more than the fire marshal. Anyway, a little more checking out in the morning, then I think you and your roomers can move back in, as long as you're willing to use the back door."

"That would be wonderful!"

"The church basement ain't no place to live." Then he looked at Jax. "You keep an eye on her."

"I intend to," Jax replied.

As she and Jazz strode back to Good Shepherd, a new feeling filled Lynn. Snow began to fall lightly, sparkling in the glow of streetlights and lamplight from within houses.

"Christmas will be here soon," Lynn remarked.

"Time flies."

"Yeah. But I was just remembering how, when I was younger, the sight of the first snow flurries filled me with such excitement. Such a sense of wonder."

Then she turned her head to look at him. "As horrible as this day has been in so many ways, I'm feeling a touch of that wonder now."

He squeezed her hand. "I may be feeling a touch of wonder, too," he answered.

A remarkable statement from him, Lynn thought. From a man who had probably known very little wonder in his life.

Back at the church basement, Lynn and Jax found her three roomers and Nancy involved in a cutthroat game of Scrabble.

"She's beating us," Will said, looking up. "All those seven-letter words!"

"At my age, young man, I have a head full of more words than you." Her eyes twinkled. "Especially since I was a legal assistant."

"No fair," Tom muttered, but the other two guys laughed.

Barry looked up from reaching in the bag for more tiles to ask Lynn, "How's the house?"

"Len said there'll be another inspection in the morning, but we may be able to move back in."

"Oh, gawd," Will said. "Back to homework. I like it better here."

Tom and Barry laughed.

Smiling again, Lynn made her way to the coffeepot and returned to the table where the huge coffee cake had amazingly lost half its volume.

"Maudc brought sandwiches," Nancy said. "In that refrigerator. Salads, too."

Lynn looked at Jax and saw him smiling. The day still held warmth and wonders despite everything.

Chapter 18

As soon as Terri heard that Lynn Macy was moving back into her house, she got ready to put her plan into action. Luke wasn't going to like it, but that was fine by her. In fact, she relished the coming event, the look that would appear on his face.

Jackson Stone liked to walk at night. Nearly every night. He'd given her the sense that he was alert, looking for something. Maybe he'd heard about the two other jurors? But why would someone have warned him all the way out here?

It didn't matter. He was probably just that way after too much combat. And the deaths would never be traced to her. Never. She'd been careful. But still, he'd been hyperaware. If he thought someone was looking to kill him, he'd never suspect Luke's current bimbo with the purple sprayed hair. Which was the whole point of her playacting.

But she needed a way to distract him, to turn his hero instincts against him. And she knew just how to do it.

Luke was born to be her foil.

The foil himself had begun to feel irritated, ego notwithstanding. Luke made up his mind that he was going to force the issue with that young woman. As a college student, she had nothing to offer him except a roll in the hay. No money, no steady job to support him and apparently no inclination to be domestic.

Imagine her wheedling that stupid jewelry out of him. Imagine that he had actually paid for it. Imagine her refusing his mild suggestion that she come to his place, just a suggestion.

Yeah, tonight or tomorrow night he was going to push it with her or drop her. See how she liked that kettle of fish.

Satisfied with his decision, he ordered another beer and was glad she wasn't there giving him doe eyes. He was beginning to distrust those doe eyes, flattering or not.

The afternoon of their return to the house, the boys departed to resume their normal schedules. Nancy took up her station in the kitchen with the teakettle near at hand. Jax made a pot of coffee.

And Lynn wandered around the house, especially the front, looking for interior damage. She could find none. Thank God.

Len showed up to tell her they had the county's go-ahead and that he'd ordered matching shingles for the roof and some siding for replacements.

"As for the gingerbread…"

Lynn groaned. "Can't do it?"

"Oh, we can do it. A guy who does woodworking said it would be fun, so he's heating up his lathe and I've given him some sturdy oak to work with. I've even got some new beadboard for the porch ceiling. It's gonna be like nothing ever happened."

"Oh, Len." Lynn started to choke up. "I have a call in to the insurance company."

Len waved a hand. "They'll take forever. I'm not worried about it. This work gets done before winter sets in. Final word."

He refused a cup of coffee and left smiling, as if very pleased with himself.

"I can't believe this," Lynn said to her mother and Jax. "I just can't believe this."

"Enjoy it," Nancy suggested. "You've got some good people taking care of you."

"I certainly do."

Jax watched as more good people showed up—Lynn's friends, including Lily Robbins, who'd been maid of honor at his buddy's wedding, and her daughter, Iris, who struck him as a pistol. Casseroles arrived along with the friends and neighbors until Nancy began fussing about where she was supposed to put them all.

Lynn laughed for the first time since the fire. "Manage it, Mom. Or I could invite everyone to sit at the refectory table in the kitchen for a supper."

"Might not be a bad idea," Nancy muttered as she limped around the kitchen, moving covered dishes. "Those boys of yours better have good appetites."

Lynn studied her mother. "Mom?"

"What?"

"How's your arthritis? You're limping."

"I didn't have my medication at the church. It'll start working soon."

"But maybe you should sit down."

Nancy shook her head firmly. "Haven't you heard? My physical therapist says it all the time. *Motion is lotion.* In other words, use it."

"Or lose it," Jax remarked.

"Exactly, young man. You Marines get it."

"Knee replacement?" Lynn suggested gently.

Nancy snorted. "The problem will have to get a lot worse before I'll endure that. Now quit worrying. Just help me figure out where to put all these casseroles. Sinful to waste food."

Many of the casseroles made their way into the upright freezer Lynn had on her mud porch. "I almost never use it," she remarked.

"It'll get a workout now. Nobody's going to cook for at least a week. And we're going to have this beautiful eggplant parmesan for dinner tonight. Although those young lads probably won't want any." Nancy put her hands on her hips. "I've noticed the mere word *eggplant* makes youngsters run for the hills."

"More for me," Jax remarked. He was enjoying all this fussing and bustling, enjoyed seeing so many people concerned about Lynn. She was far from alone in this town.

Tomorrow, he decided. He'd leave tomorrow. She'd be safe among all these people, and if he did have a killer on his tail, he'd drag that tail to the big city with him.

Nancy retired early, and Lynn looked at Jax with clear longing. "Join me upstairs?"

"Wild horses couldn't keep me away." Especially now with coming sorrow riding his shoulders. Tomorrow he was going to leave this woman. To ensure her safety. To give her space to decide that she really didn't want him in her life after all.

Because he was sure she didn't. The uniform. The uncertain life. His own mixed-up past that sometimes still made him doubt his own judgment.

This was purely sexual need on her part, he told himself as he mounted the stairs behind her. An itch being scratched. As kind and nice as she was, she was also human enough to want a man's touches. She'd never dream she might hurt him.

And he was human enough to give in to his own desires. But he had to get out to protect her from a possible killer and most certainly from a growing need that might leave her feeling bereft all over again.

Upstairs, she moved around, turning on a few lamps, starting her electric fireplace. Instantly, the room became as cozy as he was sure she had intended.

The coziness drew them together. No hesitation. Knowledge of each other's desires was strong enough to throw away any reluctance, imagined or otherwise.

He undressed her slowly with hands that almost trembled. He trailed his lips across each new bit of skin he bared, finally latching his mouth to her erect nipple and drawing a groan from her. Before he could do more, she jumped into the bed and pulled the covers up.

"Hurry up, Marine," she teased. "This gal won't wait forever."

He grinned and shed his own clothes faster than if an alert had sounded. Moments later he was under the covers with her, giving her the opportunity to explore him with her hands and mouth. To bewitch him as his loins throbbed so hard it was almost painful.

At last he rolled over, catching her wrists, his mouth

finding its way to her throat. "You're driving me to the edge of insanity."

"You aren't the only one," she whispered. "Oh, Jax, fill me. Please fill me."

He slid into her warm depths, welcomed by her heated embrace. He'd never wanted anything more.

He never would.

Later, lying in bliss beneath the comforter, the attic grown warm around them, they hugged tightly. But reality intruded. It always did.

"When are you leaving?" she asked a long time later, running a fingertip along his upper arm. Causing another shudder of desire to rocket through him.

He didn't want to answer, didn't want this time ruined.

"Jax?"

"Tomorrow," he said finally. "I have to find a place to stay and time is limited." The truth. He hoped she didn't keep pressing because he rarely lied and didn't want to start with her.

But she murmured one more question. "Will you come back sometimes?"

His heart squeezed until he didn't know if he could force a word out. "I said I would. Just as soon as I can." *If* he could. If he didn't get himself killed.

That was the truth. Sometimes an omission was necessary.

Luke stared at Terri as if she'd lost her mind. "A walk? At two in the morning? It's cold out there," he said.

She'd expected some stubbornness. She knew, however, from scoping out the situation that Stone liked his middle-of-the-night walks. She needed this opportunity and she'd figured out how to use it. How to use Luke.

"I like to look at the stars," she said, making herself pout. Although the pout wasn't all pretense. If he interfered with her...

"Oh, hell," he said.

They were leaving the bar, Luke pleasantly full of beer, Terri as clearheaded as she'd been in her entire life. "Just a short one," she said softly, running a finger along his cheek. "Then we can go warm up. At your place?"

She watched the change happen. He looked less annoyed now, and far more hopeful. "My place," he repeated. "Okay, then. A walk. But I still think you're nuts."

She managed a giggle. "Nuts is what you want."

Jax slipped out of the warm bed, his every cell reluctant to leave Lynn. "I'm going to take a walk," he said, dropping a kiss on her lips. "Just a short one."

"I can come with you."

He gazed at her, allowing himself these few stolen moments. He understood that she didn't want him out of her sight. Well, he didn't want to be, either.

"You know I like my walks. Well, my jogs."

She nodded slowly.

"Keep the bed warm for me," he said gently. "You probably won't like it when I slip like a Popsicle back under those covers, though."

That drew a laugh from her, a sound he liked to hear. "Early morning with the roof," he said as he dressed. "I know you won't be able to keep out of it."

Again she laughed. "You know me too well. But I want to come anyway." She started to throw back the covers.

Then he spoke difficult words, words that sliced them both. "No. I don't want you to come."

The sudden hurt on her face nearly killed him. Now

he'd done the last thing on earth he ever wanted to do: he'd wounded her.

But, he thought as he descended the stairs, he needed to make a target of himself this one last time. The need to clear this up was driving him harder with each passing day. The closer he drew to Lynn, the more he wanted this killer stopped.

His own skin had begun to matter a lot more to him than it ever had. Because of Lynn. Because for the first time in a long, long time, he wanted to see the sun rise on a new day. Because for the first time in forever, he wanted to build a future.

The night had grown downright cold. People would be staying indoors. Yeah, the hour helped, but even in this small town, people were out at odd hours. Staggering home too full of booze. Walking dogs.

But this was all part of the plan he'd been seeding. Nearly empty streets made an attack easier. Following the same damn path every night made him easy to find. He'd learned long ago that developing habits could be dangerous. This time it might also be helpful.

He'd been out only fifteen minutes when he heard footsteps behind him. His neck prickled but then he heard a man's voice, a woman's quiet laugh.

A couple. The killer after him wouldn't be part of a couple.

He kept walking, sensing that at least one of them was watching him. He supposed he was a matter of slight interest at that hour. But the back of his neck wouldn't stop prickling.

Let it be, he told himself. *Wait for the moment—if it comes.*

Then he heard a scuffle behind him.

* * *

Terri's moment had come. She knew how Stone would react. The fun part, aside from killing Stone, was what she was about to do to Luke.

The smile that appeared on her face was unpleasant. Ugly even.

"I don't want to go home with you," she said loudly enough to be heard.

"But you said…"

Stone's steps ahead of them had slowed.

"No, you heard what you wanted to," Terri said, her voice rising. "Leave me alone!"

"Terri…"

"Get your hands off me, you pervert!"

Stone turned. The woman was pummeling the guy. What the hell? He started back.

Terri shoved Luke hard, catching one of his feet with one of her own, causing him to stagger and grab her for balance, just as she wanted.

Stone was coming. *Ever the hero*, she thought, both satisfied and bitter. She shoved her hand into the pocket of her parka, finding the unsheathed KA-BAR. Just a few seconds and Stone would be there.

"What are you doing with a knife?" she cried at Luke, stepping back, pretending to struggle against Luke's grip. She pulled out the knife, letting it flash just briefly in the dim light.

"My God," she screamed. "What's that knife? Help!"

At this point it didn't matter if neighbors started to pull on robes to come onto their porches. She needed only a few seconds now.

"Terri," Luke shouted. "Please…"

* * *

Jax saw the knife glisten. He couldn't tell which of them held it, but it must be the guy or the woman wouldn't scream like that.

He shouted, "Stop it now!"

The woman shoved Luke again just as Jax reached her, his eyes fixed on the knife.

Then he knew.

Terri turned, ready to stab Stone just under the ribs, to drag the knife down and gut him. He was so close the outcome was inevitable.

But just as she thrust the blade toward him, only a foot away, he grabbed her forearm as quickly as a striking cobra, wrenching it until she lost her grip on the KA-BAR.

"You must be Theresa Albright," he said as he whirled her around and seized both her wrists behind her back. His tone was like ice. Or like the steel she'd just dropped.

When she heard her name, she knew it was over. Her brother would never be avenged.

Chapter 19

In the very wee hours, the Sheriff's Office swirled with activity.

Terri Albright had been escorted to a holding cell just upstairs. Luke Macy sat in a chair, still shaking from his close call with that lying woman.

Jax had given his statement more than once. The only truly upsetting part was that he'd had to call Lynn and tell her he wouldn't be back until sometime later in the morning. Twenty minutes later she'd appeared in the office, her gaze wide and worried. She took one of the chairs lined up in front of the windows and waited.

Jax wanted to go to her and reassure her, but he wasn't yet free to. Two trips to the interrogation room would probably be followed by yet another, and he'd been warned not to speak to anyone. He tried to make a help-less gesture with his hands, hoping she'd get the message that he wasn't avoiding her. She didn't respond in any way.

His earlier fury gave way to a heart-sinking sensation. How would he ever explain to her why he'd withheld so much information? Would she even care at this point?

He doubted it. He turned back to the officer whose desk he sat beside. Lynn shouldn't even be here.

Gage Dalton emerged from the back offices and waved him to come. Jax rose and followed him down the hallway, this time to the sheriff's own office.

Gage waved him to a seat. "Let's go through this again. This woman was out to kill everyone who helped get her brother convicted of war crimes, right?"

"Exactly."

"And you were informed of this by the JAG attorney who prosecuted the case?"

"Yes."

Gage sighed and tossed a pencil on his desk. "No one else knew about this."

"No."

"Why didn't you tell me about this?"

"Because there wasn't a damn thing you or anyone else could do. Hugh had no idea at first if that was what was really happening. Then investigators decided that *might* be the case. It wasn't until just lately that they figured out the killer was Albright's sister Terri. Hell, I wasn't even looking for a woman."

Gage gave a crooked smile. "We're all guilty of that mistake too often."

"*I* sure was."

Gage rocked his creaky chair slowly. "The fire at the motel? Was that her?"

Jax shrugged. "You'll have to ask her."

"She's a clam. Already demanded a lawyer. I guess she took that thing about name, rank and serial number to heart."

Jax leaned forward. "She didn't take the right things to heart."

"Apparently not." Gage sighed again. "I wager that blithering fool Luke Macy was responsible for the fire on Lynn's roof. He'll probably sing for us. As much as he knows anyway. I hope this rattled some sense into that man."

Jax's answer was dry. "I bet that's the first time he's ever had a woman draw a knife on him."

A chuckle escaped Gage. "Probably more than one wished they had. We have the number for Hugh Briggs, so we'll call him in the morning and get the full scoop from that end. At least as much as the investigators will share. In the meantime, scoot. From the look of her, I think you have some fence-mending to do with Lynn."

More than a little, Jax thought as he made his way to her through the outer office. More than a little.

He halted in front of her. "Take you home, lady?"

A minute passed before she finally stood. "Yes."

When they finally reached her house, the first light of dawn filtered through foggy air. She took a long look at him.

"You," she said, "aren't even safe off the battlefield."

Then she marched to the attic without offering him an invitation.

Nancy, wrapped in a flowered robe, appeared in the doorway of the kitchen. "Coffee, soldier? You're going to need it."

He followed her briskly, telling himself he had survived worse.

But it sure as hell didn't feel like it.

* * *

Lynn reappeared at midmorning, dressed for work. Without a word, she marched into the living room and picked up her pry bar. A minute later she was banging on walls, her thuds a counterpoint to the hammering from her porch.

"Lynn."

She stopped banging as if she sensed Jax in the doorway. "You said you were going to Denver, that you needed to find a place to live. Why are you still here?"

"Because I don't want to go."

Her arm paused midswing. "Yeah. Sure. You've been lying to me the whole time you've been here. You didn't trust me. Seems like you should have left at the beginning."

Every muscle in his body tightened at her rejection and accusation. Words, however, were far from adequate to mend this rupture. He must have taken leave of his senses, because she was right. "I didn't know at first. Then I didn't want to worry you."

"Then you should have just marched on."

He hesitated, then laid himself on the line. "I couldn't leave you."

A flimsy excuse, however true. It sounded weak to him even now. When her face remained unyielding, he turned, saying over his shoulder, "I'll be gone in an hour."

The loss of Lynn was going to stand right at the top of all his losses. A wound that might scar over but would ever be part of him.

Hell. He should have done something different. *Anything* different. He'd failed her. And himself.

Lynn turned back to the wall, beating it with the crowbar, not caring if she did additional damage. But tears began to run down her face, leaving damp trails through plaster dust.

He was leaving. For good. For the best, she argued with herself, but didn't believe it.

Tears began to turn into sobs. A man in uniform. She should have known better.

But…

She leaned against the wall as memories of her time with Jax flooded her. He was a rock-solid man, a decent man, one who had helped bring her fully back to life.

Of course he'd wanted to protect her. He'd spent his life trying to protect both his ideals and the people who depended on him. It was the kind of man he was.

She needed to accept that. Accept him. What had she wanted? Some kind of imagined perfection?

She dropped the crowbar and dashed the tears from her face. Then she marched upstairs, finding him in his room, packing his duffel.

"Where do you think you're going?" she asked.

"Denver. As you ordered."

"Oh, damn, Jax."

He straightened and faced her. "Isn't that what you want? To get this lying Marine out of your life? To return to the safety you've created for yourself?"

She winced. He was right, she *had* been trying to build a cocoon for herself. "Some safety with Luke trying to burn my house down."

One corner of his hard mouth twitched upward. "Well, apart from that jackass."

"I think he's going to be out of my hair for a while now."

Jax nodded. "He was in full confession mode, wasn't he? Wanting to disassociate himself from Theresa Albright. But that's another story for another day. All I can tell you is that when I first arrived here, I had no idea someone was after me. And when I got the first hint, it was just a hint. Nothing actionable. I also figured that if someone wanted to kill me, it'd be much easier in Denver."

She nodded and took a step toward him.

"But I was a fool," he said. "A damn fool. Every time I thought of hitting the road, I had a bazillion reasons not to leave you. *You*, Lynn. I never felt about anyone the way I felt about you."

She sighed, her heart aching and soaring all at the same time, and stepped closer. "I'm sorry I got so mad at you."

"It was understandable in the circumstances. And you're right, I can't make you safe."

"No one can. Jax…" She scoured her face with her shirtsleeve, turning damp plaster into a paste. She laughed weakly. "I'm a sight."

He crossed the two steps between them and took her into his arms. "You're a wonderful sight, Lynn. Always wonderful." He bent his head and kissed her deeply.

She was melting, she realized. Melting into him. Could she live without him? No. The realization hit her hard.

"But you have to leave," she whispered reluctantly.

"Not today, if you don't want. Not for a few more days. And I'll come back, I swear. If you want me to."

She burrowed into him. "Jax, please, don't ever leave me for good."

"I couldn't," he answered huskily. "I couldn't. I love you too much."

Her heart leaped, soaring for the heavens as she allowed her own feelings to burst through. "I love you, too. Forever."

"Start planning the wedding," he said softly. Then he swept her up in his arms and carried her up to her attic.

Downstairs, Nancy smiled knowingly and started another pot of tea.

"High time," she said to the tea bag. "High time."

* * * * *

Be sure to check out previous titles in Rachel Lee's Conard County: The Next Generation series:

Conard County Conspiracy
Hunted in Conard County
Conard County Watch
Conard County Revenge

Available now from Harlequin Romantic Suspense!

#2199 COLTON'S ROGUE INVESTIGATION
The Coltons of Colorado • by Jennifer D. Bokal

Wildlife biologist Jacqui Reyes is determined to find out who's trying to steal the wild mustangs of western Colorado. She enlists the help of true-crime podcaster, Gavin Colton. He's working on a series about his notorious father but he can't help but be drawn into Jacqui's case—or toward Jacqui herself!

#2200 CAVANAUGH JUSTICE: DEADLIEST MISSION
Cavanaugh Justice • by Marie Ferrarella

When his sister goes missing, small-town sheriff Cody Cassidy races to her home in Aurora. All he finds is heartbreak...and the steady grace of Detective Skylar Cavanaugh. Once firmly on the track of a killer, Cody and Skylar discover they have more in common than crime. But a murderer is on a killing spree that threatens their budding relationship.

#2201 PROTECTED BY THE TEXAS RANCHER
by Karen Whiddon

Rancher Trace Adkins is wary when Emma McBride shows up on his doorstep. How could he let a woman convicted of murdering her husband into his home? But he's never believed in her guilt, and the simmering attraction he's always felt toward her remains. Despite his misgivings, he agrees to let her stay until she gets on her feet, unaware that someone is after her.

#2202 REUNION AT GREYSTONE MANOR
by Bonnie Vanak

Going back to his hometown is painful, but FBI agent Roarke Calhoun has inherited a mansion, which will help save a life in crisis. But returning means facing Megan Robinson, the woman he's always loved. She also has a claim on the mansion, which puts them together in a place full of secret dangers...and a love meant to burn hot.

Was she really considering allowing herself to be
captured by the man who'd killed Amber? Even though
he'd insisted he hadn't murdered Jeremy, how did she
know for sure? She could be putting herself into the
hands of a ruthless monster.

The sound of the back door opening cut into her
thoughts.

"Hey there," Trace said, dropping into the chair next
to her, one lock of his dark hair falling over his forehead.
He looked so damn handsome her chest ached. "Are you
okay? You look upset."

If he only knew.

"Maybe a little," she admitted, well aware he'd see straight through her if she tried to claim she wasn't. In the short time they'd been together, she couldn't help but notice how attuned he'd become to her emotions. And she to his. Suddenly, she understood that if she really was going to go through with this risky plan, she wanted to make love to Trace one last time.

Moving quickly, before she allowed herself to doubt or rationalize, she turned to him. "I need you," she murmured, getting up and moving over to sit on his lap. His gaze darkened as she wrapped her arms around him. When she leaned in close and grazed her mouth across his, he met her kiss with the kind of blazing heat that made her lose all sense of rhyme or reason.

Don't miss
Protected by the Texas Rancher *by Karen Whiddon,*
available October 2022 wherever
Harlequin Romantic Suspense books and
ebooks are sold.

Harlequin.com

Get 4 FREE REWARDS!

We'll send you 2 FREE Books plus 2 FREE Mystery Gifts.

FREE
Value Over
$20

Both the **Harlequin Intrigue®** and **Harlequin® Romantic Suspense** series
feature compelling novels filled with heart-racing action-packed romance
that will keep you on the edge of your seat.

YES! Please send me 2 FREE novels from the Harlequin Intrigue or Harlequin
Romantic Suspense series and my 2 FREE gifts (gifts are worth about $10 retail).
After receiving them, if I don't wish to receive any more books, I can return the
shipping statement marked "cancel." If I don't cancel, I will receive 6 brand-new
Harlequin Intrigue Larger-Print books every month and be billed just $6.24 each
in the U.S. or $6.74 each in Canada, a savings of at least 14% off the cover price
or 4 brand-new Harlequin Romantic Suspense books every month and be billed
just $5.24 each in the U.S. or $5.99 each in Canada, a savings of at least 13% off
the cover price. It's quite a bargain! Shipping and handling is just 50¢ per book
in the U.S. and $1.25 per book in Canada.* I understand that accepting the 2
free books and gifts places me under no obligation to buy anything. I can always
return a shipment and cancel at any time by calling the number below. The free
books and gifts are mine to keep no matter what I decide.

Choose one: ☐ **Harlequin Intrigue**   ☐ **Harlequin Romantic Suspense**
                Larger-Print   (240/340 HDN GRCE)
                (199/399 HDN GRA2)

Name (please print)

Address   Apt. #

City   State/Province   Zip/Postal Code

Email: Please check this box ☐ if you would like to receive newsletters and promotional emails from Harlequin Enterprises ULC and
its affiliates. You can unsubscribe anytime.

Mail to the Harlequin Reader Service:
IN U.S.A.: P.O. Box 1341, Buffalo, NY 14240-8531
IN CANADA: P.O. Box 603, Fort Erie, Ontario L2A 5X3

Want to try 2 free books from another series? Call 1-800-873-8635 or visit www.ReaderService.com.

HARLEQUIN
PLUS

Announcing a **BRAND-NEW**
multimedia subscription service
for romance fans like you!

Read, Watch and Play.

Experience the easiest way to get
the romance content you crave.

Start your **FREE 7 DAY TRIAL** at
<u>www.harlequinplus.com/freetrial</u>.